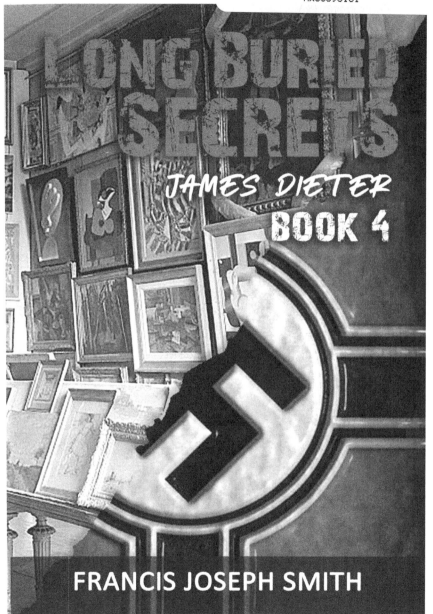

LONG BURIED SECRETS

JAMES DIETER

BOOK 4

FRANCIS JOSEPH SMITH

LONG

BURIED

SECRETS

JAMES DIETER Book 4

by

FRANCIS JOSEPH SMITH

ALSO BY FRANCIS JOSEPH SMITH:

THE VATICAN'S LAST SECRET (JAMES DIETER Book 1)

THE VATICAN'S DEADLY SECRET (JAMES DIETER Book 2)

THE VATICAN'S FINAL SECRET (JAMES DIETER Book 3)

LONG BURIED SECRETS (JAMES DIETER Book 4)

SECRETS FROM A FATHER's GRAVE (JAMES DIETER Book 5)

THE DEVILS SUITCASE

First Printing

This is a work of fiction. Names, characters, businesses, organizations, places, events, and incidents either are in the author's imagination. Any resemblance to actual persons, living or dead, events, or locales is entirely coincidental.

The Cataloging-in-Publication Data is on file at the Library of Congress.

PUBLISHED BY AMAZON

www.amazon.com

Printed in the United States of America

FACTS:

From 1936 to 1945, it is estimated the Nazi's stole an incredible one-fifth of all the artworks in Europe.

To this day it is considered the largest art theft in history.

One man, Hildebrand Gurlitt, a German art dealer, was appointed by Adolf Hitler to set aside and sell many of the art works to finance Germany's World War II effort. But Gurlitt had his own agenda, secretly amassing select pieces for himself. In the end, siphoning off over 1,500 works of art -- including masterpieces by Picasso, Matisse and Chagall -- estimated to be worth more than $3 billion in today's economy.

Upon his death in 1956, everything was bequeathed to his son, Cornelius. For more than 70 years, the artwork lay concealed in Cornelius' apartment before being discovered during a raid by Bavarian authorities for suspected tax evasion.

The art world was astonished since most of the 1,500 paintings were believed destroyed during World War II.

Even more bewildering, after simply paying taxes owed, Cornelius Gurlitt was permitted to retain all of the stolen art.

A month before his death at 81 in May 2014, Cornelius Gurlitt managed to bequeath the entire collection of stolen artwork to Bern's Museum of Fine Art.

However, Cornelius Gurlitt had amassed many enemy's while he was alive, both criminals and those in powerful government positions.

And they were about to extract their revenge...

LONG BURIED SECRETS

For my Family

CHAPTER 1

September 1938: Berlin, Germany

The intense afternoon sun beat down upon a line of well-dressed individuals waiting for flights out of Berlin's Tegel airport. The line snaked from the Lufthansa check-in counter out to the airport's sidewalk, a full 75 meters of pure desperation. Each, if they were lucky enough, were able to sit and rest on their maximum allotment of one suitcase. *And they were the fortunate ones.* Each had their own private reasons for wanting to escape. Some were so fearful of what might materialize if they stayed, paying nearly a year's salary for a Transit Visa, a necessity for leaving behind Nazi Germany. Without a Transit Visa, you were forcibly turned away. Or, even worse, imprisoned.

On the Tegel Airport tarmac stood four Lufthansa Junkers JU-52 trimotor passenger aircraft, their highly polished aluminum glistening in the sun, wingtip to wingtip, each with a destination of London, England. With an air of extreme anxiety considered the new normal in Berlin, Lufthansa's regularly scheduled service was recently increased from two to four daily flights to the British capitol. Lufthansa also deliberately increased its fares to almost double its normal rates knowing the majority of its clientele would be Jews.

Most had been waiting for hours in the hot German sun, awaiting their turn at the Lufthansa flight counter. At the counter stood two German National Police (SS) beside a flight attendant who performed double duty as desk clerk. Once they were confirmed by Lufthansa as passengers, it was the SS who actually scrutinized each passenger, then their Transit Visa and passport. If everything was in order, they were allowed to move off to an area out of sight of the other passengers.

Once out of view, a second set of SS would greet them. Only this pair had something else besides tickets and Transit Visas on their mind.

"Over here," shouted a burly SS officer.

The SS officer indicated for the middle-aged husband and wife to place their luggage on the table in front of his fellow SS officer. The officer swiftly snapped open the husband's luggage first, obviously searching for valuables. The other would simply watch the reactions of those being searched. In an area off to the left stood neat little stacks of silver ingots, gold coins, and artworks. Each obviously confiscated from fellow passengers desperately looking to leave Nazi Germany.

By now the SS had become experts in uncovering hidden compartments in suitcases and clothing. The officer meticulously felt the sides of the case before he tugged at a fabric strip that lined the inside of the suitcase. He smiled as he looked to his partner. Pulling at the piece of fabric, he could see it was recently stitched, the stitching whiter than on the other side of the case. His eyes went wide and a smile creased his face as he soon discovered a flattened piece of canvas. He realized it was a valuable piece of artwork as soon as he eyed its frayed edges. Upon unfurling, he nodded in appreciation. He then showed his discovery to his partner. "Look at the masterful strokes, the use of color. It's a Rembrandt," he said.

A highly coveted and valuable Rembrandt.

The SS officer looked to the husband in whose luggage they found the painting. "We are going to keep this for further investigation."

The man meekly protested. "But it was my late mothers."

The SS officer withdrew his Lugar from its leather holster, pointing the weapon at the man's forehead. "You are lucky I don't shoot you for smuggling. I said it is staying." He then tugged at the yellow armband on the man's coat, one required of all Jews for identification.

The husband had already lined up a buyer in London, one who was willing to pay a tidy sum. But they still required the final Exit Stamp on their passports from the German National Police before they could board one of the aircraft.

The man's wife felt compelled to speak up. "But we need to sell the painting in London so we have some money to live on," she said in a slightly raised voice.

The SS officer smiled at her and nodded as if understanding their plight. "Of course you do. I completely understand." He reached into his wallet and removed a Ten Mark bill, worth about five American dollars, rolling it up into a ball before tossing it at the wife. "That's all its worth. I don't care how you live, or where you live, as long as it's not in Germany. "

Tears welled in the woman eyes as she looked to her husband. He looked down at the marble floor to avoid her steady gaze.

The SS officer laughed aloud before he stamped both of their passports. "Now keep moving. That is unless you would rather stay? I am sure we can make some nice arrangements at Buchenwald for you. Either way, the painting stays here."

The woman started to walk towards the painting. The SS officer anticipated as much and brought the back of his hand to bare against the side of her head. The woman fell hard to the marble floor. Her husband rushed to her side. "Please, sir," he pleaded, "keep the painting." He then pulled his wife to her feet, speaking comforting words to her in Yiddish.

The SS officer handed them back their travel documents and pointed to the plane. "Now leave my country. We have no room for your kind."

The man smiled and nodded to the officers as he closed the suitcase. He then grabbed the second still unopened suitcase as both the SS officers stood admiring the painting. The husband and wife merely slipped out and walked towards one of the waiting planes.

The man's wife looked back at the loss of 250,000 English pounds. Their life savings. Her husband handed her one of the suitcases. "Carry this," he said as they cleared the terminal and walked onto the tarmac. "Don't worry. We are one of the lucky ones to escape," he said softly as they kept walking. "Many who stay will die."

"But now we have nothing to start a new life. How can we possibly survive in England?"

"Keep walking," he said. "Look depressed."

The wife shot him a menacing glance. "That is easy to do under the circumstances," she said before complying with his meager request.

At the bottom of the boarding stairs stood a Lufthansa stewardess who simply nodded to them as they walked up the boarding stairs. At the top of the steps they were greeted by yet another stewardess who pointed them to the rear of the aircraft. The husband reached their seats first, placing his suitcase in an overhead canvas sling, before placing his wife's beside his own. They both sat down with a look of relief realizing they were that much closer to freedom. Hannah looked out the window towards the terminal, eyeing the line of passengers gradually snaking their way to the aircraft.

After thirty minutes, the remainder of the seats filled with refugees just like themselves. Several more minutes passed, and with German efficiency, the stairway was pushed back, and the aircrafts door secured.

In the cockpit, the pilot checked the radiator inlet and outlets, oil cooler, and parking brake. Satisfied he set the fuel mixture to 100% before depressing the ignition button to start each engine one-by-one. Soon the wheel chocks were removed, and the pilot taxied the plane to the end of the runway. Now in takeoff position, the pilot revved the engines to maximum power, the whole aircraft shaking violently.

Suddenly the plane shot forward as if a coiled spring, barreling down the runway, the plane swiftly lifting up, now airborne.

The plane erupted into cheers.

There was no turning back now.

The husband leaned over to his wife and said, "It was a fake."

"What," she replied loudly, competing with the aircrafts engine noise.

Several of the passengers turned in their direction.

Her husband smiled at them. "First time on an aircraft," he said. "She's a bit nervous."

Each nodded in understanding before turning back.

She grabbed her husband's hand "Are you saying we still have the original painting?" A smile now creasing her face.

"Of course we do. Do you think I would let those SS pigs have our treasure? It is in your luggage. The one they didn't search."

She squeezed her husband's hand. The Germans could keep the fake Rembrandt. A masterful fake, but still a fake.

She was free. They were free. It was a new beginning.

CHAPTER 2

PRESENT DAY: MARATHON KEY – FLORIDA

Located just a leisurely drive down the Overseas Highway from Miami, it's the kind of journey that beckons you to take your time and soak in the ambiance as you start to feel, mile by mile, the stress melt away. With the Atlantic Ocean on one side of the highway and the turquoise of the Gulf of Mexico on the other, it provided a view that you could not find anywhere else.

It was also a place for the unexpected. Locals often greet the news of some particularly offbeat happening by grinning, nodding and uttering, *only in the Keys.*

The Craggy Dog Marina was a suitable fit with its Keys neighbors. At every turn, palm trees softly swayed with the continuous warm ocean breeze, each tree just tall and wide enough to provide shade up to the water's edge. To top it off, the weather hovered around a constant 85 to 90 degrees.

Life is good.

With September just beginning, only six boats lay moored to the Craggy Dog's piers, a number that could easily reach a peak of 40 when the *snowbirds* from Pennsylvania and New Jersey returned in winter. The boats currently tied up ranged from a "low-end" 23-foot King Fisher sail boat to a "high-end" 57-foot Jefferson Motor Yacht with the name *"Irish Rebel"* painted conspicuously in emerald green on its stern.

The "Irish Rebel" slept six, with a full galley, three bathrooms or *heads* in nautical speak, teak decking throughout, and a small two-person hot tub on the stern. Rumors circulated about the origin of its owner's wealth, something mysterious involving Nazi gold but unproven.

But who cares about the truth when the rumor sounds more appealing?

HAVE YOU EVER EXPERIENCED one of those days where you just wanted to curl up in your nice comfortable bed, your boat gently rocking from side-to-side, and tell the world to go to Hell?

That was just the day James Dieter was having. And it was only 7am.

It all started with an early morning phone call at zero dark thirty. Someone claimed to have his friend Eian Doherty as a hostage. They might consider letting him go if his gambling debts were paid.

Rather large gambling debts.

How many times had he warned Eian about his gambling?

He now stared into his bathroom mirror at an aging face as he applied a layer of shaving cream. Where did all of the years go he thought to himself? His brown hair, now tinged with grey. This combined with his rugged features and a 6'1, 210 pound physique he maintained from his Navy SEAL days still drew many a passing stare. However, he was entering his early forties. He had to slow down. His body could not recoup as fast from the injuries he sustained from his many exploits. Exploits just like the one he was about to get himself involved in.

He had a plane to catch out of Miami in three hours, the earliest he could find that still had availability.

His wife of six months, the Pulitzer Prize winning investigative journalist Nora Robinson, still lay sleeping. The woman slept like a rock. The early morning phone call didn't even phase her. Not even a stir. Jim stood admiring her for a few moments realizing how lucky he was. To her adoring public she was frequently compared to a young Lauren Bacall, the movie star siren of the 1940's and 50's. Nora stood 5 '8, with long shoulder length hair that seemed to constantly battle between blonde with brown roots and brown; a lithe body, and what captured men most of all were her eyes; a deep pool of blue-green that seemed to reel you in from the first instant you made eye contact.

Jim tapped her lightly on the shoulder. "Let's go, sleepyhead," he said softly. "We have a plane to catch."

Nora tossed a pillow his way. "We are off for the weekend," she replied. Her head popped out from under the blanket. "Did you say we have a plane to catch?"

"We are heading to Philly. Eian has gotten himself into a bit of trouble again. He needs our help."

Nora let out a long sigh. "James Dieter you have got to get some new friends, ones that aren't so high maintenance."

For once Jim agreed with her. "Right you are." He then pulled the blanket off Nora. "Out of bed. Now."

She tossed a second pillow at him. "I'm up."

"No, you're not." He picked her up and tossed her over his shoulder. "We have to get moving." He carried her into the yachts bathroom, or *head* in nautical speak.

"James Dieter put me down," she screamed, pounding him on his back with her fists.

Jim laid her down on the floor of the shower.

"You wouldn't dare!" Nora said defiantly.

He turned on the cold water and went back to finish packing. A smile creased his face. "Don't hog all the cold water," he shouted over his shoulder.

"I will get even with you James Dieter!" Nora shouted. "Mark my words."

"Get in line. There's a lot of people saying that," was his reply.

CHAPTER 3

Clyde's Auto body Shop
Edgemont, Pennsylvania
(15 miles west of Philadelphia)

The two-story brick building was built at the tail end of the Great Depression. Nothing special. An old rusted enamel sign proclaiming *Clyde's Auto Body* hung prominently across its two-story front. A faded promotion for White Owl Cigars was barely visible on the south side of the structure. Strangely, for an auto body shop, it lacked a garage to handle its advertised work. From its outward appearance most people would think the auto body shop was out of business. Of course, it was all a ruse. The *real* business occurred on the second floor. Poker to be exact. The only cars parked out front were luxury ones driven by the poker players inside.

Eian Doherty eyed the five-card flush in his hand, then the games pot in front of him, now up to a little over $500,000.

The marathon poker game approached its tenth hour, having started promptly at two in the afternoon of the previous day.

Eian picked up his remaining chips. "My last six thousand," he said in a slight Irish accent, placing six chips one-by-one onto the pile. "I'll call."

Eian stood just over six feet, pushing a solid 220 pounds. At one time he was considered a pretty decent boxer, even making it to the finals in tryouts for the Irish Olympic Team. However, with injuries and age he was forced to give up the sport and apply his energies into something he could really enjoy: gambling. He loved it. That and flying. However, in gambling circles, he was known as an easy mark. A whale. Luckily his job as a corporate pilot kept him, for the most part, out of the *hole* for his gambling losses. *At least most of the time.*

His choice status as a whale was the main reason for his invitation to one of the most exclusive poker games in the Philly area.

Of the ten players originally invited, only two still sat at the table: Eian and the head of the Philly Irish Mob, Mike Dolan Jr. The remaining eight players watched from afar as they smoked expensive cigars and drank single malt scotch courtesy of Dolan, the games organizer. Dolan's two goons, ex-middleweights and Golden Glove champions, provided double duty of serving and providing security for the game.

Dolan eyed Eian with contempt. "Eian, my friend," he said in a hard South Philly accent, "you know you still owe me $150k from our last game?"

Eian nodded. "I'm well aware of how much I owe," he said with an all-knowing smile. "After this game I have the strange feeling my slate will be clean. So do me the favor of showing me what a losing hand looks like."

Dolan smiled as he withdrew a .38 from its worn leather holster beneath his jacket, laying it on the table beside him. He pointed to the pot and then to Eian before laying down his cards. "I hope you can beat a full house. I really do."

Eian swallowed hard as he tossed his cards onto the table. "It's all yours, Dolan."

Dolan greedily pulled the pot of plastic chips towards his side of the table. "You win some, you lose some. Am I right, Eian?"

Eian mustered the best smile he could in response.

"But you tend to lose more than most. By my count, with your latest loss, you now owe me $220k."

"And you added that up so fast. I didn't think you had it in you."

Dolan motioned for both of his goons to stand behind Eian.

Eian realized things were starting to go downhill, *fast*. "You know I'm good for the money, Dolan."

"You told me last week you would have the money this week. Well it is time my friend. And you are not leaving until I get my cash."

One of his goons grabbed Eian from behind and jerked him up, and out of his chair. The other struck Eian three times about his face breaking his nose, blood trekking down to his mouth. Not satisfied, he started to use his stomach as if it were a punching bag. After a dozen or so blows, Eian fell to the floor clutching his ribs.

"It takes a special kind of idiot to gamble and lose week after week. And you my friend, are that idiot." Dolan walked over to him and leaned down, handing him a handkerchief. "This is bad for business, Eian. I don't want to do this but you have forced me into a corner."

The eight remaining players decided it was a good time to bid their goodbyes, exiting the room, leaving Dolan and his two goons to finish.

"See, it's just the four of us, Eian. Just us friends. Now true friends pay their debts. How do you intend to pay yours?"

Eian coughed a few times, spitting blood onto the wooden floor. "You'll get your cash," he replied with difficulty. He tried his best to smile, blood covering his teeth. He reached into his inner pocket of his suitcoat only to be stopped by one of Dolan's men. "It's just my damn cell phone," he muttered.

Dolan walked over to where Eian sat on the floor. He helped Eian by removing his cell phone for him. After several seconds, he again took pity on the man, handing him his last handkerchief. "Who are you going to call, Eian? With your track record of losses, who the hell is stupid enough to lend you any cash?"

Eian used the handkerchief to stem the blood loss from his nose before replying.

"My good friend, Jim Dieter."

LONG BURIED SECRETS

CHAPTER 4

30 June 1937: Berlin, Germany

Joseph Goebbels, Hitler's Minister of Propaganda, limped about his empty office. His limp was due to a childhood bout with polio, which left him with a deformed foot, and one leg two inches shorter than the other. Other than that, he was a small man with a large head, and a fragile body, but his voice was mesmerizing. Unlike his hero, Adolf Hitler, whose rough voice sometimes broke when he reached a fever pitch of oration, Goebbels' speech was deep and resonant; it never wavered from its carefully crafted message of German superiority and rabid anti-Semitism.

In addition, no one believed the message more than Goebbels.

When Hitler ascended to power, Goebbels assumed control over the Ministry for Public Enlightenment and Propaganda, which controlled radio, press, publishing, cinema and the other arts.

Goebbels soon subjected artists and journalists to state control and eliminated all opponents from positions of influence. He also authorized the head of *Reichskammer der Bildenden Künste* (Reich Chamber of Visual Art), to confiscate from museums and art collections throughout Germany, any art deemed degenerate. He was following the direction of his boss, Hitler. Hitler hoped to incite further revulsion against what he called the "perverse Jewish spirit" penetrating German culture.

Moreover, he said that spirt persisted in art. *Degenerate art.*

Soon over 5,000 works were seized. Masterpieces including 1,052 by Nolde, 759 by Heckel, 639 by Kirchner and 508 by Beckmann, as well as smaller numbers of works by such artists as Chagall, Ensor, Matisse, Picasso, and van Gogh.

Once seized, Goebbels ordered the paintings taken to the Reich's Bank in Berlin and stored in its vaults housed five stories below the surface to await destruction.

FAST-FORWARD THREE YEARS, the collection sat forgotten until the early days of WWII. German Armies had already conquered most of Europe but were experiencing a need for hard currency to keep its war machine running.

This is when Hildebrand Gurlitt, a German art dealer who had the ear of Adolf Hitler, first rose to prominence. Gurlitt convinced Hitler to sell the *degenerate art* on the world market. He could set the auctions up in neutral Switzerland.

Hitler saw an opportunity to not only rid himself of the artwork but also make a profit in doing so. He commissioned Gurlitt to sell the whole lot. Of course, he would have to do so slowly, piece by piece to not raise alarms in the art world.

It was the beginning of a mutually beneficial relationship, one that would enrich both, *considerably.*

CHAPTER 5

February 1945: Moscow, Soviet Union (Russia)

Stalin had just returned from a month at Yalta where he met with his Allies, Churchill, and Roosevelt. While at Yalta, Stalin made it a point to repeat previous Russian demands of wanting over $10 billion dollars in compensation for the damage his country had suffered during the Nazi invasion. Unfortunately, Churchill and Roosevelt argued amongst themselves and could not come to an agreement. Hours past, then days, with no response. Stalin was infuriated. Just before the conference was to conclude, Churchill and Roosevelt both reconvened to inform Stalin that they would turn down Stalin's request.

Stalin was no fool. He expected as much. Nevertheless, he was only acting on a grand stage. He would obtain everything he wanted and more. Even if he chose to *liberate* it. In the weeks prior to attending the Yalta conference, he established a secret "Special Committee on Germany." The Special

Committee would be responsible for confiscating valuables in the Soviet occupied territories. Stalin demanded everything of value, from entire factories to rail yards be dismantled and transported from Germany to the Soviet Union. He also required compensation for the destruction of Soviet Museums in the form of equivalent art works from enemy collections. He soon ordered all state ministries to send out "Trophy Brigades" to select suitable goods, and deliver them back to the Soviet Union.

Soon more than a hundred Trophy Brigades were formed, all dispatched to Germany, Poland, Hungary, and Czechoslovakia.

Their mission: *to steal whatever they could.*

LONG BURIED SECRETS

CHAPTER 6

23 April 1945: Berlin

Western Allied forces had already crossed the Rhine River, capturing hundreds of thousands of troops from Germany's Army Group B. Meanwhile, in the east, the Red Army had entered Austria, Hungary, Czechoslovakia, Poland, and Germany.

In the air war, strategic bombing campaigns by Allied aircraft continued to pound German territory, sometimes destroying entire cities in a single night.

There was no doubt who owned the skies over Germany.

Now Russian forces had entered Berlin proper. American, British, French, and Canadian forces were just 50 miles to the west with nothing in-between to stop them.

The Allies were concentrating their forces on Berlin. Between Russian nonstop artillery barrages from the 1st

Belorussian Front armies, and daily attacks by British & American bombers, the city was in a constant state of attack.

No one, or thing, was safe.

It was time for the rats to leave a dying ship.

HITLER ORDERED THE REMAINING valuables stored in the Reich's Bank vaults to be moved to the only place the Allies had not yet conquered, the southern German state of Bavaria. Most of the Reich's bank upper floors were destroyed during a British bombing raid back in February, but its vaults located five stories underground, lay untouched. Since the raid, SS guards were stationed 24/7 at every possible entrance to keep the curious at bay.

Hitler's order was the excuse Hildebrand Gurlitt had been patiently waiting for. For seven long years he bid his time for *just* this moment. Of course, along the way, he was careful enough to safeguard his activities to dodge any suspicion.

He had to, he had Hitler's ear when it came to art. Most of Hitler's cronies were jealous of Gurlitt's position, especially Himmler. Gurlitt was aware of Himmler's attempts to discredit him, but Hitler always curtailed any investigations into his activities. But there was incentive for Hitler to do so. If Gurlitt was exposed, Hitler's bloated Swiss Bank accounts could also be divulged.

He had what you might call a *Golden Pass*.

Nothing to look at, Gurlitt was a frail man in his late fifties. He was small in stature, on the losing end of five and a half feet; thick glasses perched on a sharp nose; balding to a point; what was left lay matted to his scalp. He and his mousey wife had a single child, Cornelius.

Now with Hitler's authority in hand, Gurlitt was one of the lucky ones and allotted three German army trucks to move the last of the "degenerate art" collection from Berlin to Bavaria. It consisted mostly of pieces he purposely held back. None of it on view since 1938.

As originally ordered by Hitler, starting in 1938, Gurlitt sold a majority of the "degenerate art" abroad to finance Germany's World War II effort. The sales had taken place mostly through auction houses in neutral Switzerland, raking in billions in sales. Of course, Gurlitt deposited *most* of the monies in Nazi Germany coffers and Hitler's secret Swiss account. But he also managed to keep a small tidy sum for himself, thinking of it as a fee for services rendered. After all, he had Hitler's backing. With no one to answer to or question his accounting, he was also able to secretly accumulate a large number of artworks for himself, including numerous masterpieces by Picasso, Matisse and Chagall to name a few. Some were hidden at his home in Munich, but most were secreted, unbeknownst to Hitler and his cronies, in the Reich's bank vaults.

GURLITT STOOD SCRATCHING his full white beard as his trucks were loaded. He expected they would soon depart, having heard reports the Russians would encircle the city in a matter of days. He resumed his count, clipboard in hand. One-by-one the precious works of art were loaded onto the trucks, minus their frames, rolled up and placed into heavy paper tubes for transport. In the distance, Russian artillery focused on the outer edge of the city, the city bracing for another ground attack that was sure to come.

The German Army Major in charge of the convoy approached Gurlitt. "That's the last of it," he said confidently before eyeing his watch. "Our pass provides us only another 40 minutes to exit the city. After that we are stuck with the rest of the rats."

"Then you better hurry, Major," he said. Gurlitt waited until the Major turned his attention to the other soldiers in the convoy before he approached his son, Cornelius, in the lead truck. "You know what you have to do," he said.

Cornelius, all of sixteen years old, nodded. Typical teenager: lanky, taller than his father, approaching five foot ten. Thin as a rail.

His father handed him an MP-40 submachine gun and two additional ammunition clips. In a low voice he said: "We will meet up at the place we agreed."

Again, his son merely nodded as he fidgeted about the trucks cabin. He knew what he had to do. His father and mothers survival lay in his hands.

The major took his place as driver in the lead truck beside Cornelius.

The major turned to Cornelius, pointing to the weapon he now held. "You might need that before we reach Bavaria."

If only he realized, thought Cornelius, merely nodding at the hardened soldier.

In a matter of minutes the three-army trucks sped off in a cloud of diesel smoke.

They would be one of the last convoys to escape Berlin.

GURLITT WATCHED AS THE trucks sped off. He wished he could have departed with them. Unfortunately, Hitler had other ideas, and had summoned him to his underground bunker one last time. Apparently, he wanted one last update on the status of the artwork. The thought had briefly crossed his mind to disregard Hitler's wishes and climb aboard with his son, but even in these last days Hitler's grasp on power was still firm. People were still terrified of Hitler's reach, Gurlitt included.

With his son safely embedded in the convoy, Gurlitt next had to worry about his wife, who, for the moment, was safe in Munich.

But for now, time was of the essence.

Gurlitt had to meet with Hitler as soon as possible and then be creative in finding an excuse to depart. Only then could he orchestrate his own escape from Berlin.

That, and he had a fortune to claim.

CHAPTER 7

23/24 April 1945: Berlin, Germany

The trucks having departed, Hildebrand Gurlitt quickly
returned to his apartment just off Potsdamer Platz, in order to
gather a few remaining items of personal interest. He also
wanted to purge his apartment of any documents that could
possibly link him to the paintings, burning them in his
fireplace. He wanted neither the Russians nor Americans to
find anything connecting him to Hitler's artwork. Satisfied he
had indeed sanitized his apartment, he departed for his 10PM
meeting with Hitler.

After several hours dodging artillery fire, he soon found
himself face-to-face with Hitler in his underground bunker.
Gurlitt informed Hitler of the paintings departure on a three-
army truck convoy to Munich. Normally a six-hour drive on
the Autobahn, but with certain sections already in Allied
hands, and bridges destroyed, additional time would be
required. Gurlitt explained to Hitler that the paintings should

reach their destination within a week. Possibly ten days. Hitler brushed aside references to the Autobahn being in Allied control. He quickly shifted his train of thought, suddenly expressing a desire to Gurlitt that the paintings be used to fund the next Reich. *The Fourth Reich.* Gurlitt alone could help finance, through the sale of the paintings, the next war. Gurlitt knew better than to contest and just allowed Hitler to continue his rant. Of course, Gurlitt had no intention of allowing the paintings out of his control. Hitler spoke for hour or so, laying out specific details, everything from whom to contact, to how the sale was to take place. Abruptly he stopped, thanked him for his service, and ordered him to escape the Russian onslaught. He then called in his personal secretary, Traudl Junge, into the room asking her to type up a document that would provide Gurlitt with unrestricted travel from Berlin to Munich. Gurlitt would be allowed to use Hitler's authority to commandeer any mode of transport he saw fit.

This in a time when roving bands of SS soldiers were shooting or hanging deserters in the streets of Berlin, above the very bunker they occupied.

Hitler performed a cursory view of the document before signing it, handing it to Gurlitt. "Be on your way before you become trapped like myself in this retched city."

GURLITT WAS LUCKY ENOUGH to link up with a small band of soldiers and civilians also looking to escape the Russian onslaught as their noose tightened around Berlin. After several days of constantly prodding the Russian defenses for a weakness, they located one in a nighttime swim across the Spree River. Once on the other side of the river, he was able to avoid capture and escape into the night.

He was alive.

And rich beyond his wildest dreams.

LONG BURIED SECRETS

CHAPTER 8

April 26, 1945:
Three kilometers east of Cheb, Czechoslovakia;
Trophy Brigade Mishka

Russian Major Vasli Petrov, using a pair of binoculars, scanned the valley before him, eyeing the single road that led into the Czechoslovakian border village of Cheb. For three days and 125 kilometers, they pursued a three-truck German convoy that had escaped Berlin and known to be traveling on the same road that lay before him. With most of the roads from Berlin to Munich already cut off, the German Army convoy had no choice but to change its route with a dip into Czechoslovakia for 30 kilometers before they could reenter Germany. Unfortunately for Petrov and his Trophy Brigade, they had orders to halt at the German border due to an agreement reached between the American and Russian governments dividing the conquered territories.

Scanning from left to right, he was able to distinguish the town's church steeple from its historical clock tower. In front of the church, the main road divided into two additional routes heading toward either Munich or Prague. Using the church as a baseline, he surveyed the road to the right, following its winding path for several kilometers. Soon he was rewarded with the three-truck convoy he sought, now approaching the church.

"We have them now!" Petrov shouted. He turned to his subordinate, Lieutenant Sergey Kuznetsov. "Form up the men. We have to catch our rats before they cross the border."

Kuznetsov laughed as he saluted. Within minutes, the ten-man unit loaded up their two ZIS-5 4x2 Russian built trucks and were in hot pursuit. The ZIS-5 was one of the standard trucks of the Red Army. But its 68 horse power engine could only muster a top speed of 45 miles per hour. Luckily, it made up for the lack of speed with its large truck bed in the rear, able to accommodate up to 20 men.

That also left plenty of room for treasure.

CHAPTER 9

April 26, 1945:
Cheb, Czechoslovakia
Trophy Brigade Mishka

Major Vasli Petrov sought to use surprise to his advantage and capture all three vehicles before they could possibly flee into Germany. They now approached the same village church where earlier he noticed the crossroads lay at its base. He realized the Germans would have to pass by this same point. Using his binoculars, he scanned the surrounding area. He looked for movement. Any movement at all. He then noticed three German trucks parked on a field of some sort, possibly a soccer pitch. Petrov had a clear view of an American soldier interrogating a German civilian. There appeared to be a small group of American soldiers gathered around them.

Petrov signaled for his column to continue. He wasn't about to have the Americans capture what was rightfully his, or more correctly, *Mother Russia's*.

CHAPTER 10

April 26, 1945: Cheb, Czechoslovakia

Sergeant Mike Dolan of Patton's Third Army led his nine-man patrol into the small Czech border town of Cheb, and there-bye exceeded his orders. His commanding officer specifically ordered him to not step foot into Czechoslovakia. The Russians were already in the area and he was under strict orders to only scout the area to the German border for any remaining German soldiers. *Do not put your men into any unnecessary danger* were his orders.

So much for orders. Dolan was looking for souvenirs. Silver dinnerware, gold jewelry, anything of value that he could take back home to Philadelphia when the war ended. Dolan was not going back as a broke, discharged soldier. That seemed to be the general theme of his unit. It was the same since they first entered Germany. In town after town they liberated, they wanted the spoils of war. Of course it was illegal to loot. Gen. Dwight D. Eisenhower had issued strict directives forbidding such thefts.

But Dolan and his *gang* had no use for Eisenhower's directive. Over the course of the previous three weeks they already confiscated enough gold, silver heirlooms, diamonds, rubies and emeralds to fill a shoe box. Using some of his pre-war contacts when he was a numbers runner for the Philly Mob, they managed to ship most of it back to a front business owned by Dolan's old bosses.

As they approached the outskirts of town, Dolan noticed three German trucks on what appeared to be the town's soccer field. Dead German soldiers lay scattered about the trucks.

Dolan indicated for two of his more experienced men to take up positions on the opposite side of the trucks. "Cover me," he said to those behind him as he advanced to the lead truck, his .45 caliber at the ready. Nobody was in the truck's cab. Dolan then approached the truck's rear, easing back the canvas flap with his weapon. He saw wood crates piled on top of each other.

Dolan turned to one of his men. "Jenson, check the other trucks."

After 30 seconds he had his answer: nothing but wooden crates.

"Sarge," yelled another one of men, a Private Lincoln. "I just found one of the German soldiers from the convoy," him dragging a young German boy behind him, the boy's overcoat two sizes too big for him. He tossed the boy down in front of Dolan.

Dolan stared at the boy, thinking he was no more than sixteen or seventeen. "You speak English?" he inquired.

The boy stood up, standing five foot ten, brushing dirt from his jacket. When he finished he nodded. "Yes, of course I do. I thought you were Russian soldiers," he replied in a near perfect English. "I could not let the Russians have what's in the trucks. Never deal with barbarians my father would say." The boy paused, wanting to know what type of soldiers he was dealing with before he provided them with any additional details.

"What happened here?" said Dolan, pointing to the dead German soldiers scattered about.

The young boy looked at him innocently enough before replying: "I killed them."

"You killed them?" Dolan laughed, turning back to his men, then to the boy. "Okay, two questions for you kid. What do you have in the trucks that is so valuable? And why did you have to kill everybody?" Dolan pointed back to the trucks, then to the dead Germans.

The boy viewed each man in Dolan's squad as they assembled around him, his gaze lacking any fear. "What if I told you my cargo is so valuable you would never have to work another day in your life?"

The soldiers started speaking excitedly amongst themselves. "Gold," shouted a young private. "Cash," shouted another before Dolan raised his arms to quiet them. "Why don't we let our new friend tell us," he said before turning to the young German boy.

The boy knew he would survive the day if he could just string them along, especially the Sergeant. He was the key. "What if I told you its more valuable than gold, or silver?"

"I'll take diamonds," shouted another soldier.

Dolan raised his arms once more before fixing a steady gaze on the boy. "Who or what is to stop us from killing you and taking what we want."

The boy shook his head. "I don't think you will. You look too smart to do that. However, if you want to die in a horrific explosion that destroys your newfound wealth, than be my guest. Only I know how to deactivate the explosives hidden in each of the trucks."

Dolans men started to back away from the trucks.

Dolan grinned. "I like this kid," he said. Maybe we can do a deal? You and me?" He pointed once again to the dead German soldiers. "I like your style."

The boy knew he had to make a deal. They had him outnumbered. They could just shoot him and take their chances with the cargo. He eagerly nodded. "How about we each get a percentage. You, Sergeant, will get twenty percent? Does that sound fair?"

Dolan was finished toying. "Okay kid, what's in the trucks that was worth killing your fellow people?"

The boy had a gut feeling about the Sergeant. In addition, he had a captive audience as he looked from soldier to soldier, each looking as if they had already spent their newfound monies. "Paintings, gentlemen. But not just any paintings. These are from Adolf Hitler's private collection. Only the best of the best."

"How much are they worth?" asked one of the soldiers.

"In your American dollars, possibly around $200 million. Maybe more. It depends on who the buyers are."

Whistles and catcalls soon ripped through the air.

Dolan had other notions. He would never have to work another day in his life if he played his cards right. His head swirled with ideas. But first things first. "All right, gentlemen, line up," he ordered his men. When he noticed them taking their time he lost his patience. "Now!" he screamed.

Each of them scrambled to line up, at arm's length. "All right boys, lose the weapons," he ordered, pointing his M-1 carbine at the group. They looked at him as if he were mad.

"But Sarge," one of them stammered.

Dolan wasted no time in shooting the man in his midsection, dropping him like a sack of potatoes.

"I said weapons on the ground! Now!" he screamed once more.

"You'll get hanged for this," said Corporal Slade. He motioned for the rest of the men to drop their weapons. They all complied.

Dolan smiled. "You'll need witnesses for that."

"You bastard!" said Slade, now realizing the predicament they were in. "Your own men?"

Dolan spoke to his new German partner. "Go and gather the weapons."

The boy performed as ordered, slinging each rifle over his shoulder before returning, dumping them beside Dolan.

"Now pick up one of the weapons for yourself."

The boy hesitated before he chose his MP-40. He expertly inventoried his bullets. Satisfied, he pointed the weapon at the soldiers.

"Anyone moves you shoot them!"

The boy looked first to him, then the soldiers. "You want me to shoot your own men?"

Dolan smiled at him. "You're right. Everybody on the ground. Slade was the first to protest. "What the hell are you doing, Dolan?" he said. "I'm not laying on the ground. Have you gone mad?"

Dolan didn't hesitate, quickly raising his M-1 and shooting him in the head. The rest of the men laid down without further protest.

MAJOR PETROV HALTED HIS little convoy. If his assumptions were correct, they were only a hundred meters or so from the Americans on the soccer pitch. He turned to his second in command: "Lieutenant Kuznetsov, I want our two trucks to burst from the woods before the Americans have time to react. We will take up a side-by-side position as we exit the woods." The Lieutenant walked over to the second truck to relay the Major's plan.

"And no unnecessary shooting," yelled the Major loud enough so all could hear.

DOLAN BEHELD HIS new partner. "How old are you, kid? And what's your name? I don't feel like calling you kid or boy all of the time."

The boy looked at him sheepishly. "Sixteen," was his reply. "And my name is Cornelius Gurlitt. My father is Hildebrand Gurlitt, Hitler's art dealer. He is the person ultimately responsible for devising this little robbery."

"Well, Cornelius, between you, me and your father, we are about to become three of the richest SOB's in the European Theater."

He barely had the words out of his mouth when Major Petrov's trucks burst out of the woods forming up side-by-side as instructed.

Dolan appeared stunned for a moment or two, initially thinking they were Germans before noticing the big red star insignia on the truck's hood and cab doors.

The Russian trucks screeched to a halt not more than 10 meters from where Dolan stood.

The Russians exited their trucks cradling their PPS43 submachine guns, pointing them in the direction of Dolan and Cornelius.

"I thought we were allies," said Dolan.

Petrov smiled at Dolan. "Until we find out who is who, my men will, shall we say, *keep the peace.*" He walked over to Dolan, extending his hand in greeting. "I am Major Vasli Petrov." Dolan, at 5 foot 10, was forced to look up at the 6 foot 5 Petrov.

"Hell of a grip you have there, buddy."

Petrov ignored him as he pointed over to the line of Russian soldiers. "And my second in command, Lieutenant Kuznetsov." Kuznetsov dipped his head in greeting.

Dolan nodded to Kuznetsov before turning his attention back to Petrov. "Sergeant Mike Dolan of Patton's Third Army. And the young lad here is Cornelius Gurlitt."

Petrov pointed to where Dolan's men lay on the ground. "A revolt of some sort."

"You could say that," Dolan replied.

One of Dolan's men shouted aloud that Dolan was trying to steal valuable paintings.

Dolan would have none of it. "Either you shut-up or you'll meet the same fate as Slade," was his reply.

The mention of paintings caught the attention of Petrov. "Please let him speak," he said.

Dolan shook his head. "No way," he replied. "He is my prisoner."

Petrov simply nodded to his men, the sound of bullets being chambered was the response.

Dolan could see they were outnumbered. "Alright, get up," he said to the soldier. "But the rest of you rats stay down on the ground."

"Come over here," said Petrov to the soldier. The soldier eyed Dolan as he walked over to the Russian. "What did you say about paintings?"

"Are you going to protect me from Dolan? He asked. "I think he wants to kill us all for what's on the trucks."

Petrov nodded. "Of course I will. We are Allies aren't we?"

The soldier felt emboldened. "These three trucks," he said, pointing to the German vehicles, "Are loaded with Hitler's paintings. Ones from his personal collection. The German kid told us."

Petrov smiled at the soldier, indicating for him to go back over to his previous position on the ground. "Don't worry you will be safe," he assured him. The soldier had a nervous scowl upon his face.

Petrov then strode over to Cornelius, halting when he stood toe-to-toe with the 5 foot 10 inch teenager, looking down at him. He removed the MP-40 from his hands and tossed it to the ground. He patted the boy on the head to intimidate him. "Is what he said true? These trucks are all loaded with Hitler's paintings? I would hope to think so because my men and I have been chasing your little convoy from just south of Berlin."

Cornelius looked to Dolan for help before realizing none was coming. "Yes, sir," he stammered. "They are from his personal collection. Very valuable. Extremely valuable."

That's exactly what he wanted to hear, confirmation that they had located something big. Especially if they were Hitler's personnel paintings. Petrov patted the boy on his head once more. "It's okay. You are safe. No one will hurt you. You may grab your weapon."

For a second or two Cornelius actually thought it may have been a trick, having heard rumors of Russians acting friendly one minute only to gun you down in the next. He looked to Dolan for help. Dolan tapped his own weapon before pointing to Cornelius's weapon.

Cornelius took Dolan's tap to mean he was backing him up if the Russian tried anything. He nodded in thanks before bending down to pick up his weapon.

"See, I mean you no harm," said Petrov to Cornelius. Petrov then looked at Dolan, winking once, before turning back to face his men. "Search each of the Americans for weapons. You also, Lieutenant Kuznetsov. Go, search them."

Dolan looked to be in shock for a moment. *He's going to kill us,* he thought to himself. *Or maybe...*

"Leave the American Sergeant alone. He can keep his weapon."

Relief suddenly flooded over Dolan, if temporarily. *But what is he up to?*

Petrov nodded to Dolan, then Cornelius. Dolan watched as Petrov slipped his safety off his weapon. Dolan followed suit, then Cornelius.

Petrov waited until all but two of his men were standing atop an American soldier, busy rummaging through their pockets, the other two of his men stood guard over the rest. He knew it was now or never. Petrov saw his opportunity as he pulled his submachine gun up and laid a quick burst into the two soldiers standing guard, they quickly fell to the ground, dead. He discharged the reminder of his weapons bullets into his soldiers searching the Americans for weapons; each fell to the ground as if they were a bag of cement, dead.

Dolan had no time to react. He stood there dumfounded as the Russian major reloaded. "What the hell are you doing?" he shouted. "You just shot and killed all of your men."

"Wasn't that the reason you already had your men laying on the ground?" he replied. "Weren't you and this boy about to do the same? To steal the paintings and divide the riches amongst the two of you?"

Dolan liked this guy. He was a man after his own tastes. Waiting for just the right opportunity, and then taking it all. "I guess you can say that," he stammered.

When the remaining American soldiers heard what was to be their fate they attempted to rise up in unison. Dolan, Cornelius, and Petrov answered them with a quick burst from their weapons. After several seconds, all were dead. Petrov took it upon himself to make sure. He walked amongst the bodies, making sure each was indeed dead.

Dolan turned to Cornelius and in a low voice said: "I guess this isn't exactly what you had planned?"

Cornelius looked at all of the dead soldiers lying about them. "No, not exactly," he stammered. "The German soldiers I killed were all S/S. They deserved to die." He then pointed over to the Americans and Russians, their bodies intertwined. "But what about all of them?"

Dolan nodded. "Well, speaking for the integrity of the men in my unit, they would have robbed their own mothers if it meant the kind of money we are talking about. So don't feel bad for them." In a low voice he continued. "And as far as the Russians, well, we might be fighting them all soon enough."

"You really think so?" he replied in a low voice not meant for Petrov to overhear. "I also didn't plan on a Russian joining our little group."

Petrov overheard what Cornelius had said. He stepped around several bodies as he walked over to where the boy stood. He wasted no time getting right to his point. "I am a capitalist at heart my young friend," he replied. Petrov then laid both his pistol and submachine gun on the ground, kicking them aside. "I mean no harm to either of you. I am but a poor soldier who has no desire to return home as a poor peasant. All I want is an equal share. Nothing more, nothing less. So, are we done bickering?"

Cornelius looked to Dolan, they both nodded.

Petrov could see everything was indeed in the past and continued. "Good. Then I think we have to do something with the bodies and then divide the paintings."

Dolan had a wide smile on his face. "I can see we are going to be lifelong business partners my new friend."

LONG BURIED SECRETS

CHAPTER 11

Present Day
Clyde's Auto body Shop
Edgemont, Pennsylvania (15 miles west of Philadelphia)

Eian sat facing Mike Dolan Jr. Behind Dolan he noticed a picture on the wall of a man in uniform. He noticed Dolan and the man looked exactly alike. Dolan followed Eian's gaze. "That's my old man," he said with a trace of pride. "It's his picture from WWII. He's also the reason I set this little game of mine in motion."

The last thing Eian wanted was to hear one of Dolan's stories. It had been a good eight hours since he had placed a call to his friend Jim Dieter for help. Eian held up his hands for Dolan to see the cuffs around his wrists. "Do you think I can get these removed? It's not like I'm going anywhere."

Dolan motioned to one of his men to remove the handcuffs from Eian's wrists. "So you think your friend will show?"

"For a friend in need? Never known him not too."

"Yeah, but will he still consider you a friend after this little stunt you pulled?"

"My losing at cards was no little stunt, Dolan." He paused a few seconds to look around the room. "I just had a bad run of luck."

Dolan laughed aloud. "Some bad run of luck. You owe me a few hundred grand. If I weren't such a nice guy, you'd be dead."

Just as the words finished leaving his mouth Jim Dieter confidently saunters in. "Well, well, if it isn't Mike Dolan," Jim says sarcastically. His wife Nora strides in behind him.

Dolan points to Nora. "I see you brought back-up."

Nora smiled. "It's all he needs for your type."

Dolan's two goons smirked for a few seconds until they saw the expression on their boss's face. Then they thought better and reached for their guns in the small of their backs, bringing them to bear on Jim and Nora.

Dolan directed his goons to put their weapons away. "We are all friends here," he said. He then indicated for Jim and Nora to sit down on two faux leather chairs against a wall lined with ceramic gas station globes of yesteryear. "It's been a few years, James Dieter. I think the last time we had dealings…"

Jim cut him off. "It was when you tried to have my father arrested for illegal parking," he replied angrily.

"That's right. He dared to park his car in my reserved spot in front of one of my finer restaurants. Silly man."

"It was a spot with a meter. There was no sign indicating anyone *owned* the spot." Jim paused for several seconds to compose himself before turning to Nora. "He has the cops on his payroll along with everyone else. So he called the local precinct and told them he wanted somebody taught a lesson. That somebody happened to be my father. He was down here visiting friends during his cancer treatments and took them to dinner. This pig had him arrested in the restaurant, in front of his friends."

"No hard feelings, Jim," said Dolan, his voice lacking any empathy. "How is your old man?"

"He died soon after his last visit."

"Sorry to hear that," replied Dolan, again lacking any empathy.

Nora had had enough. "You bastard! She yelled as she rose from her chair, coiling up her fingers into a fist. Dolan laughed at her as she took a swing at him, Dolan ducking the punch. She then kicked him in the shin, causing him to let out a curse as he fell to the ground in pain. Nora then kicked him in the ribs while he lay on the ground. "Take that you little man."

Jim jumped up to restrain her as Dolan's two goons approached.

Dolan waved them off. "Leave her alone," he said. "I deserved it." He then smiled at Jim. "You have a little fighter here. I like that. Beauty and brawn. Might come in handy where we are going."

"So you want to tell us what's going on?" replied Jim. "You obviously didn't invite us here so my wife could kick the crap out of you."

Dolan rose from his position on the floor, his shin still bothering him. "You're right. I needed a reason to get you up here from Florida, and Eian was that reason. I knew he would come to you for help. And I knew you wouldn't come if I had asked." He pointed back to the faux leather chairs. "Now I have a little story for you to hear. It's a long but potentially very lucrative story. You'll want to sit back down to enjoy this one."

Jim turned to Nora, she provided him with her *let's get this over with look* as she took a seat, followed by Jim.

Dolan waited until he had Jim and Nora's complete attention. "This is good. Now that we are all comfortable I can get on with my story. May I call you Jim and Nora?"

Jim and Nora looked at each other and just smiled, before turning back to Dolan. Nora cleared her throat as she spoke for the two of them: "I don't give a flying..," she said before stopping, correcting herself, "Just get on with your story so we all can get the hell out of here."

Jim smiled at his wife's response. "She is such an eloquent speaker. Wouldn't you agree, Dolan?"

Dolan was not use to people speaking to him in such a tone. And he sure didn't appreciate Nora kicking him in the shin and chest. He still had a bit of revenge on his mind as he casually strolled over to where Nora sat, albeit with a slight limp. "You think with your money, and that stupid Pulitzer Prize that you are better than people like me? Well think again, little fish." He slapped her across the face with the back of his hand, Nora falling hard to the floor.

Jim swiftly jumped up from his chair before striking Dolan in his gut, then with a one two combination to his head. Dolan went down hard. His two goons did not have time to react as they fumbled for their weapons, now leveled at Jim. Jim eyed them as he assisted his wife up from the floor.

"I didn't think a mobster like you had to hit a woman for his courage," he spat out at Dolan.

One of Dolan's goons helped Dolan to his feet. He brushed himself off, blood trickling down from his nose. "I apologize to you and your wife," he said. "I lost my temper. It won't happen again." He indicted for one of his goons to get Nora some ice. "I just want you two to listen to a story. Then we can all get on with our lives. Fair enough?"

The goon brought some ice wrapped in a towel. "Here you are, miss."

She thanked him before eying Dolan with suspicion. The bruise on the side of her face spoke volumes about the person that stood in front of her. "Let's just get this nightmare over with."

"Ah, but it's just beginning, my dear," Dolan replied.

"Its just beginning."

LONG BURIED SECRETS

CHAPTER 12

May, 5, 1945: Cheb, Czechoslovakia

Petrov, Dolan, and Cornelius sat around a small fire they had used to cook dinner. Potluck stew. Each had something from their rations to toss in to the pot: Petrov, potatoes; Cornelius, carrots and onions; Dolan, dried beef. Dinner now finished, Petrov passed around a bottle of Vodka. It was the end of a long day, a day that had started with them positioning the bodies where it looked as if a firefight had broken out between the Germans, Americans, and Russians. A firefight where everyone lost. Petrov and Dolan would vouch for each other's story. Cornelius, if he was to be believed, would vouch for both Petrov and Dolan. They thought it was more logical than burying the bodies and trying to cover up what had transpired. At least this version of the story sounded credible.

Now all they had to do was hide the paintings.

For this, Petrov and Dolan would require Cornelius' assistance.

Dolan passed the bottle back to Petrov before turning to Cornelius. "So your father told you he wanted the convoy to pass through this town where we now sit because fuel would be prepositioned here to refill the trucks in order to make it to your destination in Bavaria?"

Cornelius nodded.

He continued. "So you knew the convoy would have to loop into Czechoslovakia for a few miles before returning to roads leading into Germany?"

Cornelius once again nodded.

Dolan continued. "And when all of the drivers and passengers were out of trucks relieving themselves on the soccer field you just shot them where they stood.

Cornelius grinned. "I unslung my MP-40 and shot them in the backs like my father said too. They were all SS soldiers. Germany's worst. They got what they deserved."

"Yours are made out of steel, my friend!" Dolan said aloud. "You are one crazy son of a bitch!"

Petrov handed the bottle to Cornelius. "Drink a toast to those SS going to where they belong."

Cornelius took a long swig. In a second or two, his face became beet red and he started to cough.

Petrov and Dolan laughed aloud; Petrov slapped Cornelius on the back. "Is this your first-time drinking?" he asked.

Cornelius coughed once more. His voice was a bit hoarse as he replied: "Schnapps and some beer I stole from my father's private supply. Never hard liquor like your Vodka."

"Well my boy," said Dolan, "with the money we get from selling these paintings, you can buy all of the beer and schnapps you want. Hell, you can even buy the brewery where they make it." He passed around an open pack of Lucky Strikes. Cornelius declined. Petrov removed one from the pack and placed the rest into his tunic pocket.

"Sure, keep the pack," said Dolan sarcastically. He waited several minutes as Petrov lit his cigarette and apparently enjoyed the taste.

Cornelius had another sip of vodka. He looked to be acquiring a taste for the Russian's drink of choice.

Dolan realized the time was right. "Okay, since we are all a bunch of SOB's. I mean we all killed our own people for what is in the trucks, right? We all have the same drive. The same quest. None of us wants to be poor when this war is over. Am I right?"

Each nodded. "Keep going," said Petrov, "You are, as you Americans so fondly say, *on a roll.*"

"Okay," he continued. "Now how do we smuggle the paintings out of here and how do we sell them on the open market?"

Cornelius giggled as he passed the Vodka bottle back to Petrov. "My father owns a piece of property only ten kilometers from here, in Germany. It is very isolated and has its own mineshaft. It used to be a silver mine until the turn of the century when the silver ran out. That is where my father told me to store the paintings. And that is the direction I was heading when you gentlemen came upon me. Originally I was planning to drive one truck and store its contents in the mine. Possibly return for a second truck if time allowed. But now with the three of us, we can drive all three trucks to my father's mine and split our haul four ways."

Petrov and Dolan both eyed each other. They laughed aloud, thinking Cornelius was getting tipsy. "You mean three ways, my little friend, not four ways," said Petrov.

"No," Cornelius replied, "We have to include my father. He was the one who orchestrated this whole operation. He just has to make it out of Berlin before the Russians overrun the city." He looked sheepishly at Petrov. "No harm meant by what I said."

"No offense taken," Petrov replied. "Some of my people can be very nasty." He smiled at his own response.

Dolan passed the bottle back to Cornelius. "I forgot your father's name. What is it again?" asked Dolan.

"Hildebrand Gurlitt, Hitler's art dealer," he replied. "He is, or was, very famous in the art world. Not that he can paint or anything like that but he understands art and the art world. This along with the value of paintings makes him a very valuable commodity. Best of all, my father also has many connections in Switzerland. Auction Houses mostly. Connections that have enabled my mother and I to live very comfortably."

Petrov turned to look at the boy more closely than before. "You must be joking?" he said. "Hildebrand Gurlitt is your father?"

"So you have heard of him?"

Petrov knew from his Trophy Brigade briefings before he departed the Soviet Union that Hildebrand Gurlitt was in Hitler's inner circle. He was one of the top guys. Petrov was instructed by his boss before he left the Soviet Union, *follow him and you will find where the treasure is hidden.*

"Yes, I have heard of your father," Petrov replied. "And none of it was good. But how do we know you are not pulling our leg trying to save your skin by associating yourself with a well-known thief."

The boy shook his head. "No," he replied, "I am not lying. All of my proof is in the trucks."

Petrov leaned into Dolan, a wide smile on his face. In a low voice he said, "If what the boy says is true, we are not talking about a million or two in those trucks. *We are talking potentially hundreds of millions.*"

Dolan had already realized their importance. His sharp criminal mind had already derived a conclusion. He realized the Nazi's essentially had no fuel left. And what precious little fuel they did have was only doled out for high value items or to the major players. So whatever was in the trucks had to be worth some serious money. *A lot of money*. But he played along with his new business partner. "I have the whole American army on my heels. I'm assuming you likewise have the whole Russian army on your tail. So if we don't want to lose our newfound wealth we better get cracking before they arrive."

They pushed some dirt onto their fire. Within seconds, it was extinguished.

"Lead the way," said Dolan to Cornelius.

Cornelius jumped up into the first truck, Petrov in the second, Dolan followed up in the third. They all started up the trucks in unison before moving off slowly into the night.

LONG BURIED SECRETS

CHAPTER 13

May, 5, 1945: Preisdorf, Germany

Dawn was approaching as they neared the small German town of Preisdorf, a good 20 kilometers from their previous location in Cheb, Czechoslovakia. Cornelius alone knew the location of his father's property. Dolan and Petrov had no choice but to trust the young boy as they navigated what looked like, at times, *cow paths*. The 20 kilometer drive should have taken only half an hour to drive under normal circumstances but along the way they had managed to avoid known American army checkpoints courtesy of Dolan, and circumvented the main roads if they could.

Now approaching their third hour of driving, they finally passed through Preisdorf. They viewed white bed sheets hung from second story windows of homes in surrender, hoping to avoid the wrath of American soldiers operating in the area. Two kilometers west of Preisdorf, Cornelius steered his truck onto a dirt track that led to his father's property. After a minute or two of vigilant driving, they reached the entrance of the mineshaft. A thick wooden door announced its opening. Following Cornelius' lead, they each backed their vehicle up to the mine's entrance, parking side-by-side.

Time was of the essence.

Dolan hopped down and immediately took charge. "I need you to disable the explosives on the truck," he ordered Cornelius. "Then we can get moving."

Cornelius grinned at him. "There are no explosives," he replied. "I lied. I thought you would have killed me before hearing me out. At the time, I felt I had no choice."

Dolan laughed aloud. "I said it before, I like this kid."

Petrov clapped his hands together in anticipation. He walked to the rear of his truck and opened the trucks canvas flap. "Let's get busy unloading these paintings. The last thing we need is to draw attention to ourselves. Especially myself. A Russian soldier in German territory that is now under American administration."

AFTER TWO HOURS, each of the truck's precious cargo had been unloaded and stored within the confines of the mine. The thick wooden door at the mine's entrance was padlocked and camouflaged with freshly cut tree branches. For added security, Dolan placed two live hand grenades, minus their pull pins, under the branches. Anyone moving the branches and unaware of the grenades location would be dead within seconds.

With the aid of daylight, retracing their route was much easier, only taking an hour and a half versus the previous three. Once back in Cheb, Czechoslovakia, they arranged the trucks in their original spots. They then set fire to the trucks to erase any evidence of their wrongdoing.

Satisfied with the arrangement of the trucks and dead soldiers, they rested and conferred under a tall elm tree. They each agreed to meet when the war was over, knowing it could only last only another week or two.

Only then would they decide how to deal with their newfound treasure.

And if they could trust one another.

THEY HAD AN ADDITIONAL partner to deal with, Cornelius' father, Hildebrand Gurlitt. After all, Hildebrand was the architect of the heist. Now all he had to do was escape out of a war-torn Berlin. Then escape the clutches of the SS, Russian and American Armies.

And stay alive.

LONG BURIED SECRETS

CHAPTER 14

May 8th 1945: Cheb, Czechoslovakia

A convoy of six American army deuce and half's, each with a white star emblazoned boldly on its hood, pulled up to the town's sole soccer field. Soon they drove onto the field, forming up side-by-side as the drivers maneuvered to a spot where a mass of bodies lay. The bodies were allegedly the result of one of the wars only deadly American, German, and Russian encounters.

Sergeant Mike Dolan of Patton's Third Army jumped out of the lead vehicle and was soon directing the Army Investigative Unit over to the battle scene.

In front of them were the remains of three German Army vehicles, each looking as though they had been destroyed during the firefight. Beside the trucks lay bodies of the soldiers.

Opposite them stood their Russian counterparts. Major Vasli Petrov nodded to Dolan as they shook hands. Behind him were three, Russian Army ZIS-5 4x2 trucks, their drivers each standing at attention beside their respective vehicles.

After introductions, as agreed, an American second lieutenant took charge and started interviewing the Russian Major; another second lieutenant took picture after picture of the bodies.

Dolan had already provided his side of the story, now it was up to the Russian major to collaborate.

Of course, they each had already rehearsed their stories.

He and the Russian major were evidently the sole survivors.

Within the hour, each of the lieutenants had all the information they required.

The Americans had wisely brought along a two-man Graves Registration Unit with them. They reverently loaded each of the American bodies into the rear of one of their two trucks. An Army Private stood off to the side, gathering information from each of the dead soldiers' dog tags and annotating it on a clipboard.

The Russians weren't as respectful as they loaded their dead into one of the trucks, tossing each soldier onto the trucks floor, body on top of body.

The Americans then moved the German bodies to the edge of the field where they were placed side-by-side, US Army-issued blankets covering their faces. Hopefully, some of the locals would take the time to bury their own. If not, when the area was taken over by the respective military governors, they would eventually be buried.

CHAPTER 15

May 1945
American Occupation Zone, Germany

Major Vasli Petrov wasted no time contacting Dolan, only days after the independent board cleared them of any wrongdoing in the Russian, German, and American shooting. The shootings were deemed accidental. Now Petrov wanted his cut. With the war now over, he was being transferred back to the Soviet Union and obviously did not trust his new partners to uphold their end of the bargain.

As agreed, they met several days later on the German side of the German - Czechoslovakian border in a recently reopened pub. It was a pub in name alone. It still had a large gaping hole in the wall where a tank shell blasted its way through only weeks earlier. The roof had enough holes in it to warrant ten metal pots placed strategically about to catch the rainwater that leaked through. Four wooden stools sat empty at the bar. To the left, three wooden tables sat empty by a large hole where a window had been blown out. For the foreseeable future, the pub could only offer watered-down beer. In these difficult times, hard liquor was still tough to come by. *Well, just about everything was tough to come by.*

The pub's sole customer for the moment was Dolan nursing a beer. He purposely arrived early to scout the location just in case the Russian was trying to set him up. Petrov soon arrived carrying two bottles of vodka. He approached the bartender first, handing him one of the bottles. "A gift from the Russian people to you. Feel free to serve it to your customers," he said joyously.

The bartender nodded his thanks as he looked around at his empty bar.

Obviously in a very good mood, Petrov sat down with Dolan. He placed the bottle between the two of them. He took Dolan's full glass of beer and dumped it on the earthen floor. "This is better for you," he stammered, obviously drunk. He signaled the bartender for another glass. They being his only customers, the glass came without delay.

"What the hell are you doing?" said Dolan.

"Getting drunk, my American friend. And you?"

Dolan could see he was going to have his hands full.

THE BOTTLE EMPTY, they moved on to the cheap, watered down German beer. For two hours Dolan tried to talk him out of taking his share, but Petrov still insisted he receive his cut before he was transferred home.

"You will never get the paintings through your army checkpoints," Dolan warned him adamantly. "Your people are on the lookout for theft. They think everything belongs to the Government of the Soviet Union. You of all people should realize this. You would be considered just another common thief."

Petrov fumbled through his tunic before he found what he was looking for, holding up his orders and a gold embossed pass for Dolan to see. "These two pieces of paper say otherwise. They will allow me to proceed through all checkpoints unmolested."

He handed them to Dolan who eyed them skeptically. "How in the hell do I know what they say?" He said. "I can't read Russian."

Petrov smiled. "They say I am to be provided free passage through all Army checkpoints. The soldier in possession of this pass is working directly for Comrade Stalin."

Petrov signaled the bartender for another round of beer. Then he turned his attention back to Dolan. "I will be safe, my friend," he said. "You do not have to worry about Petrov."

"Okay, say you are able to get through all of the checkpoints. What will you do with the paintings in the Ukraine? They would nail you in a New York minute if you tried to sell them. And who would you sell them too? You live in a communist country. Nobody has money. You would be better off keeping your share with us."

"I will find buyers," replied Petrov confidently. "Not everyone is poor."

"Don't take this the wrong way but in the West we can find buyers in Switzerland, or even the United States. People who are looking for art. Not just any type of art mind you but exactly what we have to sell. In addition, the buyers are people who can keep a secret for a discounted price on a painting or two. They know where the paintings are from, and they still don't care."

Petrov shook his head. "I have made up my mind. I want my share or nobody will profit."

Dolan paused for several seconds. "Are you threatening me?"

"You can take it any way you want, just give me my share and we all walk away happy."

Dolan could see what Petrov planned to do. If they refused and held onto his share of artwork for a later sale, he would report them to the Allied High Commission. They would soon investigate and discover their stash of paintings. Petrov would be a hero.

Albeit, a poor hero.

DOLAN HAD NO CHOICE AND SOON contacted Cornelius. He explained the situation. Within a matter of days, the three of them had managed to load a Russian Army ZIS-5 truck with Petrov's share.

"I think you are making a big mistake, my Russian friend," said Dolan. "I would think twice if I were you. We can make countless American dollars or Swiss Francs from these paintings. We can even have your cut placed into a secret Swiss account that you could access anytime you want. It would all be on the sly. Nobody would be able to connect you to the artwork or money. You would be rich beyond your wildest dreams."

Cornelius agreed. "If your people catch you with the paintings they will first torture you, and then shoot you. But remember one thing: before that happens they will force you to divulge how you came across the paintings. Then, they will come after Dolan and myself and shoot the both of us."

"It all sounds very convincing but I have to take the chance," Petrov replied. "Neither one of you understands what it is like to live in a communist country. Unlike yourselves, once I am back in the Soviet Union they will not let me travel outside of its borders for a long time, if ever. I would never be able to collect my monies."

Truth be told, Dolan really didn't care what happened to Petrov. But he agreed with Cornelius. If Petrov were captured there was no doubt the Russian would be tortured until he had no choice but to inform on them. Taking this into account Dolan slowly reached for his holstered .45 caliber, but Petrov had anticipated as much, bringing his weapon to bear on his former partners. "Let us depart as friends," Petrov said with a slight smile. He then indicated for Dolan to toss his .45 into the bushes. "We will all be very rich soon enough. You can purchase a new one." He then climbed up and into the driver's side of the cab of his truck, waved to them, and began his long trek back to the Soviet Union, or more specifically, Ukraine.

PETROV'S CREDENTIALS DID INDEED work their magic, allowing him to pass through a total of six Russian Army checkpoints and almost 600 miles of roadway, unscathed. He merely flashed his documents and the guards, upon viewing Stalin's signature, crisply saluted and quickly waved him through. The only downfall so far was the time it took to travel the 600 miles of war-damaged roadways to the Soviet Union's border. What would have, under normal circumstances, taken 14 hours to drive, had now taken eight days. Eight days where he was forced to seek shelter, meals, and valuable petrol for his truck. No one refused him. Stalin's signature had commanders falling over themselves to assist him. Especially after Petrov indicated he was keeping a log of all who assisted him in his journey. His documents also enabled him to utilize local military units to guard the truck as he slept, eat, showered, or relaxed. Now, as he approached the Ukrainian border town of Byxo, he was so confident of his choice to take his cut and run, he could smell the money.

Maybe with his newfound wealth he would buy a new home by the Black Sea. Maybe Sochi? He had heard Stalin and members of the Politburo vacationed along its sandy banks during the cruel winter months.

Unfortunately for Petrov, much had changed in the eight days it had taken him to reach the final checkpoint on the Soviet/Ukrainian border. Stalin was on a rampage. His three top Generals who commanded the Trophy Brigades had been arrested on charges of theft. Not just theft on a small scale mind you but they had the audacity to steal entire contents of German estates and even castles, all for their personal use. They even had the boldness to ship everything back in army trucks, and in commandeered military aircraft. Stalin had his suspicions after the head of the Trophy Brigades, General Minov, was caught the week before with several valuable paintings hung in his bedroom and dining rooms. After a more methodical search, conducted by the KGB, they soon found over a million dollars' worth of rugs, silverware, and paintings scattered about his home. Stalin was livid. Now he turned on his charges, ordering everyone to be thoroughly searched upon return to the motherland. From Generals to lowly privates.

No exceptions.

PETROV HAD NO INKLING of what had transpired in the preceding eight days as he approached the final checkpoint, a KGB checkpoint at that. He handed his papers over to a young lieutenant.

"Out of the truck," the lieutenant demanded.

"I am a major," Petrov replied confidently, "You will address me as such. How dare you order me about as if I were some lowly private."

The lieutenant smiled at him before speaking. "So sorry, get the hell out of the truck, *sir.*"

Petrov sneered as he pointed to the papers. "Do you see whose signature is at the bottom of the second paper? Comrade Stalin. He will bust you down to a lowly private when he finds you have hampered my progress. Now step aside and allow me to continue."

The lieutenant nodded to Petrov. "These papers and pass have no authority over KGB checkpoints. As per Stalin's latest directive, as of three days ago, every person and vehicle is to be searched. Even your Trophy Brigades boss, General Minov was searched. And now he is in jail for theft."

Petrov turned pale, a feeling of nauseas suddenly swept over him. *This is not good,* he thought to himself. The lieutenant led him to the trucks rear.

"What is your cargo?" he demanded.

Petrov stood staring at the man for several seconds before he regained his composure. "Wooden crates of files. Many important documents."

"We will see about that." The lieutenant lowered the trucks rear gate and jumped up into the truck to perform a closer inspection of the crates.

Petrov was ready to run when two additional KGB guards suddenly appeared behind him, rifles at the ready. "Please wait where you stand, Major," said the one closest to him. "It won't take long."

AFTER THE KGB SEARCHED Petrov's truck, they easily located the paintings, each individually rolled up in cardboard tubes and placed into three separate wooden crates for their trip to his home. A quick inventory of the first crate included 75 paintings and drawings by Veronese, El Greco, Degas, Daumier, Renoir, Tintoretto, and Goya.

Petrov tried to talk his way out of the mess. "The paintings are due to arrive at the Hermitage Museum in a few days. This is all just a minor misunderstanding." The KGB swiftly placed him under arrest, taking him to a small house they had been occupying, this for a more *through* interrogation.

IN A MATTER OF 30 minutes, a bloody and beaten Petrov was overheard informing on his former partners as he was being placed into a cage normally used to transport large gorillas, liberated from a nearby zoo.

A KGB ART EXPERT was quickly dispatched from Berlin. Flown in on a captured German Fieseler Fi 156 Storch, arriving two hours after the first call was placed. Everyone knew Stalin wanted quick results but above all he wanted traitors looking to profit from the war. The art expert was a former staff member at the Soviet National Museum. In a matter of hours she surmised that the first 75 paintings were worth anywhere between $50-$60 million US dollars on the open market. But they still had another two crates with 225 paintings to inventory.

His KGB interrogators had heard enough. They dragged Petrov from the cage he was sitting in and placed him up against a stonewall before summarily executing him.

Now the KGB only had to track down the remaining 900 or so paintings. At least that's what Petrov disclosed was still in hiding.

But they knew exactly where to look.

LONG BURIED SECRETS

CHAPTER 16

May 1945: Munich Germany

After three weeks of walking, sleeping in fields, eating whatever he could scrounge, Hildebrand Gurlitt arrived home in Munich, 15 pounds lighter than when he escaped Berlin.

He never had the opportunity to use Hitler's pass, destroying it as soon as he reached the opposite banks of the Spree River. He could not risk the Russians capturing him with such a document in his possession.

Gurlitt was stunned at the devastation Allied bombings had inflicted upon its neighborhoods, particularly those around the old city. Even his favorite beer hall, *The White Mouse*, had been destroyed. Fortunately for Gurlitt, he lived some distance from the city center in a section called Bogenhausen. It was one of Munich's least devastated quarters as only a few buildings were hit, and even those by errant bombs. The Bogenhausen area consisted mostly of immense villas representing the old aristocracy. This included the stylish villa that Gurlitt and his family chose to call home.

As Gurlitt walked up the Belgian stone driveway that announced his elegant home, a sense of relief spread across his face, immediately realizing his home had escaped the bombing raids that so damaged the city center.

And that meant his family was safe.

He chose to ring the front door bell. Having not washed in weeks and living in the same set of cloths since escaping Berlin, he had the appearance of a vagrant. He knew his wife kept a small pistol for protection and the last thing he needed was being shot in his own home after traversing some 600 kilometers unscathed.

After several minutes he heard footsteps, then the porch light flickered on above his head. The curtain on the door was drawn aside several inches. Next he heard his wife, Helene, scream for joy as she yelled for her son to come downstairs. She quickly opened the door to greet her husband, having thought for weeks that he was surely dead or captured by the Russians. Despite his appearance from his weeks on the road, she embraced him.

Soon Cornelius joined his mother in clutching his father.

After several awkward minutes, they held his hands, one for each, pulling him into the house's entryway. The intoxicating smells of dinner wafted over him.

"We were just getting ready for dinner," his wife said. "You look as though you could use a good meal or two." She patted his midsection.

Hildebrand smiled. "I haven't eaten a full meal in weeks. Lead the way."

Over dinner he tried to maintain some decorum as he regaled his family of his daring escape from Berlin. When dinner concluded, he excused himself explaining he wanted to take a nice long hot bath. His wife started to clean up the dishes while Cornelius offered to get the bath ready.

When Cornelius and Hildebrand were out of earshot, Hildebrand pulled him aside. "What news of the paintings?" he asked.

Cornelius informed him of the deal he negotiated with the American and Russian.

Hildebrand was ecstatic. His son had done well. "I knew you could do it," he said, slapping his son in the back in congratulations.

IN A MATTER OF DAYS Hildebrand was promptly arrested by the American authorities who held sway as the governing authority for Bavaria.

Someone had betrayed his presence in Munich.

Gurlitt was prepared for the inevitable. His long trek from Berlin over the past few weeks had provided him with time to contemplate all possible options. He realized that as someone who had personal dealings with Adolf Hitler, the Americans would no doubt arrest him as a potential war criminal. He had accepted this.

The Americans who questioned him, a Colonel from the so-called *Monuments Men* unit, and a Lieutenant assigned as legal counsel for the 3rd Army, desired to know the whereabouts of stolen artwork. Particularly the ones identified as "degenerate art" by Hitler. They had numerous witnesses that could identify Gurlitt as Hitler's right-hand man when it came to art.

They also sought to claim Gurlitt's own extensive collection of 115 pieces of artwork openly displayed throughout his home, all thought to have been stolen.

Soon after his arrest, American Military Police showed up at Gurlitt's front door, holding orders from the American

Governor of Bavaria, General Patton, to confiscate all of the artwork in his home. His wife and Cornelius could only stand by and watch as the soldiers removed all 115 pieces of art. Luckily for them the rest lay secreted by Cornelius in Presdorf.

For days they held Hildebrand under the Allied War Powers Act. The Americans were unyielding. They interrogated Gurlitt for hours on end. Returning him to his cell only to drag him back to interrogation. This happened repeatedly. He lost all sense of time.

They also withheld the basic essentials of food and water. This, combined with everything that had transpired only days after his three-week trek from Berlin, his stomach and bowels were in an uproar. After a week of this treatment, he was a broken man. Seeing Gurlitt's condition worsening hour-by-hour his interrogators saw an opportunity. They went in for the kill, once again demanding Gurlitt turn over documentation, not only about his personal artwork, but also about the "degenerate art". They wanted to know who his customers were. Where they were from. And whom they represented. If he refused to supply this information, due to his condition, they informed him he would most likely be dead within days. Then they would have his family turned out on the street like paupers.

Gurlitt had no doubt they would strike at his family, using them as pawns. He had planned for as much.

"I'll tell you everything," said Gurlitt. "Provide me with some water and you will know what I know."

His interrogators saw it as a major breakthrough, pouring him a tin cup of water. Gurlitt took it eagerly in his hands. They waited patiently for him to compose himself. He nodded his thanks to them before speaking. "I was Hitler's art buyer, that much is true. I did keep detailed records of every transaction and who purchased what painting."

His interrogators looked at each other in congratulations. They would be the first United States Army authorities to locate any of Hitler's personal art besides the Merker's Cave find back in March.

Gurlitt went on to describe how he documented everything, whom it was stolen from, where it was stored, and eventually whom it was sold to.

"Where are the documents?" the Colonel said. "Provide those and you just might be out of our custody today."

"I stored all of them, including documentation for my personal collection in my second home, in the city of Dresden. Unfortunately all of it was destroyed during British bombing raids in February 1945. As for the so called degenerate art, I sold it all," he lied. "All proceeds going to help the German war effort."

What his interrogators did not realize was that Hildebrand Gurlitt had many powerful friends in the west. People who had purchased paintings or statues during his wartime art auctions in neutral Switzerland, most for pennies on the dollar. None of them wanted Gurlitt to disclose and identify who had purchased the stolen pieces.

When word spread of his capture, many American and English industrialists who had the ear of Allied authorities quickly sought his release. One of the more influential collectors approached General Eisenhower, the Allied Supreme Commander.

Within hours Gurlitt was released. On his documentation was a statement that he was a victim of Nazi persecution due to his Jewish heritage.

His interrogators were dumbfounded. *He was a victim?*

Soon after his release, 115 pieces in the custody of American and German authorities were returned to him. They provided him with documentation to state he had acquired them legally.

Or what could be termed *legally*, with Hildebrand Gurlitt paying pennies on the dollar to his victims who signed over ownership before being sent to concentration camps.

The remaining 1,100 or so Hitler collection pieces had been secreted by his son Cornelius, and Sergeant Mike Dolan in a mine on property owned by Hildebrand Gurlitt.

He now realized they were about to become very rich.

Very rich indeed.

CHAPTER 17

May 1945: Moscow

JOSEPH STALIN PACED ABOUT his ornately decorated Kremlin office with the prowess of a tiger. He was furious. He soon picked up a silver paperweight, presented to him by the people of Stalingrad, flinging it at a gilded mirror behind his desk, the mirror shattering into thousands of tiny pieces. "Are you telling me some little piss ant Army major decided to steal artwork destined for the Soviet Union?" he demanded of General Pastekov, his commander of Operation Eastward.

Stalin had ordered Pastekov to systematically round up all of the greatest art treasures stored in the Russian-occupied sector of Germany and ship them back to Russia. Twelve trains and three cargo planes carried about two and a half million works of art to Moscow, Leningrad and elsewhere. The haul was referred to as "trophy art," as in trophies of victory.

"You bring me that bastard, alive," he demanded, his face turning crimson. "Do you understand?"

General Pastekov was well aware of Stalin's mood swings. He saluted. "Our KGB captured him on the Ukrainian border. But…," he stammered.

"Don't you but me," he screamed. "Make it so, or it will be you who is taking the next train to our far eastern lands."

"…he had partners."

"What do you mean *had* partners," he demanded.

"The KGB have already executed the major. He is dead. The major had an American soldier and two German nationals as his partners. One of whom was Hitler's private art collector. They all reside in the newly created American Occupation Zone in Germany. We just can't charge across the border and demand the paintings, Comrade Stalin."

"It's our artwork. Nobody else's. It's owned by the Soviet people. *Our people*."

Stalin's eyes narrowed as he stared at his General. He allowed several seconds to pass before he looked away. "Then we can deal with the rest of his crew. We will eliminate them one by one until I get what is mine!"

CHAPTER 18

August 1945: Moscow

Comfortably seated behind his plain wooden desk, Stalin eyed the two gangly men who stood at attention in front of him. They had recently changed from their army uniforms into ill-fitting civilian clothing.

"You are two of the best agents General Pastekov could provide me?" He barked. "You can't even dress like spies! You look like two refugees." He pointed to their baggy pants and mismatched suitcoats. 'How do plan to infiltrate the American zone and kill the bastards who have the rest of my paintings?"

The taller of the two continued to stare straight ahead as he responded. "But Comrade Stalin, we were instructed to look like refugees in order to blend in."

Stalin suppressed the need to grin. "Then you have succeeded." He stood up and walked over to a side table where an aide had earlier laid out two Tokarev TT-33 semi-automatic pistols. Beside them lay two magazines containing 7.62×25mm cartridges. Stalin picked up one pistol and expertly slid the magazine into its handle before repeating the process for the second pistol.

Satisfied, he then picked up both pistols and walked over to where the two men stood.

"Normally I would never hand a loaded weapon to anyone. But we must establish trust between us, don't we?" He said, handing each a pistol. Stalin previously had forbad weapons in his presence since an assassination attempt two years earlier by a junior officer. Now everyone had to submit to a thorough search of their person before entering his office, even his leading generals.

"Thank-you, Comrade Stalin," they both replied in unison.

Stalin realized that General Pastekov was waiting in the outer office, him conveniently having the next appointment. "So the general has filled you in on what needs to be accomplished? To steal back the paintings from the American soldier and the two Germans?"

"Yes, sir," they replied once more in unison.

"Good," he said, turning to take his place behind his desk. "Then tell me how you plan to accomplish this mission."

Each looked to his weapon, removing the safety in one quick action. The taller of the two smiled at Stalin, raising his pistol and pointing it at the tyrant of the Soviet Union. "The General said if we killed you, he would reward us beyond our wildest dreams." He pointed to his weapon and to that of his cohort. "I guess we now have been provided with that very opportunity by none other, then yourself."

Stalin slowly reached under his desk where he had secreted a Tokarev pistol taped to the bottom of his desk drawer. Only his was loaded with real bullets. "The general is a smart man. He knew there would only be the three of us in my office due to the delicate nature of this assignment." He slowly eased his pistol from its hiding spot and, carefully keeping it hidden, aiming it up through the desk at where the first soldier stood.

The second soldier spoke up. "The general was afraid he was going to jail due to his theft of goods from Germany. So he used us to get to you."

Stalin smiled at them both. "I guess you have me. May I be permitted to provide you with a word of warning? Right now the two of you are in a very powerful position. Maybe I could offer you something in return for not murdering your premier?"

"We could not trust you to follow through if you did."

"The general told you this?"

"Yes, the general has been very good to us."

"Then why don't you shoot me and get this charade over with?" He demanded.

"It's not that simple," said the first soldier. He pointed down to the intercom on Stalin's desk. "First I want you to tell your secretary to allow General Pastekov into your office."

Stalin smiled at them. "So the general wants to personally see me executed? Maybe he even wants to do it himself? I don't blame him." He pushed the first button on his intercom. "Tell General Pastekov to enter," he ordered.

Within seconds, the General was standing beside his two assassins. He had contempt in his voice as he spoke to Stalin. "You thought you would kill me," he said, "but it is I who will have you killed. I have always detested you. The whole General staff detests you. You are nothing but a career criminal who bullied his way to the top of the pile. Now, your time is done." He turned to his two men. "Shoot the dog."

Two soft clicks were heard in response. Followed by two more. Each of the men now realized their guns were empty.

The general realized the desperate situation he was now in, the tables reversed. "I don't believe this."

It was Stalin's turn. He slowly raised his own weapon from its hidden location under the desk, a wide grin on his face as he laid the weapon down on top of his desk as if daring them to act. He knew the general would try something underhanded such as this. *Or hoped he would.*

"Don't just stand there, get him," the general ordered his two assassins.

Stalin was quicker, picking up his weapon and swiftly shooting both of the soldiers with a bullet to the head, each dropping to the floor, dead.

He then turned the gun on the general. "Any last words?"

The general straightened his tunic top and brushed his hair back. "I have no regrets. Do with me what you will. But you will always be a bastard to me!"

Stalin shot him dead with a single bullet to his head.

His office door came crashing in as his outer office guards burst into the room, weapons at the ready. Stalin indicated he was okay.

He then signaled for his aide to enter.

"I want you to suspend the operation to steal the paintings from the American and the two Germans. We will wait until I can at least trust someone on my general staff to carry out a simple order without one of them trying to assassinate me."

IN TIME, STALIN passed on the paintings, content with what his Trophy Brigades had already stolen. He had enough plunder.

What he really desired were people he could trust.

CHAPTER 19

Present Day: Clyde's Auto Body, Edgemont PA

Dolan enjoyed having the floor, speaking down to Nora and
Jim. "You are both smart people so I can skip with the details
and just go with the basics. A little history for you. Early spy
stuff. The predecessor to the CIA was the OSS or Office of
Strategic Services. They set up shop back in 1943. By the end
of 1945 they were receiving over half of their funding from
captured Nazi treasure hoards. What they found, they kept. The
old finders, keeper's rule. As the war was ending, and even in
the years just after, say 1946 and 1947, they uncovered major
treasure hoards such as paintings, gold, sometimes even cash.
They were worse than the Russians in stealing stuff."

Nora and Jim appeared bored.

Dolan noticed the disinterested expression upon their
faces. "Trust me, its gets better. Just hear me out. He walked
around to his coat and pulled out a pack of Camels. He offered
them around the room, everyone declined. He put one in his

mouth and one of his goons obliged his boss and produced a lighter. He was more at ease now, exhaling a ring of smoke before continuing. "My father, God bless his soul, was a numbers runner for the Philly Irish mob back in the late thirties, early forties. Believe it or not, he was one of the few who never got pinched by the cops. He was low level, but he had a lot of gumption. Unlike his cohorts, he never had an arrest record, so unfortunately he was eligible for military service. Just when he was moving up in the Philly organization, he was drafted. Fast forward three years and he's an Army Sergeant assigned as a forward scout to old blood and guts Patton's Third Army.

Towards the end of the war in Europe, I'm talking like the last day or two, my dad and what was left of his platoon stumbled upon a three truck Nazi convoy parked in a field. Alongside the trucks, lay five dead German soldiers, and one survivor. My Dad said the lucky bastard was just a kid not older than sixteen. He was dressed in street clothes and evidently was not a soldier. After a few minutes of interrogation the German kid informs my dad about the contents of the truck. Are you ready for this? *It's Hitler's personnel painting collection.* Or sort of his personal collection. It's all the paintings that Hitler said was "degenerate art". What he really did was use it as an excuse to confiscate the paintings. Picture a Philly mobster stumbling upon a bunch of stolen art. It basically fell in his lap."

Now Dolan had Jim and Nora's complete attention. Jim had heard rumors of such a collection but the paintings were supposedly destroyed in a bombing raid towards the end of WWII. If what Dolan was saying is true and he had proof these artifacts survived, the value would be in the billions of dollars.

Jim's interest was piqued. "What happened to the German boy in your story?" he asked Dolan.

Dolan smiled at Jim. "So I have your attention? I knew once you heard a portion of the story you would be intrigued."

"A portion?" asked Jim in reply.

"Oh yes, allow me to continue. When my dad and his platoon came across the German kid, he had just shot five German soldiers. His own people. Well, not really soldiers but Nazi's, those SS types. When questioned by my father the boy admitted to shooting them. He explained he had to get rid of the witnesses and that he didn't like Nazi's. Of course, my father took an instant liking to the boy. Within minutes, a Russian platoon shows up. But they are not your ordinary Russian soldiers, these were part of Stalin's Trophy Brigades. They were looking for anything of value to bring back to Russia. So here is my dad with his fellow American soldiers meeting up with Russian soldiers, and this German boy, all standing around with three trucks full of enough stolen artwork to make them all rich beyond their wildest dreams."

Dolan smiled as he excused himself to fill up his empty glass with two fingers of Scotch, followed by two pieces of ice.

"You can't pause now," said Nora, she was just as fascinated as Jim and Eian. Even the two goons looked absorbed in the story.

Dolan knew he had them right where he wanted. Unfortunately he required the pretense of their friend Eian, being in trouble. If not, they would have never left Florida. At least not for Dolan's purposes. They wouldn't have accepted his calls. Now, he had his proverbial hooks in them.

He nodded to Nora as he continued. "Everybody's standing around the dead Germans and the trucks full of art. Dad and the Russian officer send their men to make sure the Germans were actually dead. Of course it was all a ruse. While they were checking, Dad, the German boy and the Russian shoot them all in cold blood. No witnesses except for the three of them."

"Oh, my God," exclaims Nora. "They were butchers."

"More like entrepreneurs, Nora," Dolan replied smugly. "My Dad now only had two partners instead of potentially 15 to 20. Moreover, of those, he knew somebody would eventually slip up or even worse rat them out to the authorities. Now, in one swoop, only three partners. But all in all, less witnesses."

"I still say they were murderers," said Nora. "They could have simply divided up the paintings and each would have been millionaires."

Eian and Jim nodded in agreement.

Dolan held up his hand to quiet them. "Please allow me finish the story."

Jim was the first to speak. "Let the man finish, I'm interested in where the story is going."

Dolan smiled at him as he continued. "So here they are with all of these expensive paintings in the middle of nowhere. Now what do they do? My Dad knows there is no possible way he could bring back his share of the paintings to the US and not get caught. So the German boy shares the details of where he was heading before my Dad and the Russian surprised him. They come to find out the boy's father owns an old mine in Bavaria, just a few miles away across the border from where they were standing. The German boy, my dad, and the Russian major, using the German trucks, transport the paintings to the mine in Germany. Luckily for them within a few weeks it becomes part of the American Occupation Zone."

He takes a sip of his Scotch, savors it for a few seconds before continuing.

"Several weeks go by and the Russian Major contacts my Dad and the German boy. He informs them that he must return to the Soviet Union and wants his cut of the paintings to take with him. Now my father and the German boy had a feeling from the start of their partnership that the Russian Major was going to be the weak link in the chain. Luckily for my father, the German boy's father, had somehow made it out of Berlin and returned to Munich. So between the three of them, they devised a plan to screw the Russian out of his cut. Well, at least a portion of his cut. They managed to pull the old bait and switch on the Russian and had reproductions made up for 20 of the more expensive paintings that were slated to be part of his share.

There were plenty of forgers out of work. The German boy's father personally knew several from their work with the Gestapo. Within weeks, they had 20 Old Masters forged. When the time came, they helped the Russian Major load his share of close to 300 paintings. He had no way of knowing that the 20 most expensive had been switched. How could he? He was no expert. Within weeks the poor schlep was nabbed by his own government as he tried to transport his plunder back to the Soviet Union. I heard he actually made it to the last checkpoint on the border when they caught him. The Russians quickly put him to death and confiscated his share of the paintings. Fakes and all."

He took another sip of his scotch before continuing. "That left my dad, the German kid and his father. Over the years they managed to sell off paintings one at a time in Switzerland to not arouse suspicion. Most were private collectors whom didn't care about the artworks provenance. It would be for their own viewing pleasure. The German boy's father died in the 1950's and the boy was caught in 2010 while on his way to sell a painting in Switzerland. But in-between they each made many millions. The government then searched Cornelius's apartment and found almost a thousand paintings that had been stolen during the war. Of course they confiscated them, but in the end the German courts ruled they were owned by the man and the confiscation was ruled unlawful. So believe it or not the government returned most of his paintings. They had no law, and still to this day have no law on returning treasures appropriated during war. The German boy, Cornelius, lived until 2014 and when he croaked, he screwed my Dad, or me, since Dad died in 2010, out of my share of the paintings. His Will stipulated that upon his death the paintings were to be donated to a Museum in Bern, Switzerland. That included my father's share of the stash."

"Now the Russians, after they confiscated Major Vasli Petrov's paintings in 1945, put them on display in various museums around the Soviet Union, including the Hermitage. They had no idea that the 20 Old World Masters were fakes. Evidently they were excellent reproductions because they fooled the experts for years. And this is why I need your help. The three of you are known as experts in the field of recovering WWII related treasures."

Jim tapped Nora on the knee. "Did you know we were considered experts in WWII related treasures?"

Dolan expected as much. He indicated to one of his goons to place a shot past Nora's head. The goon raised his 38 took aim, and pulled the trigger. A loud explosion was heard in the small confines of the room as the bullet flashed by her head, imbedding in the plaster wall behind her.

Jim leapt up at Dolan but the second goon was ready and landed a blow to his gut, knocking Jim back into his chair. "If I were you, I'd stay down, boy," the goon said with a smile, albeit missing several of his teeth.

Dolan took it all in stride as he sipped his scotch. After several seconds, he looked to Jim, Nora, and Eian. "That bullet was an attention getter. May I continue my story? Maybe this time without interruption?"

Jim rubbed where the second goon had landed his blow. "I'm going to get even with that monkey of yours," he replied through clinched teeth.

Eian knew how ruthless Dolan could be and tried to defuse the situation. "His place, his rules," he said.

"Well thank-you, Eian," said Dolan. "First smart thing you said today." He continued. "Now like I said before I was so rudely interrupted, the three of you are known as experts. That is exactly what I need, experts, because art is not my field of expertise. I work the Philly area, to include South Jersey. If you want to talk about gambling, small personal loans, or maybe some political issues, no problem. However, Europe and its art world are not on my radar. I don't know the turf."

Dolan held up his empty glass. One of his goons took the hint and grabbed the bottle of Scotch from the bar, refilling his glass.

Dolan continued. "What really has me worried is how the Russians recently found out about the fake paintings my dad and the other two Germans provided the Russian major. They think I have the original paintings. That is why I need you, your wife, and Eian to help me. The Russians think my Dad smuggled paintings back to the US and placed them in hiding. But he chose, unwisely I might add, to allow his partners, the Germans, to keep them hidden in the small German town of Preisdorf until he needed some money."

"Preisdorf?" Jim inquired.

"It's where the mine is located. But in 2010 my father died. Cornelius used that as an excuse to move everything from Preisdorf to his apartment."

"I take it he didn't trust you?" snapped Eian, having hung back on commenting for most of the story. "I wonder why?"

Jim cut him off. "How did they sell the stolen paintings?"

"Once they agreed on which painting to sell, Cornelius would take the train down to Switzerland and sell a painting in one of the many auction houses in Zurich or the auction house would arrange a private sale for a higher piece of the action."

Suddenly Dolan realized he had gone too far, too late. In laying everything out for his new partners, he inadvertently exposed to his goons that the Russians sought the info. Not only that, he had laid bare how his father and Cornelius sold the paintings. His goons could potentially sell the information back to the Russians. Hell, it's what he would do if in the same position. He slowly reached around to the small of his back and quickly withdrew his .38 caliber. His two goons could not react in time before he shot each of them in the head, both falling hard to the floor.

Jim and Nora sought safety on the floor, pulling Eian down with them. "Looks like a chip off the old block," said

Jim. "First his father does the same to his platoon, now the son to his own people."

Dolan placed the handgun on the table in front of him. "It's okay," he said. "I'm not looking to harm my new friends. Especially ones that are going to make me rich."

They looked around to make sure nothing else was about to transpire.

In a low voice Nora turned to Eian and said: "This guy's nuts."

Eian replied in an equally low voice, not wanting to be overheard by Dolan. "I just play cards with him. He's no friend of mine."

Jim, Nora and Eian eyed Dolan as he walked over to the main wall separating the bar from the card room. He seemed to be staring at a painting as if it were the first time viewing it before he promptly removed it from the wall, tossing it onto the table in front of him. "A quick art lesson for the unsophisticated."

They each looked over to where Dolan's two goons lay sprawled on the floor.

He followed their gaze. "Don't be silly, I have more where they came from. Now get up off the floor. I'm not going to hurt you. I want to show you something."

They gathered around the table, Jim closest to the .38 in case Dolan had any more devious intentions.

Dolan started speaking as if a professor. "Presently, famous artworks are copied by the dozens in places like Chengdu, China. They have artists lined up easel to easel. Orders come in from the various websites and they go to work. You even have 3D digital printers that can produce a reproduction that can look like just like the original. It's done every day. Now to spot a fake you have to look at the colors in the painting – not all paint colors were available in the past. That's why savvy buyers will bring a color chart to see if they spot a color that wasn't available in the era the artwork was painted."

He pointed to the painting that lay on the table. "Flip that painting over," he said to Nora. "Look at the surface it is painted on. How does it sit on that? How does it feel and does it look aged enough? Is it nailed or stapled. Nails were only used before 1940, staples after that."

Nora tossed the painting down on the table. "Any more magic tricks, Dolan?"

Dolan smiled at Nora. "As a matter of fact, yes. You and your husband are going to recover everything I am owed. By now I think you realize this was all carefully orchestrated to get two of the best WWII treasure hunters to work for me."

"Three," said Eian. "Three of the best."

"Excuse, me," Dolan replied, "three."

Nora eyed Dolan with contempt. "Couldn't you just have asked us to help? Did you have to kidnap our friend?"

"Why? Would you have helped me if I did? We aren't exactly the best of friends." Dolan stared at Nora for several seconds and said, "I didn't think so."

Jim looked to his friend, Eian, then to Dolan. "Eian's part of our team. We will require his services to even have a decent chance of recovering the art."

"I expected as much," said Dolan. "You can have him. I know where he lives. For that matter, I know where you and your lovely wife live. Even what dock your boat is tied up to."

"We don't like to work under the guise of veiled threats, Mr. Dolan," said Jim, the anger in him rising.

Dolan held up his hands. "No threats. Just stating a simple fact. My point is don't try and run from me. Now down to the simple stuff. I am fronting you $500k in walking money to get things moving. You can hire whomever you want but only share the pertinent details with them. I also expect a daily update on your progress and more importantly, your whereabouts. Is that understood?"

Jim looked to Nora and Eian, each nodding in return. "Agreed, but only in part," replied Jim. "We will need you to acquire some equipment for us."

Dolan turned his hands over, revealing his palms. "What can I do for the great, James Dieter?"

"First of all we will require an assortment of small arms with accompanying ammunition. Smoke grenades, Stun grenades, and most importantly the use of a private jet that Eian will pilot."

Dolan nodded in agreement to the requests. "Is that all?" he said sarcastically.

"No. If we are to do this for you, we also need you to secure the release of someone from prison."

"Federal, State or local?" he responded as though it were an everyday request.

"State," Jim replied.

"Charges?" asked Dolan.

"Robbery, no weapon used. He is a second story man. Never hurt a fly. He is also a forger. Best in the business. And he has a lot of good connections."

Dolan nodded. "Done, and done. I will have to call in a few favors. Grease the palms. Give me his name and I'll have him out within the week."

As Jim wrote down the name, he was already planning his own double-cross.

CHAPTER 20

Collegeville PA

State Correctional Institution – Phoenix, a medium-security prison located 32 miles northwest of Philadelphia, had the responsibility for confining inmates from the Philadelphia Metropolitan area.

Within its walls were convicts whose crimes ranged from burglary, assault, armed robbery, up to mass murders.

Not exactly the kind of people you would want to bring home to meet Mom.

It also had the distinction of holding one Charles "Chuck" Denny. One of the country's best second story burglars, and an equally impressive master forger. His work was well known to all who operated in the trade. Rumor on the street said that some of his best work hung in two of Philadelphia's most prestigious museums: The Philadelphia Art Museum, and The Barnes Museum. Of course, this was unbeknownst to its caretakers. *He was that good.* He could study a painting, whether in a museum's gallery or of a photo, and produce a copy within a day. A master copy in two. He could nail the painting down to the direction of the brush strokes. A real savant.

But he also enjoyed committing burglary. He had a passion for it.

At an early age, he realized that 90% of all homeowners never locked their second story windows. Made the work very easy for him. He would never carry tools with him. Didn't have too. All he had to do was find a home with a ladder laying around, usually by a garden shed. Prop it up on the back of the house and enter through an unlocked window. He would be in and out in less than five minutes. Sometimes even while the family ate dinner downstairs. Unfortunately for him, one day an officer on a routine patrol caught him red-handed.

Now he was two years into a six-year stretch.

Chuck sat in his solitary six by nine cell, tugging at his 3-day salt and pepper goatee with one hand as he applied cyan blue to a portrait of a little girl. It was a portrait to cull a favor with one of the guards. The guard had promised Chuck a carton of smokes, a bottle of Scotch, and fresh fruit. He desired something better than prison food. He was desperate, having already added 20 pounds to a frame that was 6'1, 150 pounds soaking wet during his 2nd story days. Now he looked in the mirror and saw a plump old man of fifty-five. In his prime, his friends used to call him *Stretch* but with this diet, in four years, they will be calling him *Chunks*.

The guard came by to check on his portrait. Chuck was just adding his finishing touches to it. "There you go my friend," he said as he handed the portrait to the guard. "It is still wet so be careful."

The guard looked at the portrait, then the picture, comparing the two. "I can't believe you did this," he said, his voice rising in gratitude. "It looks exactly like my daughter! I mean, exactly! I would have paid three grand if I had to pay someone on the outside to do this." The guard gratefully handed Chuck his payment: a brown paper bag containing a carton of smokes, a bottle of Scotch, and some fresh fruit. "You are truly very talented."

"Thanks. Tell your friends."

"Oh," the guard said absently, still staring at the portrait. "The warden sent me to bring you to his office."

The last time Chuck had the pleasure of visiting the warden was his indoctrination to prison life. "You don't happen to know why, do you?" he inquired softly. He knew nothing good came from a visit to the warden's office. "I've been minding my own business, not bothering a soul."

The guard smiled at him. "Don't worry about it. I think it might be good news. At least that is what I have heard through the guard rumor mill. Something about the governor approving you for an early parole. Knocked four years off your sentence. So if I were you, I'd get a head start on packing up your stuff."

Chuck eyed the guard, then the interior of his dismal cell. "You're not pulling my chain are you?"

"No. Pretty sure it's all on the up and up. If the rumor is to be believed, somebody named James Dieter managed to pull a few strings in the governor's office. Or somebody he knew owed somebody something."

Chuck sat back in his chair for a few moments, pondering what the guard had just said. He knew no one would mention James Dieter's name unless it was all true. They couldn't. No one knew he had connections to James Dieter. Therefore, the rumor had to be true.

That could only mean one thing.

He had a *very* special job for him.

CHAPTER 21

Philadelphia, PA: University of Pennsylvania

Mention the name Benjamin Franklin and people think of the many titles associated with the man: inventor, printer, scientist, and most notably, politician.

But not many people realize he was also *an educator*.

In 1749, the esteemed Mr. Franklin organized 24 trustees from the surrounding Philadelphia area to form an institution of higher education. He dreamed of a school operating at a level such as Harvard, Saint Johns, and Yale, three of the United States' earliest operating colleges. By 1751, his dream gained traction, opening its doors to children of the gentry and working class alike as the Academy and Charitable School in the Province of Pennsylvania, or the future *University of Pennsylvania*. Of course, it was unanimous that Franklin should serve as its first president, doing so until 1755, and continuing to serve as a very active trustee until his death in 1790.

In the years after its founding, many former students felt a sort of gratitude to the University that had been the source of their prestigious education. They wanted to give something back. Franklin, never one to miss an opportunity, asked many to bestow something of significance back to the University when they felt comfortable in their situation. He even took it a step further by specifying the types of donations the University would welcome: artwork or money.

Donate they did.

From Franklin's Presidency to the present, many alumnae have elected to donate monies, paintings, and sculptures to their beloved *U of P*. Through these donations, the University quickly expanded to 302-acres—boasting more than 200 buildings, most of sturdy, ivy clad brick. Of course, the new buildings would require only the best artwork to adorn its prestigious walls. Nothing less was acceptable. This led to the birth of the University of Pennsylvania Art Collection, one of the largest, not only for a University, but in the world. In 266 years the collection has grown to include over 8,000 artworks, most of it donated from wealthy benefactors, who were, at one time or another, former students. All of it prized, some more than others. The collection of paintings, sculptures, photography, and decorative arts are spread across 100 University locations.

As everyone is familiar, where you have valuable art you also have someone wanting to remove it for his or her own personal collection. Hence the need for the fourth largest police force in the state of Pennsylvania. In addition, with the kind of money the University had hanging on its walls, they also employed the latest in high tech gear such as vibration detectors, displays to detect even the slightest of pressure changes, and saturation infrared and microwave motion detectors. Instead of just focusing on entrances and exits, it operated a fully-saturated system that left no blind spots – making it nearly impossible to physically enter, externally hack, or disable the system.

Its security measures are one of the main reasons why they have never experienced a major theft.

That and they always hired ever-vigilant curators. The latest in a long line of observant stewards including one that will occasionally sleep on the main museum floor in a sleeping bag just to be one with her *charges.*

Like many enterprises, the University did not recognize the talent they had on their staff, nor did they compensate Summer Larson fairly.

Then if you add in two children attending a prestigious high school, and her in the initial stages of what looked to be a very nasty divorce, money was tight. This left Summer Larson vulnerable.

Extremely vulnerable.

That is why Mike Dolan Jr. steered Jim Dieter in her direction.

PROFESSOR SUMMER LARSON WAS hunched over an 1854 oil on canvas painting of *"George Washington Rallying the Troops at Monmouth,"* that lay horizontal on two wooden horses. With a skill gained over her 22 years, she carefully removed years of accumulated grit from its aged canvas. As curator of the University of Pennsylvania Art Collection, she had no reason to be on the floor performing the 'dirty' work in art speak. She had over 20 employees who specialized in everything from forgery to art restoration. It would have been easy enough for her to assign one of them to finish the tedious task. However, she enjoyed getting her hands dirty, and it also had the secondary benefit of taking her mind off her personal problems.

Unfortunately, for Summer, her primary job was pushing paper and appealing to rich benefactors. For years she tried to treat those areas as minor nuisances. And for years the University President and Summer went back and forth in disagreement. Normally she relented, realizing there was a time and place for gravelling. Gravelling and looking the part went hand-in-hand when you were a museum curator. When required she could also dress for the occasion. At 5'10, 132 pounds soaking wet, with long blond hair, many a wealthy patron had approached her at one of the countless University functions, or *beg-a-thons*, testing her marriage vows. Of course, she innocently ignored them all. Now, in the process of a nasty divorce due to a philandering former husband, she wished she had accepted a few of the *opportunities*.

JIM DIETER STRODE into the *cluttered room*, as least that's what Summer Larson's secretary called it, looking for Ms. Larson. He was immediately overwhelmed by the smell of emulsion cleaner and varnish in a room that was the size of a three-car garage. The security guard who escorted him pointed over to the corner of the room where Summer was working. "That would be her, sir," he said. "I'll just stand over here by the door in case you need anything."

Jim nodded in thanks. However, he knew the guard wasn't just standing there for his sake. He wanted to make sure nothing was touched. He immediately understood why as he walked passed and marveled at a Kazimir Malevich, a Piet Mondrian, and a Picasso, each awaiting touch-up or rework. The three paintings alone had to be worth at least $15 million at auction. He stopped to admire the Mondrian with his use of reds, blues and whites. He stood there transfixed for several minutes not realizing Summer Larson had noticed her visitor and walked over to stand beside him.

She interrupted his train of thought. "I think the original varnish should be respected and should never be altered or removed as the artist themselves placed it there. It's something we try and ingrain into our students, if the artist themselves placed it there then leave it, respect the artist's technique. Just one of the many teachings here at the university. We have a reputation to uphold at U or P and we don't want any of our students to ruin any originals in the name of restoration."

Jim turned to see a women in her early forties but who could easily pass for someone in her thirties. She had a kind of understated beauty; perhaps it was because she was so disarmingly unaware of her good looks.

She pointed back to the painting he had been admiring. "As time passes, oil paintings tend to darken due to the accumulation of dirt and yellowing of the protective varnish layer. Art restoration has always been tricky, as conservationists try to remove buildup without damaging original material. It can be tough to separate the original layers from the gunk with a scalpel."

"It is all fascinating," he said. "I would like nothing more than to discuss removing gunk from paintings with you but I know you are a busy woman." He held out his hand in greeting. "James Dieter," he said.

"I see you are still the cocky one." Summer smiled as she gently pushed his hand aside, laughing aloud. "For two people who have met before I would think a hug would be more appropriate. Don't you think?" Without another word, she embraced him.

Jim was taken back for a moment. "I'm sorry, I truly don't mind being hugged by a beautiful woman, but have we met before?"

Summer shook her head. "And I thought I was memorable. You really know how to deflate a girl's ego, Mr. James Dieter. All right, it's up to me. Think back to your senior year at a Naval Academy Dance. The girls from U of P were invited down due to something about not enough women at the Academy for partners. I guess they did not want the guys dancing with the guys. That wouldn't look right to the Admirals."

Jim quickly noticed when she smiled and laughed, you couldn't help but smile along too, even if it was just on the inside.

After several more seconds of him trying to recollect their meeting, his eyes lit up. For a moment he looked embarrassed. Jim shook his head. "I don't believe this! It is you!"

"In the flesh. Just like I was all those years ago. And you never called. I waited, but you never called."

Jim held up his hands. "My uniform went into the wash with your number. Honest. I even tried to find you through the school. I tried for a couple weeks before I graduated and shipped out to Basic Underwater Demolition/SEAL school at Coronado. But that was before the internet and all of those search tools."

"All I'm hearing is blah, blah, blah. Excuses, excuses. You really hurt me, James Dieter. We spent seven hours just talking when we met. For me, you stuck out. It took me months to get over you. I started comparing everyone I met to you." She paused for a moment, dabbing her eyes as an old memory surfaced. "You even called me Miss Seasonal. You know, *because my name is Summer.*"

Jim felt like he walked through the wrong door and couldn't go back. "No, no. I remember," he said truthfully. "You haven't changed a bit. You are still as beautiful as the day I met you. And I did try to find you."

"It was night when we met, not day, and I have changed. More weight, hair turning gray, not to mention two teenagers and a future ex-husband who finds enjoyment in stressing me out."

Jim pointed to his own head. "Join the club. Some gray. No paunch yet. I just married last year. No kids yet. But the job is stressful enough."

He was still as handsome as the night they met. She quickly dashed the thought. She smiled once more. "My secretary said it was important. You required the services of an art expert." Summer paused before allowing her arms to take a sweep of the room. "This is my kingdom. How can I help an old acquaintance who dumped me?"

"Ouch, you don't give up," Jim said holding up his hands in surrender.

"My apologies. Last shot, I promise. Seriously, how can I help?"

Jim looked back at the guard, then to Summer. "I don't know how to say this without coming across sounding as if I'm a thief."

"You're a big boy. I'm sure you can push through. My advice is to just come out and say it."

"And you're still a smart ass."

"Takes one to know one."

"All right, here I go. I periodically work in the recovery of lost items. It is literally something I fell into. I won't lie, I have made a lot of money doing it. Lately most of my work has been associated with WWII items. Specifically, items stolen by the Nazis."

"Wait a minute," said Summer. "Weren't you one of the people who found that horde of Nazi diamonds and gold? I think they called it the Bormann Treasure."

Jim simply nodded.

"And you gave it all back?"

Once again he nodded. "I was called a fool by a lot of people after that one. *A lot.*"

"More like a hero. I hear you reunited a lot of families with valuables they had stolen from them during the war."

"Well, most of it was delivered to their families, since most, if not all died in the concentration camps."

"You are a decent human being, James Dieter. Most of the people today live by the adage, *finders' keepers.* Yet you gave it back."

"Most of it. We did get a small finder's fee for our time and effort."

Summer smiled. "So what can I do to help you or your team? I hope it has something to do with buried treasure. By the way, how did you come across my name? Who suggested I could be of help?"

"I can't say who recommended you. They just said you were the best at what you do, and that you needed the cash."

"Divorce sucks. Cash I could use. Only lawyers seem to profit from another's misfortune."

"So maybe we can help each other? It seems my team and I have reached a point where we need someone with both your expertise and possibly access to tools of the trade. Now my team and I have, shall we say, uncovered some lost Nazi artwork worth in the vicinity of $2 billion. We require somebody who could provide some on-site advice on the works authenticity."

Summer stood staring at Jim, a look of shock gracing her face. "Did I hear you correctly when you said *two billion*? With a capital B? And, is it all legal? Sounds to me like the art should be in a museum."

Jim nodded. "It's overseas and in regards to a museum, well, that's where we require your assistance. All in all, it would only require a few weeks of your time."

Summers curiosity was piqued. How could it not be? This was the dream of every curator. Recovery of lost artwork.

She did not answer with a no, so Jim continued. "The job pays $200k, along with first class hotels. Three weeks tops. Money might help with your teenager's future college tuition."

Summer smiled. "Two-hundred thousand? As in dollars? Not pesos? Are you sure it's not the old dump the ex-girlfriend guilt pay?"

"I thought you said no more shots were coming my way?"

"You threw me a softball, so I had to swing."

"Okay, my bad."

Summer pointed back to her work. "Can you provide me with a couple of days to finish this? I just can't up and leave."

"A few days I can spare."

"Then you have yourself a teammate."

CHAPTER 22

Present Day: Moscow, Russia

A rain induced haze intermittently obscured the Kremlin's distinctive "onion dome" as the early evening showers moved obligingly from one unsuspecting area to yet another. This simple act of nature allowed the government complex to appear in full view, presenting one with a sheer sense of awe when viewed from afar.

The streets were missing its normal traffic. With the upcoming Army Day celebrations, many officials were settling in for a three-day weekend at one of their *dachas* outside the city's limits.

Within the walls of the Kremlin, one building stood out from its peers due to the presence of heavily armed guards milling nearby: the Premier's offices. Russia's answer to the White House Oval Office. Occupying the entire seventh floor, the Russian Premier's office was like stepping onto a Hollywood set that blended both Russia's past and present.

Walls lined with Estonian birch. Floors covered with hand woven rugs from Turkmenistan. Glass mosaics from Siberia. All leading to a hand-built mahogany conference table from the Urals that could easily seat 25 if tasked. At its top was the Russian Premier's desk, also hand-built out of mahogany. Together they effectively formed a T-shape. The Premier's desk was positioned as if a presiding judge passing judgement of those who would gather around the tables highly polished top. Behind the Premier's desk, mounted to the wall, were four stag's heads, ranging from an 11 pointer to a 24, each shot by the man who now occupied the chair behind the desk, Alexi Sherinko.

The room stood empty except for Sherinko and his Deputy, Alexander Bortnikov. Earlier, Bortnikov's had his aides deposit two wooden crates on the conference table. Each crate measured ½ meter by ½ meter. He turned to Sherinko. "I have something for you to see, my friend," he said, his voice cracking with enthusiasm. He approached the first crate, and removed the top. Inside each crate were ten cardboard tubes, each containing a single painting. He reached in and selected a tube labeled *Józef Brandt - A Hunting Trip,* carefully withdrawing a painting from its tube and unrolling it in front of Sherinko.

Sherinko was a huge admirer of the arts, preferring the Old Masters to impressionists. He even took several art courses at University, studying artists from the 1700-1800's. He removed his glasses from his shirt pocket. He considered the painting for several minutes, even running his fingers along the edges. "Is this a Brandt?" he said, looking up to Bortnikov for confirmation.

Bortnikov smiled as he nodded. "I thought I could fool you on that one."

"Never on a Brandt," he replied. "Look at the brush strokes. The technique. The man was a true artist. I'd say its worth around $40-50 million on the open market."

Once again, Bortnikov nodded. "You are correct. That is if we could sell something supposedly destroyed during World War II, the great patriotic war." He pointed to the painting, then the wooden crates. "If I may, a little back story for all of these paintings before you."

It was Sherinko's turn to nod.

"As I already mentioned, the whole world thinks this painting disappeared in WWII, along with many others. Let us regress back to the time of the bastard, Stalin. We know he sent out Treasure Hunting Units towards the end of the war seeking to steal anything of value from Germany, Poland, Hungary, and Czechoslovakia. Using Stalin's authority, the Treasure Hunting Units were able to confiscate thousands of pieces of art. The very painting sitting in front of you was stolen in the last days of the war. This is the reason I requested this meeting."

Sherinko looked up at his deputy, his eyes narrowed. "This isn't another one of your schemes to strike back at the Americans in some devious way? Is it?" he said, referring to Bortnikov's last attempt. He put together a plan to undermine the German and American alliance by selling cheap natural gas to the Germans against America's wishes.

"In a way it is. But please indulge me for a few minutes. It has the potential to be the most lucrative minutes of both your life, and mine."

Sherinko looked down at the painting in front of him. "You said this was stolen?" he said, knowing it came from the vaults of the Hermitage, never having been displayed to the public."

"Yes, it was, but please keep it. Think of it as a down payment for a venture I have planned. I will do all of the work, and I was hoping you would just provide the resources."

Sherinko looked extremely pleased as he picked up the painting, admiring it even more now. "Please continue," he said, his eyes never leaving the painting.

Bortnikov knew the painting sealed the deal. He continued. "My story begins with one of our Army Majors in 1945, during the last days of the war. This particular major was assigned to one of the many Treasure Hunting Units combing through Eastern Europe searching for anything of value. Just before the German surrender, the little thief struck a deal with an American soldier and a German boy whose father was Hitler's personnel art dealer. Between the four of them, they managed to steal over a thousand paintings from Hitler's private collection. But our Major was impatient. He was stupid enough to confiscate an Army truck, load up his share of the paintings, and head back to his village in the Ukraine. Of course, the KGB seized him when he approached the Ukrainian border. The case quickly reached Stalin's attention due to the paintings being from Hitler's personal collection. At the time, the major's share was worth in excess of $200 million American dollars."

He moved nearer his friend before continuing. "Stalin was able to deal with the major but not the American nor the father and son team. They were in the relative safety of the American Occupation Zone. They were also wise enough to remove the remainder of the paintings and transport them to a safer location after our major departed. They did not trust him. They knew he would get caught. We actually think one of the partners may have been the anonymous source who notified the KGB."

Sherinko smirked as he looked at his friend. "Tell me, how did that ruthless bastard Stalin deal with the major?"

"The KGB shot him before Stalin could. But Stalin imprisoned his whole family."

"The bastard was even more ruthless than I am," Sherinko replied.

Bortnikov continued. "These paintings," he said, pointing at the two crates, "they represent only a small fraction of what was stolen. The rest are in the Hermitage's basement vaults."

"So how many paintings are we talking about?"

"In just the basement of the Hermitage, close to 300 were originally confiscated from the major."

"And what about the rest of the paintings? The 300 is only one-fourth of the original collection stolen. What did the German father and son team and the American do with their share?

"That's why I am here today, sir. One of our people, in the states, just informed us that an American treasure hunter named James Dieter is helping the American soldier's son, Mike Dolan, in possibly acquiring the rest of the paintings."

Sherinko's face turned white. "Let me get this straight. Are we speaking of the same James Dieter who stole all of the Bormann gold that was rightfully ours? The same James Dieter that hurt our Hezbollah Allies in Lebanon?"

Bortnikov nodded. "The same person. Now he has an accomplice, his wife. She's a Pulitzer Prize winning newspaper reporter." He shook his head. "*A newspaper reporter*. This is why we have to acquire the paintings. If just to beat that meddling fool Dieter and his wife."

Bortnikov removed additional canvases from the crates, laying them in front of his boss. "I propose that we allow James Dieter and his team do all of the dirty work for us. They take all of the risks. When they complete their heist we simply slip in and steal the paintings from him. Once we have the paintings, we put them up for auction in areas we know won't give a damn about the paintings provenance. This way we are not raising any alarms in the art establishment. Another option is to sell them through our security services to private collectors. Focus on specific collectors that will keep the art locked up for their own private viewing."

Bortnikov pushed another painting closer to his friend. "Think of it. This one, bold, masterful stroke can potentially enrich us close to a billion dollars."

Sherinko smiled at his friend. He was no idiot. Of course he recognized the potential. However, he also wanted to strike back at James Dieter. "I want this operation to proceed," he said. "You will have at your disposal, all the usual people and resources. Use them wisely."

Bortnikov knew the true meaning of *use them wisely*. It meant to keep Sherinko's name out of all correspondence, and all blame resides with Bortnikov. Everything. Any leaks and Bortnikov would be dead. Any blowback and Bortnikov would be dead. Sherinko may be his close friend but he would eliminate his own mother for chance at a billion dollars.

Bortnikov called in the Presidential guards from the anteroom. "Take these crates back to the airport and make sure they reach the Hermitage in Saint Petersburg tonight. And be careful."

He then approached Sherinko with an out stretched hand. "There is plenty more where these came from. We just have to follow James Dieter and his wife." The beauty of the plan is they will do all the work and we collect the prize.

Sherinko shook his hand and smiled. "Handle them any way you want. I don't care. Either way, they're dead."

LONG BURIED SECRETS

CHAPTER 23

Present day: Collegeville PA
Phoenix Correctional Institute

Charles "Chuck" Denny, walking papers in hand, watched as the prisons black iron gate swung majestically open. Dressed in the same clothes he wore the day he started his sentence, a pair of faded dungarees and a worn tee shirt, he walked out a free man.

Eian stood waiting for him and waved him over to the stretch limousine he hired for the occasion. He handed Chuck a cold bottle of beer, and then hugged him.

"Don't hug too hard," Chuck said in a strong south Philly accent. "I did just get out of prison. Might mean we are engaged or something," he said lightheartedly.

"I can see prison didn't take away your sense of humor."

"I needed something on the inside to keep me going." Chuck put the cold bottle up to his lips, and in one long swig emptied it of its golden liquid. He then handed the empty bottle back to Eian. "Now Jim wouldn't go to all of this trouble to get me sprung if it weren't for something really important. So where is the great James Dieter? I was expecting his ugly ass to pick me up."

Eian handed him another cold one. "We can talk in the limo on the way back to Philly."

"Hold on a second. Before I get in that limo, you need to tell me what the hell is going on?"

Eian nodded. "Fair enough. Jim potentially has a job for you. One that involves a big payday. Enough so you can retire. He said you could think of it as your very last job."

"Okay, you piqued my interest. Who would I be working with?"

"Summer Larson. She works for …"

Chuck cut him off. "I know who Summer is. If she is involved I have a feeling this is an art related job. Something high-end."

Eian nodded.

"Theft or forgery?"

"A little of both."

"Summer knows several art forgers. With her connections as University of Pennsylvania Curator, she is familiar with some shady characters. On the forgery side of the house, she knows people who can pop out a copy of a masterpiece in a day."

"So, you in?" Eian asks.

Chuck put the second bottle of beer to his lips and tilted his head back, drinking it all in one swig. He then tossed it against the stone wall of the prison, the bottle shattering. "Hope they can't throw me back in jail for littering."

"I doubt it. They have bigger fish to fry."

A sly look appeared on Chuck's face. "This car go past any strip clubs? It's been a long two years since I've seen a beautiful woman. Hell, for that matter, *any woman*."

Eian knew they had him. "Get in. I'm sure the driver can find a few."

LONG BURIED SECRETS

CHAPTER 24

Present Day: Moscow, Russia

Alexander Bortnikov summoned Sergei Liugo, the head of Russia's military intelligence service, commonly known by the Russian acronym GRU, to his office.

Bortnikov rose from his desk to greet Sergei, shaking his hand firmly, then ushering him over to where two plush leather chairs sat in front of a roaring fire. "Sit down my friend," he said.

After his discussion with Sherinko, Bortnikov was quick to realize he required just the right specialists for his operation to succeed. In addition, he knew only the GRU were the only organization who could handle such a delicate mission. The GRU, with their main responsibilities laying in suppling intelligence to the Russian president, had just the right mix of highly trained personnel at their disposal. That and they were familiar with *performing dirty work when required.*

After pleasantries were exchanged, Bortnikov wasted no time. He began to lay out an intelligence operation he envisioned in the West, one that would focus on the Americans, James Dieter and Mike Dolan. Bortnikov even supplied the locations the subjects would visit courtesy of a well-placed source. When he finished he leaned over and picked up a bottle of Vodka from the floor. Beside him, on a side table, were two small crystal glasses. He poured generously into each, handing one to Sergei.

Bortnikov continued. "There is to be no official sanctioning of the operation. Your people obviously have protection at any of our embassies, but are on their own once they leave the grounds."

"That is to be expected. My people know the risks of the job."

He raised his glass in toast. "To getting back what Stalin originally planned to steal in 1945."

They drained their glasses. Bortnikov refilled them.

Sergei spoke assuredly. "I will put my two best operatives on the job. I have a husband and wife team that should blend in nicely."

"Good, very good, Sergei. I knew I could count on you. Speed is of the essence. I need you to have the operation up and running within the next 24 hours. From what our insider tells us, our foes will be moving very swiftly. We will have to be in place before they arrive."

Bortnikov once again raised his glass, looking directly at Sergei. "To, your, health," he said, emphasizing each word.

Sergei understood the true meaning of the toast.

Succeed or you will be dead.

WITHIN AN HOUR Sergei Liugo had his two best operatives, the husband and wife team of Yuri and Lana Velismo, standing at attention in front of his desk. They had been pulled from an operation tailing a possible spy operating out of the American Embassy.

In less than ten minutes he explained the operation in full detail to them.

"You will be in Switzerland by tomorrow," said Sergei. "You will meet our main GRU contact at our Embassy and he will outfit you with anything you may require. By then we should also have additional information available on the two Americans you will be surveilling."

Yuri and Lana simply nodded.

"If you have to eliminate either one of these people, don't plan on coming home. We want this to be a clean operation. Do you understand me? Clean! The President will disavow you if otherwise. He has no desire for an incident with the Americans. They will just go and eliminate two of our people in retaliation."

"Understood, sir," they both barked mechanically.

Sergei knew they would follow his orders to the letter. They were both ex-military. Yuri was a former Special Operations Forces, 3rd Guards Spetsnaz Brigade operator. Equivalent to the British SAS or American SEALs. His wife, Lana, was once a noted physicist with the Rocket Forces. Now she operated as an assassin within GRU's foreign department with six kills to her credit.

Nether relished failure.

"My I ask a question, sir?" inquired Lana, still staring straight ahead.

Sergei smiled at Lana. He envied Yuri. His wife was both smart and beautiful. "But of course," he replied. "And please, stand at ease, both of you."

"What if they fire upon us?" she inquired. "Can we engage?"

Sergei shook his head. "You should not provide them cause to fire on you. You are not to be seen, nor heard, just observe them until the time comes when you can relieve them of our product." He stood and walked around to where they both stood. "But if they do show hostile intent, I would use some of that hand-to-hand combat training you both are so well known for."

With that, he pointed towards the door. "I wish you both much success. Enjoy Switzerland, I hear it's wonderful this time of year."

CHAPTER 25

Philadelphia PA
University of Pennsylvania

Summer cleared one of the chairs in her office of a stack of
paperwork, looking for a free spot before finally giving up and
placing it on the floor. "I thought computers were supposed to
be our salvation and do away with paperwork?"

Jim looked around at her windowless office, then the
papers stacked on the floor around the room. He counted at
least six empty styrofoam coffee cups on her cluttered desk,
and possibly a frameless Picasso. "Your office looks worse
like a rats nest," he chided her.

She motioned for him to sit. "The maid hasn't been here in
weeks. She might even be buried under some of this clutter."

Jim waited until Summer took a seat behind her desk
before continuing. "I have a straight out of the gate question
for you. As head curator of one of the largest university art

endowments in the world, I have to know how you came across the dark side of forgers and art thieves?"

Summer pondered her response for a few moments. "Those type of people gravitate toward the arts. They tend to frequent the museum to view the art or attend one of our many free lectures given by our graduate students. They can't stay away. It's in their blood."

"Like a hit for a junkie?"

"Exactly! I once had a person who volunteered to assist in our restoration area. It is a dirty job and each year our budget restraints always have us in constant need of volunteers. This particular person said he just wanted to be near the history, the artists, and the many stories their pieces tell. A real history buff. History we have, money not so much. We performed a complete background check on the guy. Came back squeaky clean. No reason to doubt his intentions. He volunteered with us for almost 10 years. Great work ethic. Always volunteered for the dirty assignments. Come to find out the guy was stealing pigments to make his own paints, and stealing canvases' to paint on. Not your ordinary pigment or canvas mind you, some of our special ones are from the 1700 and 1800's. A forger's dream. A master forger could beat the standard artwork testing due to them having access to original pigments and canvas. All due to our first University President, Ben Franklin, himself a printer and sometime aspiring artist. He was also a notorious spend thrift. He used to buy in bulk to cut costs. We still use original pigments and canvas he procured to help in restoration."

Jim was dumbfounded. "I can't believe you still have original supplies from hundreds of years ago. Don't they tend to expire?"

"Great question. I thought the same until I dealt with our paint expert. Actually, he is a Doctor of Color Science Research. And no, I did not make that title up."

"You're pulling my leg."

"No, serious. There is actually a Doctorate degree in the field of Color Science. I call him Dr. Paint. Anyway, a quick education in paints. Now paint as we know it wasn't produced commercially until the mid-1800's. Up to that, artists mixed their own paint by grinding pigment into oil. We still have pigments and oils from the 1700's. Painters back in the day use to mix it fresh every day since it had a tendency to harden after a few hours. Older paints consist of small grains of pigment suspended in oil. To the naked eye, it appears smooth. On a microscopic level, particles of pigment are suspended in oil. Think of fruit in a Jello mold. Then contact with the air causes oils to oxidize and crosslink. The paint sets and hardens over time with different pigments drying at different rates." She paused for a few seconds. "You getting all of this?"

Jim smiled. "So I think what you are telling me is because of your vast stock pile of paints, the university can not only restore the paintings but also we have the means to make forgeries? Forgeries that can fool almost any expert?"

Summer nodded. "You hungry?" She said. Before he could respond, she was leading him outside the building. Once outside, Summer pointed toward a line of food trucks or as the locals referred to them, *Roach Coaches*. "I love the Chicken Curry from this one particular truck. Do you mind?"

"Lead the way. This is your territory."

Summer walked up to a battered panel truck covered in large Chinese characters from top to bottom. The area was empty due to the lunch hour rush ending over an hour ago. "Ni hao," she said to a middle-aged Chinese man who smiled at her from his perch in the trucks window. "Hello."

"Jim allow me to introduce you to Mr. Zhang Wei. He makes the best Chinese food in all of Philly."

Jim nodded to the man.

"Ms. Summer set me up in food truck business last year," Zhang Wei replied in halting English. "We do very well. She very good to my wife and me."

Summer placed an order for two chicken curries and pulled Jim aside to a picnic table to await their food.

"You set this guy up in business? Aren't you the nice little refugee helper. Didn't picture you as a big humanitarian."

"Cut the crap, Jim. It was either that or report him to the police. You see that guy, Mr. Wei, *he was my volunteer.*"

"You mean…"

"Yep, you just met the art forger. This guy has done everything from Michelangelo to Rembrandt. Of course courtesy of my labs products."

"I'll be damned. And you didn't involve the police?"

"No. I didn't think it was right. He didn't sell any of his paintings, he just wanted them for his own collection. When he first showed me, I was floored. I couldn't believe the quality of his work. Of course I confiscated his works to use as teaching tools. In return, I provided him with this *opportunity*." Summer pointed to the truck. "But he also owes me. He owes me big time. And from what he has shared with me, he has friends who can help."

Zhang called out to Summer. "Food ready."

Summer and Jim walked up to the truck. "Mr. Wei, can we talk privately?"

Zhang said something to his wife in Chinese and exited the back door of his truck. "You will like my curry," he said to Jim.

"I am sure I will."

Summer indicated for Zhang Wei to sit at the picnic table. "Mr. Wei, remember last year when I didn't turn you in to the police for stealing my pigments and canvas?"

He looked to the ground in shame. "Yes, and you were always so nice to me. It was a bad time. I love to paint. Especially Old Masters. They are so elegant."

Summer nodded in agreement. "Well, we need your help. Jim and I have some potentially lucrative work for you. Art work. Forgeries to be exact. Of course you would have full use of my lab."

"And you will be paid generously," Jim interjected.

He looked at them as if someone had returned his long lost dog. His eyes suddenly teared up. He continued in his broken English, "I will gladly assist you. I owe you so much." He then pointed to his truck, his wife waving at them. "You name the time and place."

Jim pushed a piece of paper across to Zhang. It contained a list of 15 of the world's top missing paintings from World War II, a thumbnail picture beside the name. "Do you recognize these paintings?"

Zhang studied them for a few minutes. "I recognize all but these three," he said, pointing to the three. "I studied at the National Art Institute of China. Very prestigious. I have much knowledge on the timeframe of these works of art."

"I'm sure you have, Zhang," said Jim. "Could you do a forgery of each? Given enough time?"

"Of course I could," He replied as if insulted. "I could also have three other artists assist with the work. He contemplated the list for several more minutes. "If we have full access to your materials, I would say three days, maybe four, tops."

Jim smiled at Zhang's confidence. "I also have a man that is being released from prison this week. A forger. Really a master forger. I want him to help you with the artists' signatures and the paintings Provenance on the reverse side. We will require the forgeries to pass any inspection."

"I will await your instructions. When you are ready let me know. I will contact the others."

Summer touched Zhang's hand. "I will reach out to you tomorrow to get started."

TWO PICNIC TABLES AWAY sat a man in green doctor's scrubs. He had ordered food from another lunch truck when Summer and Jim approached the Chinese food truck. He discretely pointed a one inch listening device in the direction of where Jim, Summer and Zhang sat. A clear wire ran from the device to his ear, enabling him to listen to every word they said. When the discussion with the cook from the white truck was complete, he tossed a full soda can and a half-eaten burger in the wastebasket. He then pulled his cell phone from his pocket.

"They are up and running," he said in guttural Russian. "Put our people in-place to watch their next move. But don't harm anyone. *At least not yet*. Their time will come."

LONG BURIED SECRETS

CHAPTER 26

Philadelphia PA
Airport Embassy Suites Hotel

Jim strolled into the living room portion of the hotel suite from his adjoining room. An older man, in ill-fitting clothes, with a salt and pepper goatee and a dour face accompanied him. The older man almost fit the mold of your average middle-aged male, minus the paunch.

"Everyone," said Jim rather loudly, trying to get them to settle down. He could see they were enjoying the free mini-bar he provided. "I would like to have your attention please."

Nora, Eian, Summer, and Zhang Wei stopped their discussions midsentence. "Must be important to stop the Happy Hour," said Nora. "Who's your friend?"

"I don't mean to interrupt your Happy Hour but I would like to introduce a new member to our team: Charles "Chuck" Denny. Chuck is our famous second story burglar and master forger. This gentleman has paintings hanging in top museums and galleries around the world. And the museums don't even know they are fake."

"You better watch out, after that introduction he might want to charge us more than he is slated to make," said Nora.

Everyone laughed aloud.

Chuck decided to take a seat where he could keep his back to the wall but still have a clear view of all in the room. After two years in prison, he still had trust issues.

Jim handed him a bottle of beer. "Chuck let me introduce you to your new teammates. He walked over to stand behind Eian. Of course you already know Eian Doherty, our pilot and former IRA gunman. I hear he took you on a side trip from prison for some entertainment?"

"You could call it that," said Chuck. "Well deserved after two years."

Jim moved behind Summer. "This is Summer Larson, University of Pennsylvania Museum curator, and the only one amongst us with actual art cred."

Chuck grinned. "I have heard your name mentioned in many art related circles. All good I assure you."

Jim then moved to stand behind Zhang. "This is Zhang Wei, like yourself, a master forger. According to Summer he is the real deal. Zhang also has several accomplices that work for him and they will be assisting him with his work and ultimately, with our mission. Don't worry, they will not get a cut out of our pot. Zhang will be covering their fees from his own share."

Zhang smiled at the group. "No worries, they work cheap. All are family."

"Nice to meet you Zhang," said Chuck. "If Summer says you are a master forger, who am I to doubt her. I look forward to working with you."

Jim proceeded to where Nora sat. "Last but not least, my beautiful wife, Nora Robinson. Pulitzer Prize winning journalist and my better half. Obviously, you don't get a Pulitzer unless you are very good at following leads."

Chuck nodded to her. "In prison I have nothing but time on my hands so I read a lot. Of all the journalists I've read, I have to say you are one of my favorites."

"Thank-you," said Nora, blushing a bit. "Always nice to meet a fan."

"I am just grateful to be free," said Chuck. He now turned to Jim, his bottle half-raised. "Thank you for getting me paroled and for the stretch limousine that picked me up at the gates of prison. That was a nice touch of class."

"That's the way we tend to operate," replied Jim. "First-class for our people," pausing for a few seconds, "especially when it's on Mike Dolan's dime." Jim pointed over to an empty chair. "That's where Mike Dolan would be sitting if we had invited him to attend our little gathering. Just in case you are unaware, Mike Dolan is head of the Philly Irish Mob. He also both initiated the job we are to embark on and had you freed from prison."

"I know the man from reputation alone. I also know nobody moves in Philly without his say so. But I do owe the man a debt of gratitude for his orchestrating my freedom."

Jim nodded. "Now you may be asking yourself what do we expect from you?"

"Doesn't bother me what you have in store. Just name it. You know my capabilities. I owe you people."

"Let's see if you still feel the same way after I go over the operation with you?"

Over the course of the next ten minutes, Jim explained their job in detail. When he was finished, he grabbed a beer and sat back down beside Chuck. Silence gripped the room for a few moments as Chuck digested all Jim had shared.

It didn't take long for Chuck to formulate his opinion. "I'm operating with a bunch of loons! You are crazier than I am. So I should fit right in," he says laughing and shaking his head.

Jim slapped him on the back in congratulations. He raised his beer, the group following his lead. "To getting back what those Nazi bastards stole, and returning the paintings to their rightful owners."

Eian added to Jim's toast. "And to screwing Dolan out of his share."

"Here, here," they replied in unison.

After Jim finished his beer, his thoughts quickly turned to Dolan. He knew he was a scheming career criminal who would try and recover everything his father stole. *Everything.* He also knew Dolan to be a double crossing murderer who would allow no one to stand in his way.

Jim was not going to let Dolan profit a dime from the paintings. That is where Chuck and Zhang would apply their talents, assisted by Summer.

Together with Nora and Eian, they would put the kibosh on Dolan's plan to keep the paintings for himself.

Jim spoke up once more. "Okay, assignments. Eian, tomorrow I want you to take Chuck shopping. He requires a new wardrobe to wear in Europe. Especially after being locked up for the past few years." He tossed over a rolled-up bundle of bills whose bank paper label read ten thousand dollars. "He also requires some special tools. He can fill you in on the specifics. Then I want you to make sure our aircraft is ready for departure in 48 hours from now. You are in charge of making sure the Manifest is correct. Lastly, you are the pilot so all drinking stops tonight."

"Got you covered, boss," he replied

Chuck grinned. "I gained a few pounds in prison. Could use some new attire."

"Just one of the benefits of using Mike Dolan's money," Jim replied."

Next, he turned his attention to Summer. "I need you to get Zhang Wei access to your lab starting tomorrow. Zhang and his accomplices will need to start work right away. I also need you to call in some favors within your academic community. We will require as much information on the Bern Museum as you can get. No detail is too small. Then I want you back here tomorrow night, passport in hand, bags packed for 2-3 weeks."

"I have to get my soon to be ex-husband to watch our two teenagers. Should be fun for him. But can do. No worries."

Jim turned to his wife. "Nora, I need you to grill your newspaper contacts for info on the town of Bern and its surroundings. Anything we should know, especially about the people and politicians. Find out if there is anyone who could cause us problems."

"Shouldn't be an issue."

"Meanwhile, I will make sure our sponsor, Mike Dolan, is in the dark as much as possible. Unfortunately, he wants to be part of the operation and will meet with us in Bern sometime over the course of the next two weeks. I am going to wing it and tell him about how we intend to acquire his artwork. Of course, it will be all lies. He's getting nothing back."

Everyone in the room clapped and whistled.

OUTSIDE THEIR HOTEL room, in the hallway, a young woman wearing a stolen hotel maids blue shirt had been able to record the entire conversation between Jim and his team using a state-of-the-art TACRON Door Eavesdropper. The device was capable of hearing through doors and walls up to six inches in thickness. It was also small enough to fit into the palm of her hand and as thin as a credit card. Satisfied she had indeed gained everything her boss required, she slipped the device back into her purse. Then at a fast pace, she moved down the hall, removing a blood wig from her head as she went, and slipping out of her maids shirt, dumping both into a trashcan by the elevator. Once on the elevator she hit redial on her cell. In seconds, her boss picked up. "I have it," she said smugly.

"Were you able to record their entire plan?" her boss responded.

"Everything from start to finish. They had no idea I was even in the hallway."

"I need to hear their plan before my next meeting."

"On my way to you as we speak."

JIM OPENED HIS hotel rooms door and walked into the hallway. Fifteen feet away a red fire extinguisher hung from the wall. He reached down and removed a small black disc on the outer wall of the extinguishers tank before placing it in his pocket.

Jim had his suspicions and planted the camera on the hallways fire extinguisher when he checked in. Once in place he simply monitored it from Nora's laptop.

Luckily, they were able to catch the young woman in the blood wig listening in on their discussion. From that point on, they simply acted out the entire scene for her.

In effect, they played her.

Once Jim closed the door, he nodded to his assembled group.

"Okay, now we can stop the acting. Bern, Switzerland in two days. Let's start with our arrival."

It was time to get down to the details.

The real details.

CHAPTER 27

Present Day: Bern, Switzerland

Jim and Nora decided to splurge a little and sought only the finest accommodations for their fellow teammates. They booked everyone into the Hotel Weiss, conveniently located directly across the street from their target: the Museum of Fine Arts Bern. The Hotel Weiss was not just any hotel mind you, but one that specialized in Old World luxury, *not unlike the paintings they were going to steal*. Erected in 1813, the hotel proudly boasted it provided accommodations for such notable historic figures as Goethe, Wagner and Brahms. Its original character and charm included heavy woods and white Italian marble throughout its interior. It even possessed an indoor swimming pool filled with thermal water from the hotel's own spring. Who could ask for more?

Now they just had to focus on their target.

FROM AN ARCHITECTURAL perspective, the Museum of Fine Arts Bern combined historical Baroque with modern Swiss elements for an overall attractive setting. You could also see it in the smile of its Master Curator, Christian Lasseter, as he stood proudly just outside the Museum's new Gurlitt Wing, named after their prime benefactor, Cornelius Gurlitt. Christian could be seen daily, greeting tourists or during his daily stroll around the exterior of the Museum just to pick-up trash. Nevertheless, he was an old-time curator, known to be fervently against the installation of any security systems that would impede the experience of a visitor to the Museum.

He preferred human interaction, and that meant human guards, not alarms.

Of course, the museum had many masterpieces besides the Gurlitt collection. It housed and displayed over 50,000 masterpieces covering 800 years of art history. In addition to works by renowned Swiss artists Albert Anker and Ferdinand Hodler, there were works by Dalì, Monet, Vincent van Gogh, Kandinsky and Pablo Picasso.

In addition to the masterpieces, there were approximately 48,000 sketches, prints, photographs, videos and films.

Truly an impressive collection.

At least it would be *if all of its Gurlitt collection were authentic.*

SUMMER LARSEN STROLLED slowly through the main galleries, not wanting to attract much attention, pausing only when needed. She was well versed in the many ways to spot a fake painting, but this doesn't stop forgeries from slipping into famous art collections. It has been noted that over 10% of most museums' collections were forgeries, known or unbeknownst to its owners.

When it came to forgeries, she had seen it all: tea bags that had been dabbed onto the canvas to age it; nicotine sprayed over it to make the canvas seem older; oven aging; sauna aging; you name it she came across it. In addition, a few incriminating details that a potential forger could miss. One example would be the existence of staples. You would not find them on a painting produced in the 1800's.

However, technology has caught up with the times. Summer also used, courtesy of Chuck, Google Glasses that he modified with a vastly improved processor and 3D stereo monolithic capability. The improved processor allowed Summer to upload her color stick to the glasses. With the color stick uploaded, they were able to deduce what colors were available in the timeframe the picture was painted. She simply stared at a picture and the glasses scanned it. Within seconds, the glasses would identify color irregularities. For an additional capability, the 3D stereo monolithic allowed her to penetrate the surface of the painting to the canvas below, viewing the actual sketch that the artist had followed to paint the portrait. In a forgery, the sketch would mostly be absent.

SUMMER ANNOTATED in her notebook the paintings she assumed to be copies. For several paintings, she required a second look with the Google Glasses for confirmation she was correct in her assumptions.

As planned, she met Jim met across the street in a small café. He was on his third cup of coffee when she strolled in and over to where he sat. He pointed to the seat across from him.

"Well?"

Summer sat down, a broad smile creased her face. She handed Jim her notes. "I have to give kudo's to Chuck and his modified Google Glasses. They worked perfectly. I now have photos of every painting on display in the Gurlitt wing. Between my analysis and the glasses, I would say that 35 of the 300 they currently have on display are fakes. Each of the 35 are on the low end of the value scale. My best estimate is in the $100K to $500K price range."

Jim paged through her notes. "You mean to tell me you were able to deduce all of this in only two days? Something the museum's own experts say are all originals?"

"Like I said, with the glasses Chuck modified, yes. You see, the museum wants them to be the originals. People pay big money to see these paintings. People won't pay big bucks for reproductions."

"So you are saying they are aware that over 10% of the paintings are fakes?"

Summer smiled at Jim. "That's my expert opinion."

Jim smiled right back at her. "This could work to our advantage."

At a second table across from them sat Charles "Chuck" Denny. He too had strolled around the museum, sometimes walking right past Summer unnoticed. Only he was not admiring the artwork; Chuck was studying the guard rotation, positioning of the cameras, and when possible, identifying possible laser detectors embedded in the walls and floors. He waited until Jim motioned for him to join them.

Chuck handed Jim his notes. "For all of the things you hear about the Swiss, you know, modern, very precise. Well, in regards to the museum security systems, it is stuck in the 1970's. It is a joke. I could break in and take what I want any time after closing."

Jim looked to Summer, then Chuck. "Could you do it repeatedly? Over the course of several days? Preferably a holiday weekend?"

"If I can locate the electrical main going to the museum, and cut the power, I could walk in and out like it was a department store," Chuck replied confidently. "Take your pick of what you want."

"What about an electrical backup system?" inquired Jim. "Like a generator to provide secondary power to the alarm systems?"

Chuck nodded at him. "Yes, they have a rather large diesel generator that would kick on in the event of a power outage. It is supposed to keep power flowing to all of the security systems. However, if it has no petrol, it will not come online. They made the mistake of surrounding the generator with arborvitaes to make it look more aesthetic. The arborvitaes will actually provide me a decent cover when I simply drain the generator of its fuel. It does not get any simpler: no fuel, no power. So, like I said, if I can cut the electrical main providing power to the museum and the backup generator has no fuel to operate, I could walk in and out."

Jim smiled widely. "Well the plan is to take the originals and replace them with forgeries that have been masterfully created by you, Summer, and Zhang and his friends. We only want a selected group of paintings, not all of them. Forty-five to fifty; don't want to be too greedy. Since Summer has already identified the reproductions in the galleries. We will stay clear of those."

"What about Dolan?" replied Summer. "Didn't you say he sought the entire collection?"

"Dolan will take what we give him. As far as we are concerned, we will concentrate on high value items. However, in order to make this happen we will require up to 100 reproductions completed in 11 days. Really, its 50 paintings doubled. So, two of each painting. One with your original pigments and oils, the second painting of a lower grade. The lower grade ones only have to meet minimum standards. Ones that could be passed off to an amateur. Is that doable?"

Summer nodded. "I'm sure Zhang and his crew, with the appropriate materials, aided by Chuck and myself, can reach that number." She turned to Chuck. "What do you think?"

"First I have to inquire as to how many people are helping Zhang? The reproductions are the key. I can steal anything, but we need something to hang back in its place."

Summer quickly called Zhang on her cell phone. In a matter of seconds, she had her answer. Four. All experts like himself."

"Fifty Old Master pieces, times two, for 100 pieces in 11 days? Divided by Zhang plus his four, myself, and Summer assisting. Yes, it's doable. Would I recommend it? Hell no. But you are the boss. You're footing the bill and paying my salary."

Jim held up his hand to stop him. "So, are you saying we require additional time? Or it can't be done?"

Chuck shook his head. "I must be getting too old. I'm starting to doubt my own abilities. In my younger days, I could have painted 50 masters in 11 days if I had the proper tools and conditions. But for this operation to work we will need everything to proceed like clockwork."

Summer concurred. "You have my word. I will have everything in-place back in Philadelphia. Between you, me and Zhang and his crew, we have enough talent to get the job done possibly ahead of schedule."

"Prison really screwed with my mind. I tend to doubt myself more and more. If Summer is confident, then I'm on-board. We will get it done."

Jim rapped his knuckles on the wood tabletop. "Love it when a plan comes together! I knew you would come around." He looked to see who was in earshot before deciding to continue.

"All right this is how we are going to proceed…"

JIM DIDN'T REALIZE the old woman sitting three tables away reading the newspaper, *or pretending to read the newspaper,* was listening in on their conversation. On top of her table was an oversized pocketbook. Inside there was a parabolic microphone pointed directly at Jim's table, secretly recording everything Jim, Summer, and Chuck had been discussing.

She watched as Jim paid the tab, and each of them departed.

She quickly did the same.

And then called her boss.

CHAPTER 28

Zurich, Switzerland

Yuri and Lana Velismo strolled out of the Russian Embassy with a one-meter long duffel bag in tow. Inside the bag were 50,000 Euro's, two 9mm Beretta pistols with accompanying silencers, two sets of night vision gear, a pair of 10x50 binoculars, a parabolic microphone for eavesdropping, four fragmentation grenades, two smoke grenades, and ten disposable cell phones.

Just enough product to start a small war.

As instructed, they approached a late model, blue, 4-door Opel parked across the street from the Embassy, and used the cars fob to open the trunk, swiftly stashing their gear.

Yuri and Lana had landed two hours earlier at a private airport north of Zurich, one frequented by the diplomatic crowds. Soon after their arrival, they provided a private briefing about their mission, to the Ambassador and his GRU aide. Upon its conclusion, the proverbial doors were flung open to the embassy's arsenal. They were offered access to everything from common pistols up to anti-tank type weapons. Obviously, they declined the heavy stuff. It was a well-known secret, *wink-wink*, in diplomatic circles that the Russians kept an arsenal at each of its Embassies. *Of course only for self-defense purposes.*

Within minutes, Yuri had inputted their coordinates into his iPhone but stopped short of requesting final directions. He turned to Lana who sat in the driver's seat, motioning back to the car's trunk. "How far do you think we could get on 50,000 Euros?"

Lana smiled at him as she put the car into gear. "Yuri, think about it for a moment. We are in Switzerland, stupid. The world's most expensive country. It might last us a week, but our government would track us down in a matter of weeks, if not days."

"Just a thought," he replied. "Never seen that much money before. Would be nice to one day have a bank account that large. Think of it, no more dirty work, just relaxing on a beach somewhere."

Lana steered the car towards the north/south highway entrance ramp. She was already two steps ahead of him, her own wheels turning, as she merged onto the highway and accelerated, following the signs to Bern.

Who said they couldn't keep one or two of the paintings for themselves?

LONG BURIED SECRETS

CHAPTER 29

Bern, Switzerland

Jim had just completed his fourth tour of the Museum. Nora's third. Chuck's fourth. The museum staff did not consider this uncommon because the display was extensive. Some visitors were even known to spend their entire vacation touring the museum, returning day after day.

On each of their visits, Jim and Nora discreetly used their cell phones to photograph the guards on duty. Chuck used his to record the security system and the guard's security room. By the fourth day, between the three of them, they had managed photos of all 25 guards, exact locations of the alarm panels, cameras, generator, and the security station.

With all the information in hand, they were able to assemble a primitive guard schedule and define the security layout.

Next, they proceeded to figure out who would probably be working the night they intended to remove the paintings.

"OKAY, I THINK we can concentrate on at least these three security guards," said Jim, the photos spread out in front of them. "They look to be the youngest. With youth comes indiscretion. That and they most likely will hit a pub or two after work."

Nora and Summer laughed aloud. "Speaking from experience?"

"Aren't you two the funny ones," he replied. "You mean to tell me in your younger misspent youth neither of you ladies hit the pubs after work?"

Chuck decided to chime in. "I lived above one. Does that count?"

Jim shook his head and pointed back to pictures of the three youngest guards. "Now all we have to do is follow them to a local pub they frequent. That is where we have Nora and Summer chat them up and buy a few rounds. Make them talkative."

Nora looked to Summer. "I guess we are the proverbial bait."

Summer nodded. "A girls got to do, what a girls got to do."

Jim smiled at them both. "Beauty always captures a man's heart. *That and a* few *rounds of drinks won't hurt.*"

"Throwing your wife to the wolves?" Nora replied.

"It's only for an hour or so. I want you two to have a map of the museum spread out on a table. Act a little bewildered."

"You mean the old maiden in distress routine?" replied Summer.

"I like her, Jim," said Nora. "She gives it right back."

Jim looked to Chuck for help but he just raised his hands in surrender. "I do security."

Jim shook his head. "Where's Eian when I need him?"

"He's still at the airport having the aircraft serviced for our flight home," said Chuck.

Jim pointed back to the map. "Ladies, if you could start off with acquiring some basic tips. The usual stuff: What is the best time to visit? Recommended artworks to see? Then buy a few rounds to get them to really open up. Try to find out what their normal routine is when the museum closes at night. Do they hang out in the security room? Or are they positioned at various locations around the museum?"

"We have it, Jim," said Nora. "Between us, we will own those guards."

Jim next turned to Chuck. "All right, where do we stand for security?"

Chuck rose from his seat carrying a rolled up map. He unfurled it on top of the table, and then placed two empty wine bottles on each end to keep it from rolling back up. "I spent a portion of my day walking around and becoming familiar with the area. What I discovered is the museum is typical by European museum standards. By typical I mean all electrical power comes from an outside source." He pointed down at the map. "I went to city hall and was able to make a copy of a streets department map. If you look at the manhole covers, they indicate a letter *E* for electrical and the letter *A* stands for sewage or *das abwasser* in German. Now if you look at all of the ones within 200 feet of the Museum, you see only one with an E on it." He used his forefinger to emphasize the manhole cover. "I walked by it earlier today and located this particular one in an alley beside a trash dumpster. I was able to pry it up and look in without anyone noticing me. When I looked in the manhole, about two feet below me, I saw one line, and it went in the direction of the Museum. It has to be for the museum's electrical power."

Jim patted Chuck on the back. "And this is why Chuck is on the team. Great recon."

"I'm not done yet," he replied. "When you want the power cut, all I have to do is use some common hair spray and a candle lighter, between the two they act as a torch. I simply burn off the wires insulation and drop in a few pieces of metal and boom, the area goes dark. Since I will have already drained the fuel from the diesel generator there will no back-up power. "

Jim looked to Nora and Summer. "Now you see why we needed this man." He turned to Chuck. "You are the man of the hour. Remind me never to invite you over to our house for dinner or drinks."

Everyone laughed.

Jim lays a diagram of the museum on top of Chucks. "I think I might have found a potential point of entry," he said, pointing to a side window in an older section that connected with the new Gurlitt wing. "It only has a heavy-duty cage covering the window for security. It is potentially the weak link. If we can gain access, we should only require about two hours to remove the paintings we have identified, replace them with our reproductions. From there we load the truck and hit the road to the airport where Eian flies us back to the states before anyone becomes aware."

Chuck looked to each of them. "The key is the guards. They will have at least four or five on duty, all heavily armed. I think that is the main reason for the rinky dink security system. They have placed all of their faith in the armed guards."

Jim stood up and rolled up the maps.

"Alright people. We are a go."

CHAPTER 30

Jim could overhear Summer and Nora in the hotel's hallway, chortling like two schoolgirls. He looked at his watch. It was almost 1am. He placed the book he was reading on the nightstand as he rose from his chair. He walked over to the room's door and peaked through its security pinhole. They evidently were having trouble inserting the room's key card into the door slot. He overheard more than a few choice words being used.

Jim opened the door for the two of them. "Good evening," he said sarcastically, "or should I say, *good morning*?"

"Don't mind my husband," said Nora, blowing past Jim and walking over to where a bottle of merlot sat on top of the bar. "Sometimes he can be such a bore." She held the wine bottle up for Summer to see. "I told you it was here."

Jim waved Summer in from the hallway. "You might as well join your partner in crime."

A loud pop was heard as the cork exited the bottle. "Success," said Nora, her words slightly slurred. She poured Summer a glass, then a glass for herself.

"I thought you would be out for an hour or two," he said, pointing to the room's clock. "In case you haven't noticed, it's been four hours."

"I told you he was no fun," said Nora.

Summer burst out laughing. "You were definitely right on that one."

Jim shook his head at his wife's antics. "I'm fun. I'm lots of fun. Hell, I put the F in fun. I just think we should stick to a schedule," defending himself.

"No fun. No fun. No fun," they chanted in unison.

Jim held up his arms in surrender. "Never argue with a drunk, and absolutely never argue with two."

Nora put her glass of wine down for the moment, grabbing her purse. "Now if you would have simply asked us if we accomplished our mission," she replied smartly, "you would have been rewarded with this." She held aloft a sheet of white notepaper.

She handed it to him. "Here you are, sir."

He quickly skimmed what she had written. "This is the mother lode!" he said excitedly. "You have names, schedules, positions where they stand, rotations."

Nora nodded. "The young guards bought us drinks all night. They hoped they were getting lucky. But we led them on. For a couple of older women we still have it." She high-fived Summer.

"Still got it," Summer replied.

"We even said we would meet them next week for drinks." Nora looked to Jim. "But we lied."

"My bad," said Jim. He pointed to the piece of paper. "This is 10 out of 10, ladies."

"I would say you have to go a little higher on your scale," chimed in Summer, her words also starting to slur. "We found out the guards are ardent video gamers and just happen to play in the security room when they work the overnight shift. *All five guards in one location.* They take over all of the security screens for video games. *Translation: No screens covering the floors nor guards patrolling the floors.*"

Jim couldn't believe their luck. He walked into the bathroom to get each of them a glass of water. When he returned they were both passed out on the room's sofa. He managed two blankets from the room closet and placed one over each.

He appropriated the rest of the bottle of wine, pouring its remaining contents into one big glass for himself.

This is going to work, he thought to himself.

This is really going to work!

WHAT JIM NOR HIS teammates realized was that the museum was hiding their issues in plain sight: *the museum was running low on funds.* The financial strain from building the new Gurlitt Wing left the museum in poor financial condition. Almost bankrupted them. Basic repairs and annual maintenance were being pushed further and further back.

The museum also put all new upgrades on hold. They originally had 120 infrared motion detectors placed discreetly about the museum but only 35 were still in working order. The remainder were left up as some form of visual deterrent. The ones that did work were all hooked up to the building's electrical grid. If power went out the entire security system was affected. An antiquated monitoring system consisting of twelve cameras placed around the building's perimeter provided the extent of the exterior security.

There were no cameras installed within the actual museum due to the board of trustees stating such equipment in the building would be too expensive. Therefore, they simply hired additional security guards. Most museums require their security guards to make hourly phone calls to the police to indicate all was well. However, with five armed guards on hand for the nightshift, the Bern museum thought that to be pointless. The board also denied a request from the security director to increase the guards' salaries in a bid to attract more qualified applicants for the job. The current guards were paid slightly above minimum wage. Therefore, you get what you pay for: guards who didn't make the scheduled rounds and played video games in the security room.

So one power outage, and if you could contain the guards in one area, you could steal whatever you wanted.

And get away with it.

CHAPTER 31

It was approaching 8am when there was a knock at the door.

"Room service," was announced from the hallway.

Jim opened the door to find a uniformed waiter standing behind a rolling cart filled with an assortment of breakfast items, a big pot of coffee in its middle. He handed the waiter a 20-franc tip. "I'll take it from here," he said. "Don't want you to see the two bears I have sleeping on my couch."

The waiter smiled as he quickly pocketed the 20. "If there is anything else I can do for you please don't hesitate to ask."

Jim pulled the cart into the room, wheeling it over to a small dining table by the room's window. "Time to rise and shine, ladies," he said. "Breakfast is served."

Nora and Summer looked to be in the same position they passed out in the night before.

Another knock at the door. Jim looked through the security pinhole. "Just Chuck," he said. "He's here for breakfast." He opened the door.

Chuck entered already showered and shaved ready to start the day. "I see somebody is going to have a hangover today." He continued past them, walking over to where Jim was pouring coffee for everyone.

"Late night for the ladies?" Chuck said to Jim.

"You know it," he replied. "They were a hot mess last night."

Nora was first to rise, Summer shortly followed. "Lots of black coffee, please," Nora demanded. "Now I know why I stopped going to bars."

Jim corralled them in. "Today is an early day for a reason," he said excitedly. "I sent Eian to the airport about half an hour ago to get the jet ready. I want Summer and Chuck to fly back today in order to get started on the reproductions."

"So soon?" asked Nora. "I thought we all had a few more days of surveillance to complete?"

"Like I said last night, you both hit the mother lode. Schedule is moving to the left. So I want everyone to have a nice breakfast before Summer and Chuck check out of the hotel and head for the airport."

Jim turned to Summer. "I need you to identify the top fifty paintings by value. Minus the reproductions. When you do, send a JPEG File to Zhang so he can get started on the low end reproductions."

Summer nodded. "Zhang and his crew can meet us when we land in Philadelphia. From the airport, the campus is only 15 minutes away."

"Are you sure Zhang and his crew won't garner any undue attention wandering around campus?"

Summer shook her head. "No worries. The Museum rents a warehouse that doubles as a bunkroom for the many graduate students who perform volunteer work. Usually from other universities. It's only two blocks from campus. It has a staff kitchen, showers, and bunk beds. Zhang and his crew will essentially live there 24/7. Right now, no one is using it and I am the only one with a key. I can arrange for pigments to be delivered to meet our schedule. We all know the paints have to be mixed the old-fashioned way, daily."

Chuck nodded in agreement. "I can get some sleep on the plane in order to be ready to go when we land."

Jim handed cups of coffee to Summer and Nora. "That's leaves Nora and myself to tie up loose ends around here and keep the ball rolling. We only have 11 days to go. Let's make them count."

CHAPTER 32

Philadelphia

Eian maneuvered the Bombardier Learjet 35A jet aircraft into a slot reserved for visiting aircraft at Atlantic Aviation, away from the prying eyes of the International and Domestic terminals' passengers. The flight took a little longer than he expected with a head wind forcing him to stop for fuel in Gander, Newfoundland. With a range of only 2,700 miles, it was the best rental they could get on such short notice. Of course, next time, with Dolan's money, he would rent the Gulfstream 550.

Eian looked over to Summer as she slept in the co-pilot's seat. "Time to get up little darling," he said in his best Irish brogue.

"We there already?" was her reply, brushing sleep from her eyes.

"What do you mean already? You slept almost the whole way. I had to do all of the work."

She smiled at him. "You wouldn't want me to miss my beauty sleep. Would you?"

Eian laughed at her. "Go wake our partner in the back while I finish up here."

Summer walked back to see Chuck sprawled across two seats, feet dangling in the aisle.

He heard her approach. "I'm up," he barked. "Where's the coffee?"

"You and me both. I'm on it," she replied.

Two minutes later, she handed him a white Styrofoam cup full of hot coffee.

"You're the good one, aren't you?" was his response.

Eian finished his duties and ventured out of the cockpit.

Summer stopped him. "Where will you be while we are painting?" she inquired innocently.

"I might visit a few friends."

"Don't think so," said Summer and Chuck in unison. "Jim said to keep an eye on you to make sure you don't visit any of your usual haunts."

"Did he now?" was his reply.

"Got a bunk with your name on it. Right beside Chucks."

Zhang suddenly appeared at the open aircraft door, a US Customs Agent right behind him. "Welcome home," he said.

The US Customs agent walked on board after Zhang. Outside three of his cohorts were opening panels; a fourth was leading a drug-sniffing dog through its routine. "Good evening," he said. "We are spot checking. You and your passengers have been selected for the full search."

The agent looked up to the cockpit, than the rear of the aircraft. "Just the three of you?"

Eian nodded. "Just us three lost souls."

"No problem. We should have you out of here in ten or fifteen minutes. Could I get each of you to exit the aircraft and stand in front of your luggage?" After they departed, the agent proceeded to search the aircraft's galley.

Each stood by their luggage as the handler allowed his dog to search the aircraft. Satisfied, the handler directed the dog to their luggage.

Eian turned to Summer and Chuck, just out of earshot of one of the agents checking the aircraft's wheel well. "I hope we don't encounter this group when we come home with all of our goodies."

The lead agent walked over to them, handing Eian, as the pilot, an official looking piece of paper clearing them. "You are good-to-go my friends. Enjoy Philadelphia."

Eian thanked the agents as they departed. He then turned his attention to Zhang. "Let's get the hell out of here."

"I have transportation waiting for you," he said, pointing over to a white mini-van, his crew already waiting inside.

Summer looked to the van, and then to Eian and Chuck. "Looks like it's going to be tight squeeze gentlemen. I'm up front, shotgun."

In minutes they were off to the warehouse.

They only had 11 days to work their magic.

The clock was ticking.

CHAPTER 33

Bern, Switzerland

Yuri and Lana were able to reach Bern in only 60 minutes using the A1 Motorway. Of course, Lana insisted on driving, reaching speeds in excess of 150 kilometers per hour over the flawless Swiss highway. It would have been higher but the Embassy vehicle started to shake and rattle at 150, forcing her to drop down to the posted speed limit of 120. To cover the same distance back home in Russia could have taken them hours due to the atrocious state of their public roadways. It wasn't uncommon for a driver in Russia to carry two or three spare tires if traveling long distance.

Lana pulled up the granite circular drive that announced the Hotel Weiss, one of the area's top hotels. A uniformed valet opened the door for her, holding out his white gloved hands for her keys.

"Herzlich willkommen," he said with a smile, *welcome.*

"Are you sure about this," said Yuri, noting the extravagance of the exterior. "We are supposed to be operating a little more discretely. Maybe a budget hotel would better suit us?"

She ignored him as she allowed the bellman to remove their bags from the back seat.

The bellman then pointed to the trunk.

"Do not open the trunk," she commanded. That is the last place she wanted exposed. She would have to resuscitate the poor man if he saw their weapons cache.

Yuri shook his head. "Are you sure about this?" She leaned into Yuri as they walked up the red velvet carpeted steps, arm-in-arm. "We have 50,000 euro's in our bag and I have no intention of returning... *most of it.*"

ENTERING THEIR SUITE, a complimentary chilled bottle of champagne sat in an ice bucket on the nightstand.

Yuri handed the bellman a 10 franc tip while Lana popped open the champagne. "Tomorrow we start work. Tonight we have a second honeymoon."

The bellman smiled as he winked at Yuri. "Have a great night, sir," closing the door behind him.

Walking down the hall the bellman heard glasses clink and loud laughter. He reached for his phone as he approached the elevators, texting a message to his contact:

They have arrived.

CHAPTER 34

Hotel Weiss: Bern, Switzerland

It was a long and tiring day. Chuck, Summer, and Eian had departed over twelve hours ago. Soon after, Jim and Nora scouted possible locations for a nighttime approach of the museum. They double and triple checked avenues of approach and escape. After lunch they drove to Zurich and hopefully away from prying eyes. They sought to acquire some common tools, and shop for black clothing for each member of the team. Driving to Zurich to gather the necessary supplies prevents any connection to their purchases so near where a robbery was committed. They made it back to their suite in time to shower and collapse into bed.

Jim lay in bed staring at the ceiling. He couldn't stop his mind from playing possible entry points into the museum over and over again. He nudged Nora. "You awake."

"I am now," was her sarcastic reply.

"I can't sleep," said Jim.

"Well, try harder. It's almost midnight."

On the nightstand, Jim's cell phone rang unexpectedly.

He looked at the caller ID but it was clear. "That's strange," he said. "Nothing is showing."

"Answer it," said Nora, "it might be from our people in Philly."

"Hello," he said hesitantly. He heard several metallic clicks, then a ping. He held his hand over the phones mouthpiece. "Sounds like an old-fashioned scrambler."

Nora was still in bed, resting on her elbow. She silently mouthed, "Are you kidding me?"

"James Dieter?" inquired a strong male voice on the other end. For the moment Jim couldn't place the accent.

"Yes," he replied.

"I am a ghost from your past, my friend."

Jim still had no recollection of the voice.

"Jim," said the voice, "Its Benny. Benny Machaim."

Benny Machaim paced the sparse confines of his office. The head of Mossad, Israeli intelligences equivalent of the CIA, he worked unusual hours, sometimes living in his office for days on end. Standing five foot five, head shaven bald, lean and fit from his prior exploits as a Shayetet 13 commando, an elite naval commando unit of the Israeli Navy, he was still a force to be reckoned with.

"Benny," he replied a bit surprised. "How are you, my friend?"

"I am, as you Americans are fond of saying, busy as usual."

Jim was considered a *Friend of Israel* due to the assistance he and Nora had previously provided, returning lost diamonds and gold to its rightful owners, Holocaust victims. It is a status very few are able to achieve.

Nora held up her hands in a *what gives* pose. Jim looked to his wife and hunched his shoulders. He continued: "I'm surprised you still remember me."

"Don't be silly. How could I not remember you and your lovely wife? The two of you helped us right some wrongs committed a long time ago. We will never forget you. It's funny but I was just speaking with our mutual friend, Solomon Nubelman. You remember Solomon?"

"Of course I do," replied Jim. "You helped him with his hit list."

Benny ignored the comment, pressing on. "He still lives in Salzburg with his family, living each day like it is his last. Still strolls along the Salzach River every day."

"I'm sure Solomon is enjoying those grand kids."

Benny interrupted him. "His granddaughter just had her first. He now has his first *great* grandchild."

"He must be very happy, indeed."

"For all the poor man has been through, yes he is. To see your own parents die in a concentration camp, his father in his own arms. However, he saw where the Germans hid their diamonds as they abandoned the camp. In addition, he used his money to get even. But enough of the reminiscing, Mr. James Dieter. This is a serious call."

Jim looked to the clock once more. It read midnight. "It must be something serious for you to call me at this hour of the night. What is it, one o'clock in the morning where you are?"

"Yes, it is. My work never stops, Jim. You of all people know that."

Of course he did. Jim remembered one of his contacts saying Benny kept a cot in the office so he wouldn't miss a thing.

"I hear you are working on recovering some artwork?"

Jim looked at Nora, then his phone, before replying. "Benny, you never stop surprising me. But to answer your question, yes. Paintings. Art that most thought was destroyed in WWII."

Benny nodded in understanding in his empty office. "You must be talking about the Gurlitt collection?"

Jim was dumbfounded. "How did you know that?"

"What, I don't have people too? What I can tell you is that little pig and his father stole more art than most of the top Nazi's put together. Even Goring if you can believe it. We know Gurlitt was the top buyer and seller of art during the war. He worked under direct commission of Hitler himself."

"I should have known you would be on top of this one. However, I can tell you this, there were four little pigs involved in the theft at the end of the war. The two Gurlitt's, an American named Dolan, and a Russian named Petrov. The Russian took his cut not long after the four of them divided the treasure. He was caught smuggling it back to Russia by the KGB and shot soon after he identified his partners. His portion of the paintings wound up being confiscated and sent to a few different museums. I heard Stalin picked some of the choicest paintings to hang in his offices."

Benny looked at the picture of his wife and two children on his desk. "And allow me to ask something: Why do you know so much about this particular theft?"

"That's the reason Nora and I are in Bern. We are working a job for the son of the American from the war. The older Dolan died a few years back but not before relaying the story to his son. These are not the best of people."

Benny shook his head in his empty office. "I have to question some of the people you are acquainted with, Jim."

"No, you have it all wrong. He is not a friend nor an acquaintance. He sort of kidnapped my friend Eian. You remember Eian? He helped us on the last job."

"Of course I do. He is an excellent pilot. However, you have to explain how he *sort of kidnapped Eian?* How do you sort of kidnap someone?"

"Long story, short version. Eian owed a lot of money to Dolan and then he lured Nora and myself into his spider web and it went downhill from there. All of that aside. You just provided me with an idea. An idea to help us with the art job. In the end, it is going to benefit some of your people from WWII. Well, a lot of your people. Maybe you could provide some assistance?"

"For anyone else, yes, it would be an imposition. However, for you my friend, the proverbial vault is open. What can we do for you?"

"Can we meet? Here in Bern?"

After an awkward pause, Benny replied: "I am not allowed in Bern at the moment. The Swiss didn't like something I did a few months ago. Seems I hurt them in the pocketbook. How about Salzburg?"

"Salzburg, Austria works," replied Jim.

"Okay, Hotel Schloss Mönchstein. They have an excellent bar with a glass dome over it."

Benny looked at his on-line calendar. "How about in four days? Say Thursday?"

"I have to move a few things on my schedule but I can make that happen."

"Now for the reason I called. Two things. First. You have two Russian agents on your tail. They are staying in the same hotel. They go by the names Yuri and Lana Velismo. Married couple. They may be using an alias. Evidently your art job is gaining some notoriety."

Jim looked nervously to Nora before replying to Benny. "I can't believe this. We've tried our best to keep our job under wraps."

"I think you have a rat on Dolan's team. They in-turn are feeding info to the Russians. Of course, we have the ability to intercept most of the Russian communications traffic. These games go round-and-round. So we are all one big happy family."

"I owe you one for this. Thanks."

"That's not all. You may find yourself ever deeper in debt to me. I find myself visiting Iran tomorrow, of course undercover. They would never willingly allow me to enter. It seems the Russians not only have Yuri and Lana Velismo on your tail but they are importing some hit men from Iran to assist them. They just happen to be the same people I will be visiting tomorrow. They are some part-time art dealers who double as very nasty international hit men. They are on our radar for some work they performed in the Sini last year. Killed a few of our people. So I find myself in the position to help not only my country but also my good friend, James Dieter. It is my hope to try to persuade them to back down from working with the Russians. If I am not successful, then there is always plan B."

"You mean they disappear?"

"Disappear is such a nasty word. Let us say they are going to meet some of their past relatives."

"It does sound better when you say it that way."

"Jim, a word of warning. It appears the word is on the street and everyone wants a piece of your little project."

Jim just shook his head. "I can't believe this. Whatever happened to honesty among governments and thieves?"

Benny laughed aloud at the analogy. "That's for politicians above my paygrade to decide. I work for the people. For my country. Definitely not for the money. With that said, I leave tomorrow. And I will meet you in Salzburg on Thursday."

"Done. See you at the Hotel Schloss Mönchstein's bar. Drinks are my treat. And be careful."

CHAPTER 35

Tehran, Iran - 3:25pm

Benny and two of his top agents waited silently on a side street in a middle-class neighborhood in northern Tehran. They had flown in via Cairo that morning on forged Egyptian passports.

His two agents sat patiently on a stolen motorbike as Benny stood watching their targets only 50 meters from where he stood. He eyed a late-model white Renault with a middle-aged man and a younger woman in deep discussion. Benny was waiting for several people to leave the immediate area near the car. He was operating under orders to avoid injuring innocent bystanders. After several minutes, the street was clear.

Benny tapped the driver of the motorbike on the shoulder, indicating they were good-to-go.

The agent on the rear of the motor bike pulled a SIG Sauer P226 from a black backpack then handed the cloth backpack to Benny. Benny then indicated for the driver to proceed at a slow, 15 kilometer per hour speed just as they had rehearsed the day before. Slowly they approached the Renault, the motorbike diver stopping adjacent to the car's driver. The agent on the rear of the bike aimed first at the passenger then the driver, a quick double tap for each, killing both instantly.

The agent on the rear of the motor bike quickly jumped down from the bike, scouring the inner area of the car, before removing documents and a leather briefcase. Satisfied they had recovered everything, they promptly sped off in a cloud of smoke.

Neighbors in the immediate area clearly overheard the sound of glass breaking. Some of them even dared to rush out to see what had occurred.

An older woman draped in a black shawl cautiously approached the scene. She first viewed the driver's side window broken. Then as she edged closer she saw two bodies, both slumped over, evidently dead. She kissed her prayer beads before waving to her husband who was still standing on their home's wooden porch. "Call the police," she screamed.

HIS TWO AGENTS on the motorbike were clear.

Satisfied their targets were dead, Benny promptly walked to his awaiting car.

Within hours, semi-official Iranian news agencies were reporting the murders of a Lebanese art dealer called Habib Dawood with ties to the Lebanese group Hezbollah -- and his daughter, Mariam.

And there the story rested, until a flurry of activity on obscure social media accounts tied the hit to Mossad, claiming that the victims were not Lebanese, but rather one of the most important figures in al Qaeda -- Abu Mohammed al-Masri -- and his daughter, the widow of Osama bin Laden's son Hamza.

The original reports about the mysterious Dawood seemed suspect because there was no record of a Lebanese art dealer by the name of Habib Dawood, nor anyone with a similar spelling. Nor was there a eulogy in Lebanon -- for either him or his daughter. In addition, there was nothing in pro-Hezbollah media in Lebanon to verify the identity of the victims.

Twenty-four hours later an agency called Shamshad News, which described itself as an Afghanistan-based radio and television news outlet, also claimed that al-Masri had been killed in Tehran. But the Iranian authorities remained silent.

Within days of the killing unnamed Iranian officials said the Israeli Mossad did indeed carry out the attack.

It was noted that the dead were guests in Iran trying to assemble a group of art experts for a mission somewhere in Europe, possibly Bern, Switzerland, hoping to enrich the depleted al Qaeda and Hezbollah coffers.

Thanks to Benny, the only thing they would be enriching was the ground they were buried in.

CHAPTER 36

Jerusalem: Mossad HQ

Benny ensured his translators worked through the night on the documents his men had confiscated from the car in Teheran.

What they eventually uncovered deeply disturbed him, or at least, how it concerned his friend. He reached for his cell phone. In seconds, he connected with Jim.

"Jim, its Benny. I am afraid I have some good news-bad news for you. Good news is everything went according to plan yesterday and you have no more worries from the targets in Iran nor Lebanon, at least not for the fore seeable future. But there is still time. They have long memories."

"Thanks for that one," replied Jim. "I know we really pissed off the Hezbollah when we went for the Bormann gold and stole it from under their very noses." He paused for several seconds. "But let's hear the bad news."

"Well, our targets were carrying documents that I had my people translate. Luckily I can share this information with you because it does not affect our state. According to the documents, the Swiss Government has every intention of moving the Gurlitt collection to a temporary location in Zurich in nine days. This will undoubtedly force the Russians to hedge their bets. So with the people we eliminated in Iran now out of the big picture, the Russians will be forced to rely solely on their two agents staying in your hotel. They will probably try to steal from you what you in-turn steal from the museum. There is also the possibility the Russians will try to use the international courts to file a case against the Swiss for possession of stolen artwork. The court case will probably go nowhere, but as you can see, the possibility of a court case has forced the Swiss hand. They will move the art until this blows over. Out of sight, out of mind. I can tell you this, once it's in a Zurich vault you will never get it. They will place it 200 feet underground."

"I can't believe it! We just finalized our plan to hit the Museum within the next eleven days. Now we have to go back to the drawing board."

Benny paused for a few seconds. "I still owe you. Any way I can help, just call. You have my number."

"Benny, as usual whenever I speak with you it is an education."

"I will take that as a complement my friend. Besides, I don't mind planting little seeds in your head if they are going to develop into something beneficial."

"This is all great info, Benny. I am going to run this pass my team. I think that makes Thursday's meeting even more important. I will see you at the Hotel Schloss Mönchstein's bar. Remember drinks are on me."

LONG BURIED SECRETS

CHAPTER 37

After he hung up with Benny, Jim checked the time. He noted it was a six-hour time difference. Summer, Eian, Chuck, Zhang, along with Zhang's crew should still be working or getting close to finishing for the day.

Nora poured him a drink from the mini bar. "We might as well celebrate Benny ridding the earth of those terrorists. Scotch on the rocks for you, sir." She searched the well-stocked fridge until she found something to suit her own taste. "Vino for me."

She filled her glass with a merlot 'mini' bottle and then raised it in toast. "Cheers, to getting that monkey off our backs."

"Two monkeys really. They doubled as hit persons *and* art thieves."

They both took a decent sip of their respective drinks.

Let's FaceTime with the group," said Jim.

In a matter a seconds Nora had Summer on the other line. She placed the cell phone on the glass table in front of them propped up on a book so they could see everyone. "We have news. Jim thought it best to call at this late hour to keep you abreast of recent developments."

Eian sat down beside Summer. "Jim, they have kidnapped me. Won't let me out of the warehouse."

Jim laughed aloud. "They are only following orders, Eian," he replied. "I didn't want you sliding any deeper into debt. But on a serious note. We are going to require your services sooner than we thought."

"I'm ready to go right now," he responded. "Free me, please."

By now Chuck, Zhang and his crew had joined Summer and Eian.

"How are you on the paintings?" Jim inquired. Nora refreshed his drink then her own. She waved to everyone.

"We are actually ahead of schedule," replied Summer, looking at her cohorts sitting around her. "We have all 50 of the high-end reproductions complete and in the drying ovens. We should have the remaining low-end reproductions complete in about four or five days."

Jim looked to Nora. "You want me to tell them or do you what too?"

Nora smiled at him. "Let me."

Jim clicked his glass to hers. "My lovely wife has something to say to you all."

"Oh boy. I feel a fastball coming straight at me," said Summer.

Nora smiled at everyone. "We have good news, and somewhat good news," she began. "Good news is a highly placed friend of Jim's called to tell us that he was able to avert someone trying to kill us. That is, Jim and I."

"That would definitely be classified under the good news column," said Chuck.

"Thanks, Chuck," he replied. "It had to do with a job Nora, Eian, and myself had worked on last year. The Bormann gold job."

Eian chimed in. "One less person wants me dead: only 29 to go."

Summer looked at Eian. "Give us some time. That list may grow."

Jim covered his face with his hands to hide his reaction. "I see you are still making friends, Eian."

"You know me, Jim. Never one to sit idly on the sidelines. Such a lovely personality."

Nora put a halt to the banter. "Okay. Let me please continue."

"Floor is all yours," said Summer.

"Now for the semi-good news. Jim's friend also informed us that the Swiss intend on moving the Gurlitt collection within the next nine to ten days."

A series of groans was heard on the other end of the call. Zhang could be overheard interpreting the news to his crew. Soon an argument broke out in Chinese. Zhang evidently calmed them down by offering more of his share. The argument stopped."

Eian was first to speak. "So how can we help?"

Jim continued. "We need you to work through the next couple of nights and finish as many as possible. The whole plan has changed. We are moving up our timetable for the museum. I potentially have someone to assist us with inside info on the move. I am meeting with him soon in Salzburg. I want you to fly Summer and Chuck back to Bern three days from now. Nora will fill you in on the details when you get here. If you still have paintings that are not done, then I need

Zhang and his crew to continue working on what remains. He can then overnight the paintings to us. They will all stay in Philadelphia at the warehouse in case we need something else completed."

Zhang nodded. "We will do as you say, Jim."

"All right then. See you in about 72 hours."

CHAPTER 38

Jim and Nora woke the next morning with a new vigor most likely attributed to the information Benny shared about the Russian interlopers staying in the same hotel. It was one late night call they didn't mind receiving. His call did make them realize one thing: the word was truly on the street. But how long would it take to reach the proper authorities?

They had no idea the Russians, besides having their own agents trail them, had contracted with al Qaeda and Hezbollah to possibly kill them. That was a wake-up. With Benny and his agents eliminating the two assassins in Iran, that left the Russians and Mike Dolan to deal with. *At least that they knew about.* It's always good to know who your enemies are. Especially when you're competing for the same products. In this case, very expensive artwork.

Jim had a meeting scheduled with Benny later in the day in Salzburg. That left a few hours for him and Nora to toy with the Russians before he had to depart for the airport. Maybe test their mettle.

Jim rang down to the Valet and asked them to have their car ready in 15 minutes.

He then let the system work its magic.

LONG BURIED SECRETS

CHAPTER 39

Bern, Switzerland

Yuri and Lana Velismo had made the most of their time at the Hotel Weiss. They spoiled themselves for the first two days with several in-room meals and a couple's massage. They even spent time in the hotel's luxurious spa where Lana tried to talk Yuri into his first pedicure. Of course he declined, preferring to sit in the sauna while Lana had her toes done.

But now it was time to get to work. They had a schedule to keep.

They wasted no time discretely spreading around some of the euros they had converted into Swiss Francs. First, the room service captain, then the concierge, the valet, and finally the head of the cleaning staff. All were in jobs that were notoriously underpaid and each appreciated the padded envelope containing 500 Swiss Francs that Yuri had provided them. Soon enough they had Jim and Nora's daily itinerary, car description and license plate, and even their dinner reservations. They were even notified when Jim or Nora walked past the front desk.

Clearly it was money well spent.

YURI's CELL PHONE rang to the Rolling Stones song, *I Can't Get No Satisfaction*. It was the Valet. He called to inform Yuri that the Dieter's had requested their car be delivered in front of the hotel in 15 minutes. Yuri thanked him and requested the same of their car.

Their first solid lead. It's time to see what they are up too, thought Yuri. He yelled to Lana who was still in the shower. "Lana, they are on the move. Let's cut it short."

JIM AND NORA WALKED arm-in-arm past the front desk, each dressed smartly as if attending a business meeting.

The front desk clerk smiled, "Guten Morgan," she said, *Good Morning* in German. The hotel staff appreciated its guests taking the extra step to dress to impress. After all, The Hotel Weiss had a reputation of stuffiness to uphold.

They were quickly followed by Yuri and Lana dressed in a more relaxed ensemble of jeans, tee shirts, and sneaks. Lana's long brown hair was still damp, having rushed her shower and having little time to use the blow dryer. The front desk clerk nodded to them as he was now busy checking in a guest.

Both couples stood out front of the hotel, at a distance, awaiting their respective vehicles. Lana casually eyed Nora, knowing that she was a winner of a Pulitzer Prize for her writing; but could she shoot someone in cold blood or fight a man in hand-to-hand combat? Yuri likewise observed Jim. He knew him to be an ex-Navy SEAL and most likely a worthy advisory.

Only time would tell.

Jim and Nora's car came out of the hotel's underground garage first. The valet left the engine running as he ran around to the passenger side door and opened it for Nora. She smiled at him in thanks.

Jim looked to Nora in the passenger seat. "That has to be them," he said. "I detected a Russian accent as they spoke between themselves."

"Should we wait until their car comes out of the garage," said Nora, a big grin evident upon her face. "Possibly give them a fighting chance?"

"Look at you. Are you starting to enjoy this?"

"A little excitement will never hurt anyone."

Jim eyed the car as it came out the garage. He drove slowly for three blocks, eyeing them in his car's rear view mirror, waiting until they were seated in their car. "Okay, it's go time. Let's take them on a little sight-seeing tour."

LANA ONCE AGAIN ASSUMED the driving duties. Yuri was relegated to the passenger seat. "Hold on," she said, the car accelerating forward in a desire to catch up. "I see them about three blocks ahead."

Yuri pulled up the city map on his cell phone, hoping to get an idea of where they were going. "Looks like they are heading out of the city."

JIM HAD NO DESIRE to lose his tail. He spotted them only two blocks behind them. "Okay, first turn coming up." He made a right-hand turn, went one block, and then made another, and another until he came full circle.

Nora had pulled up the Bern city map on her phone. "Okay, make a left at the next light and then merge onto Schanzlistrasse, it goes right in front of the Casino."

Jim turned as requested, watching in his rear mirror for his tail to do the same. "Right behind us. What's next?"

"They have a Bear Garden for brown bears and a Cathedral from the 1400's. Which one?"

"Definitely the Cathedral. We can take the heathens to church."

"Oh, I like that. Make a left at the Casinoplatz and two blocks up on your right you will see the church spires."

"Then I'm going to pull in and park."

FROM ONE BLOCK BEHIND, Lana tailed Jim's car.

"Where are they going, Yuri? Talk to me."

Yuri consulted his cell phone map of Bern. "Looks like either the Cathedral or the Bear Park."

"He's pulling over into the Cathedral parking lot."

"Follow him," said Yuri. "Just maintain a little distance. I don't think they made us yet."

Lana waited as Jim approached the parking attendant before driving closer.

JIM TURNED INTO THE PARKING lot for the Cathedral, driving up to the parking attendant's booth. "This country is expensive. Twenty-five francs to park? What's that, like $30 back in the states?

"Something like that," Nora replied. "I have an idea. Pay the attendant fifty francs. Tell him you are paying for the car behind us."

"Oh, I like that. Good one."

He handed the attendant a fifty-franc note and told him what he wanted to do. At first the attendant was confused, but he soon understood Jim's intent.

The lot was relatively empty, with the early morning crowds that were normally associated with tour buses had yet to show. They found a space by the front of the lot and parked. Quickly exiting their car, they moved at a fast pace into the cathedral.

"HURRY UP," SAID YURI. They are already walking into the cathedral."

Lana pulled up to the parking attendant's booth. Yuri already had twenty-five francs ready for her to pay for parking.

The attendant merely waved them in. "The car before you already paid for your parking," he said, a big grin noticeable on his face. "Never have come across that before. Very nice people."

"We've been made," said Lana and Yuri at the same time.

They parked a few spots over from Jim and Nora's car.

They soon joined them in the cathedral.

WHEN JIM AND NORA first entered the cathedral, and were out of view from the parking lot, they ran up the steps to the balcony with the intent of watching their Russian tails come in.

Soon enough, Lana and Yuri came walking in. They stood just below Jim and Nora, scanning the relatively empty cathedral. They quickly decided it was best to separate. Jim and Nora watched as Yuri opened the confessional doors on the right-hand side, Lana did the same on the left-hand side.

Jim tapped Nora on the arm, a smirk upon his face. "Let's get out of here."

"This is too much," was her reply.

"Not if they decide to start shooting it won't be."

They walked back down the steps, pausing at the front door. Nora picked up a hardback book that was for sale in the rear of the church. She eyed Lana and Yuri as they walked up the aisle, now by the front of the cathedral, a good 50 meters away.

"Shall I?" she said, ready to drop the book on the floor.

"Go for it," replied Jim.

Two seconds later the sound of the hardback book echoed throughout the silent cathedral.

It had the desired effect as Lana and Yuri both turned to the sound in time to watch Jim and Nora exit.

Lana pointed to the back. Yuri nodded and started running. In a matter of seconds, both were leaving the cathedral.

Jim and Nora drove towards the rear of the parking lot, exiting just as Lana and Yuri ran to their car.

"Wait until they catch up," said Nora looking back, making sure they were spotted.

"Okay they have us," she said. Nora watched as they were now only a block behind them. "The days too early to end our fun. What do you say we try something else?"

She consulted the map on her phone, looking for something of interest. "Oh this will be a good one."

"For whom?" responded Jim. "Us or them?"

"Oh, definitely us," she chuckled. "Okay, in one block you are going to pull into a police station parking lot," pointing to a small parking lot off to his left.

"Are you sure about this? A police station?"

"Trust me. I'm going to walk in and only ask for directions. But you never know, maybe something else will materialize. Most importantly, the Russians won't have a clue as to why I'm in there. Make them think a bit."

Jim could only smile. "Smart and beautiful," he said.

"We are so rare," was her response.

YURI SAW THEM first. "Off to your left. Pull in," he commanded. "Is that a police station? Why are they going into a police station?"

"Who cares, just take notes." Lana backed their car into an empty spot five rows from Jim's car.

Yuri used his notepad and annotated the time and place. "Looks like just the woman is going in."

In a minute or two Nora came walking out. For a moment, it almost looked like she smiled in their direction.

Lana banged her hands on the cars steering wheel. "Did you see her? They are treating this as though it's some type of game."

They eyed Jim's car for several moments, Nora still standing at the passenger side door. In another minute or so, a police officer walked out of the station. Nora pointed to Lana and Yuri's car. He waved in acknowledgement and now approached the Russian's car.

"What's going on, Yuri?" said Lana as the officer drew near. "Something's not right."

Yuri tried to ignore the approaching officer, fumbling on his phone.

A tapping sound on Yuri's passenger side window caught them both by surprise. He turned to see the officer indicating for him to roll down his window.

"Yes, officer," Yuri said in English, "Can I help you with something? I hope we didn't do anything wrong?"

They both watched as Jim and Nora pulled out and onto the main street and sped off.

The officer handed them a pamphlet with a picture of a sleeping dog, a cat resting within its paws. "No, no, you did nothing wrong," the officer replied in English with a minor French accent. "Your friends that just left," he pointed to Jim and Nora's car, now almost out of sight, "said that you would like to donate to our station charity. The woman gave us a 50-franc note. Most generous of her. The woman said that you are big animal shelter supporters." He pointed to the pamphlet. "We have adopted the shelter as our station's charity. We all give what we can."

Lana saw that Jim and Nora's car was now out of sight, long gone. "Give the officer a 50 franc note, Yuri," she said in a frustrated voice.

Yuri dug through his pockets, finding only 100's. "I only have 100's," he said in desperation to Lana.

"Just give him the hundred," she said slowly and deliberately.

After the officer took his money and departed, Lana once again banged her hands on the steering wheel. "They won the first round," she said, "Well played."

Yuri pulled out a small iPad. "Should I activate the GPS Tracker on their car?"

Lana smiled at him. "I didn't think we would have a need for it. But yes, turn it on."

CHAPTER 40

"Do you think we lost them?" asked Nora, looking back at the police station parking lot.

Jim laughed aloud. "That was a classic move. You mean to tell me you just walked in and were able to spot the pet charity poster?"

Nora turned back around in her seat, facing forward. "I walked in with the full intention of asking which way to the Bern Art Museum. However, when I saw the poster of the two pets and a collection jar beneath it, I quickly put two and two together. I walked up to the officer on duty and handed him a 50-franc note and said I wanted to donate to the pet charity listed on the poster. He told me I was most generous. That's when I told him our two friends were outside and would also like to donate. But they had disabilities and, if it would not be too much of an imposition, could he walk out and accept the donation himself? He was most helpful and soon followed me out the door. You saw what happened after that."

"That was a genius move," he said.

"Like I said earlier, so few of us."

Jim leaned over and offered her a peck on the cheek. "So true." He noticed a restaurant. "Let's get something to eat while our two friends drive around town searching for us. Then you can drive me to the airport for my flight to Salzburg."

ONLY ONE BLOCK AWAY sat Lana and Yuri in their car, a GPS receiver in Yuri's hand. They eyed Jim and Nora sitting at a table by the window in the restaurant.

"Looks like the bribe we paid the valet turned out to be money well spent," said Yuri.

Twenty-four hours ago, the valet had informed Yuri and Lana where he had parked Jim and Nora's car. Yuri wasted no time in discreetly placing a GPS transmitter under the rear bumper.

"Next we have to bug the interior of their car," said Yuri.

"And bring our service weapons," replied Lana. "This is the last time they will treat this as a game."

LONG BURIED SECRETS

CHAPTER 41

Salzburg, Austria

Evening was approaching as Jim sat down in the Hotel Schloss Mönchstein's well-appointed lobby. After his short flight from Bern he was intent on catching up on some e-mails on his iPhone.

As Jim pulled out his phone, a well-dressed gentleman strode up unannounced and sat down in a chair that backed up to Jim's.

"You keep some strange company, Jim Dieter," said Benny in a low voice from behind. He placed his cell phone to his ear as if speaking to someone. "Have you encountered the Russians I warned you about?"

Jim half turned in his chair. He picked up on Benny's deception and did the same, placing his phone to his ear. "Still the master at arriving unannounced."

"The Russians want you dead. Well, dead after they find out what your plans are for the paintings. My guess is that they have connected the hit we performed in Tehran to the paintings."

"So they are aware Mossad might be assisting us?"

Benny dropped the charade as he placed his phone on the chair beside him. A cryptic smile suddenly appeared on his face. "I knew I shouldn't have called you," he said jokingly but tinged with a hint of seriousness. He then picked up his phone and walked around to sit beside Jim. He extended his hand in greeting. "What am I getting the Mossad involved in? *Hell, what am I getting involved in?*"

Jim shook his friend's hand enthusiastically. "It's good to see you too," he replied sarcastically.

"Yes, yes. Of course it's good to see you."

"My apologies for dragging you up to Salzburg but I needed to speak with you in person. It's definitely something we could not discuss on the phone." Jim casually surveyed the area about them before continuing. "When my wife Nora and I helped you with the Bormann gold, you had mentioned that I had one chit, anytime, anywhere, all I had to do was call."

Benny looked to the ornate ceiling, admiring the hand-stamped tin panels. He then nodded. "For a Friend of Israel, anytime, anywhere."

Jim looked directly at Benny. "Well today I am calling in that chit."

"I presume it must be something big?"

"No, not really," said Jim, before pausing for a few seconds. "Well, maybe. I may need some help from you and someone from our past."

"So my elimination of your enemies in Iran was not the favor you hoped for?"

Jim stopped him for a second. "Wait a minute. I think they were enemies to us both. You have to provide me a free pass on that one."

Benny smiled. "Okay, you are given a free pass on that one. So let me get this straight. Not only do you require my assistance, but you also need a friend's assistance?" He paused dramatically for several seconds, scanning the hotel's lobby before answering. "For the friend part, whom did you have in mind?"

"Do you think Solomon Nubelman would be willing to assist us in a little deception?"

"Solomon Nubelman? You are the one who helped him. Because of you, he was able to fulfill a promise he made to himself as a nine-year-old in a concentration camp after watching his father die in his arms. Moreover, that promise was to extract revenge on his enemies from the war. I don't think Solomon would have an issue, at all. You have to remember that he is getting up there in the years but then again, who isn't? Yes, I think for you, he would be willing to do anything."

"Can you arrange a meeting between the three of us?"

"That is a simple request." Benny held up his index finger, indicating for Jim to wait a second. He then searched his phone for a number before placing the phone to his ear. He obviously had Solomon's private number. After several rings, the phone connected. "Solomon. Benny here. Shalom my old friend. I hope your family is doing well. Listen, this is a business call, so I am cutting short on the formalities just this once. Now the reason I am calling you, it concerns an associate of ours. I happen to be sitting beside James Dieter. You remember him?" Several seconds passed as Solomon spoke to Benny. "I know your memory is still sharp as a tack and I knew you would never forget our friend. I just had to ask. He is the reason why I am calling. We are sitting in Salzburg at this very moment and would like to pay you a visit. I will provide you the reason in-person, not over the phone."

Obviously, Solomon had concurred.

"Thirty minutes would be fine. Shalom."

Jim searched Benny's face. "Well, are we good?"

Benny nodded. "He is sending a car for us. He said he would go to his grave for you."

"Well, let's hope it doesn't have to come to that."

LONG BURIED SECRETS

CHAPTER 42

Philadelphia International Airport
Atlantic Aviation Services ramp

Eian sat in the cockpit, conducting the final pre-flight of his Gulfstream 550 rental aircraft for their journey back to Bern. He didn't expect to be flying so soon, but since Jim's call to Summer, telling them to finish and get to Europe, it had been a whirlwind. They rushed to finish the last painting, only taking it out of the curing oven less than an hour ago. After which they loaded the van and headed straight for the airport.

Eian scanned the cockpit's instruments for any indication of fault before re-setting a few circuit breakers and testing the fuel indicators. Satisfied, he called back to Summer. "I'm good-to-go," he said. He then tapped his watch. "Times a ticking."

Summer was busy helping Chuck and Zhang load the reproductions into the aircraft. "Alright," she replied. "We are moving as fast as we can. We should be ready in five minutes."

That's all Eian wanted to hear. "I'm holding you to that." He quickly turned his attention to the sky and the cloud cover, contacting the control tower asking for the latest weather report.

Summer rolled her eyes. She turned to Chuck and Zhang. "Give somebody a little power…"

AT THE EDGE of the airport fence line, a woman aimed her parabolic listening device at Eian's aircraft. She was getting her monies worth out of the device, using it for the second time in two weeks. Some of the audible was broken up but she was able to acquire enough information to make an informed decision. She pulled out her cell phone, typing a short message to her boss. *They are leaving now. Loading complete.*

She watched as their plane departed. She then drove her rental car to the return lot.

She had a plane to catch to Europe.

CHAPTER 43

Salzburg, Austria

Solomon stood waiting at the top of the stone steps to his manor house as the Rolls Royce Phantom VI pulled into the portico. The car's driver quickly jumped out of the car and raced around to open the door for Jim and Benny.

Jim was amused. "Some class, wouldn't you say?"

"That's Solomon," Benny replied, he's like the President of Austria. *Only they like Solomon.*"

"Gentlemen," said Solomon, holding out his arms wide in greeting, a bear like hug first for Benny, then for Jim. For someone in his late eighties they were surprised at his strength. "It's nice to finally meet you in person, Mr. Dieter."

"Please, call me Jim."

"And you shall call me Solomon. I had the chef prepare us a light dinner by the pool. There we can discuss how I may be of service to you both."

The manor house consisted of a main four-story building in historical Tudor style that, according to the carving above the stone arch, dated to 1710. Anchoring both ends were faux castle keeps.

As they walked through the double doors, two servants dressed in 17th century period costume held the doors ajar for them.

Jim looked around the marbled entry room and had to ask. "Excuse me Solomon, but how big is this place? It's absolutely massive!"

Solomon halted the procession for a moment, speaking in German to the younger of the two servants. After several seconds, he seemed satisfied. "You'll have to excuse me, I'm not aware of all the particulars of the house, even after living here for five years. To answer your question Jim, just under 10,000 square feet, but if you include the ten-car garage and the riding stables, about 14,000 square feet. This house is so enormous there are certain parts I haven't visited in months." He turned and indicated for the servants to lead the way. "Please, this way. We don't want the food to get cold and possibly alienate the chef." He smiled before he said in a low voice, "He's French and has a bad attitude, but the man can cook!"

Jim and Benny both laughed aloud at his candor.

The lite dinner was more of a buffet; a six-foot table covered in assorted hot and cold dishes, cheeses, and vegetables. A second table held an assortment of decadent desserts. On one side stood the chef, impeccably dressed in his whites topped with a toque blanche, or white hat, and with his carving knife at the ready.

Benny turned to Jim, "I hope today is not the day you chose to start your diet."

Jim stood in amazement. "I feel like royalty," he said.

Benny nodded. "As a friend of Solomon's, *you are royalty.*"

DINNER COMPLETE. It was time for business. Solomon, Benny, and Jim strolled the grounds smoking Cuban cigars and drinking an Austrian Cabernet out of hand-carved crystal goblets. Benny was first to speak. "Solomon, on our way over to your beautiful home, Jim and I discussed a role we hoped you could play for us? This role could aid in the return of stolen artwork, priceless works seized during the war. Jim's plan is to return all pieces to their rightful owners. Very similar to your own situation."

Without so much as a second elapsing, Solomon agreed. "What can I do to assist?" He replied anxiously.

"But it could be dangerous," said Jim.

Benny nodded in agreement.

Solomon took a long pull on his cigar, waited several seconds before exhaling. He had a look of seriousness upon his face as he spoke. "Gentlemen, are you saying it's potentially more dangerous than the German concentration camp I was literally raised in? The one where my parents died? Hell, my own father died in my arms. If I can, at my age, still possess a way to strike back at those bastards, then count me in."

Benny patted Solomon on the back in thanks.

Jim raised his glass in appreciation.

Solomon turned to Benny and Jim, with a hint of seriousness he said: *"Do I get to shoot anybody?"*

CHAPTER 44

Salzburg, Austria

A sudden chill in the nighttime air forced them to move indoors. They now sat in the manor houses library, occupying three plush leather chairs that faced a roaring fire.

"Tell me how I can help?" queried Solomon. "I have many friends scattered throughout Europe, many in high places who owe me considerably. That is, if the job you have is indeed in Europe?"

Benny grinned as he turned to Jim. "I think the man is opening the proverbial vault to you."

"Very kind of you, Solomon," said Jim. He was already prepared to respond. "Do you have any contacts in the Swiss or Russian governments?"

"Many," he responded. "How high up do you want to go?"

Jim took a sip of his wine before replying. "The top floor."

Solomon pulled out his cell phone, then a pair of reading glasses. "I can't read a damn thing without these. I not only feel old, *I am old*."

Benny and Jim laughed aloud as they each pulled out their own reading glasses for his benefit, showing Solomon he was not alone.

"Okay. For Switzerland, I have the President of the Swiss Confederation, which is effectively the leader of the country, Lisanetta Tuttleson, on speed dial. And as for Russia, the Defense Minister, Sergey Mastacov, I also have his personal number on speed dial. Unfortunately, the President of Russia chooses not to deal with people such as myself."

"His loss, our gain," said Benny. He then turned to Jim, a smile creeping across his face. "I told you he had some powerful and prominent friends."

Jim again held up his glass. "Solomon, when Benny first told me you were an influential man, I thought he might have been laying it on a bit thick in regards to the people you were acquainted with," replied Jim.

Solomon nodded. "Jim, it's amazing what money and high-end parties will do. Especially when you donate to their favorite causes, *usually themselves*."

Solomon suddenly stood and walked to the fire, grabbing a brass poker from the stand. He half-turned to Jim and Benny as he kneeled on the wood floor in front of the flames. "So, what can an old man like Solomon Nubelman do to help his friends screw some Nazi bastards in their graves?"

Jim turned to Benny, then Solomon. "Well, in order for our plan to work, the services we will require of you…"

CHAPTER 45

Salzburg, Austria

Benny and Jim had departed over an hour ago. Solomon had his limo driver take Benny to the airport and Jim back to his hotel.

Now it was time to contemplate in silence. Solomon was still sitting in front of his fireplace. He stared at its embers as he nursed his wine, considering what they had discussed.

Not many people can say they had the privilege to have entertained the head of Mossad in their home, let alone him asking for assistance on a certain project.

He was briefly interrupted by his butler, Damir, with him pouring the last of the wine into his glass.

"Danke schon, Damir," said Solomon or *Thank-you*. "You can be on your way. I'm just going to rest here for the time being."

"Very well, sir," he replied. "Your wife is in bed reading. All of the staff have left for the night. The chef will be back in the morning to make breakfast. Before I leave, I will set the manor alarm. I bid you goodnight, sir."

Solomon watched as Damir departed the room. He then rose to place a small log on the embers. In a matter of minutes, the flames were decent enough to place a second log diagonally across the first. Sitting back in his chair, he allowed his mind to wander. He was in a state of melancholy as he thought of his father. He would be proud of him and how he had hunted down their enemies, his ridding the earth of Nazis one-by-one. And from living in squalor to one of the richest men in Europe. *Wish he could have lived to see it all,* he thought, as he took another sip of wine.

"Enough," he said aloud. "Time to get to work." He pulled out his cell phone from his shirt pocket and looked at the time. Nine pm. He hit the speed dial for the personal cell number of the President of the Swiss Confederation. Within seconds, she picked up.

"Solomon," Lisanetta Tuttleson said, "I am so happy to hear from you. I was just thinking of you."

SOLOMON HAD JUST bid goodnight to President Tuttleson, and then he called Jim at his hotel.

"I have news on the first art shipment," he said excitedly. "It will be shipped in a white, non-descript transit van to not attract attention. Just one van with two guards, one driving, the other a passenger. Before shipment, the paintings will all be taken out of their frames, rolled up for storage in telescoping tubes, and then placed in travel bins. The first shipment is departing at 9am Tuesday, five days from now."

Jim was astounded. "The President just up and told you about the shipment? No questions as to why you wanted to know?"

"It's all in the presentation, my friend. She is aware of my background as an art enthusiast. I simply informed her that I heard from a friend that the Gurlitt collection was being taken down for so-called maintenance. It was just a casual conversation that I steered her to. Then I inquired about her grandchildren, and it progressed up to my latest art acquisition. I told her I would like to have it placed on loan in the Bern gallery in her honor. That is when she informed me of the Gurlitt collection was being moved and not for the purposes of maintenance. It was just a casual conversation between friends."

"Hell of a conversation. She just laid out the museum's whole plan to you."

He smiled. "What can I say? People like to open up to a kind old man. Now, I will call the Russian Defense Minister to see if he has any information on the people they have sent after you."

"And how will you swing the conversation to the Gurlitt collection?"

"The same as the Swiss President. I will ask about his family and soon after that inform him of my desire to donate a painting to the Hermitage Museum in his name. That should stir up some discussion. I will also invite him and his wife to this year's Salzburg Christmas festival as my personal guests."

"Solomon, it sounds like you have everything well in hand," replied Jim. "I won't hold you up any longer. Call me as soon as you hear anything. And thank-you, Solomon, for all of your assistance."

Solomon wouldn't hear of it. "No, thank-you, James Dieter. Benny informed me of the real reason why you are doing this. You truly are a man of God."

Jim blushed on his end. "I wouldn't go that far Solomon. I'm just doing what's right."

A SLENDER MAN GAINED access to the manor house through an unlocked window in the servant's quarters, this prior to the butler setting the alarm as he departed for the night. He was dressed in black from head-to-toe. Once in, he proceeded to the second floor, following Solomon's booming voice as he was evidently speaking on his cell phone. In the hallway, outside of the library, the slender man eyed Solomon sitting comfortably in his chair by the fireplace. Patiently he waited until Solomon had concluded his phone conversations: one with the President of the Swiss Confederation, which he only caught the tail end of, and the second with the Russian

Defense Minister. That had extra meaning for him but he would need to address that at a more appropriate time. Using cunning gained from years of training, the man eased into the library, dangling a homemade garret between his hands. Slowly he approached the chair from the rear were Solomon sat, sipping his glass of wine. The room was quiet except for the crackling of the fire. The man sought a position directly behind Solomon. He waited until Solomon had finished his wine and had placed his glass on a side table. In a matter of seconds the garrote was around Solomon's neck, the slender man pulling back with such an excessive force it quickly crushed Solomon's windpipe. He gasped and struggled for almost 30 seconds before his body went limp. Luckily, for Solomon, his death had been quick, but that was all part of the slender man's plan. Wasting no time, he quickly proceeded over to the fireplace, stroking the fire until it was once again blazing. Using the hook side of the fireplace poker he yanked the logs onto the room's wood floor, its embers scattering onto the antique oriental rug.

The man stood back for few moments, waiting until the rug caught fire. Within seconds the fire began to spread. Since time was of the essence, the man pulled Solomon onto the floor not far from the fireplace, positioning him face down. He then placed the fireplace poker into his right hand as though Solomon's last moments were spent tending to the fire.

The fire now spread to the rooms' heavy drapery. It would not be long until the whole house would be engulfed. The man looked around the room for a smoke detector, noticing one above the entranceway. Moving a chair into place, he used it as a stool to remove the smoke detectors battery, pocketing it before placing the detector back into its original position, then the chair.

Satisfied, he was quick to leave the same way he had come in, through an unlocked window. Once outside, he hastily walked towards where he had parked his car on a side street just outside of Solomon's compound. As he walked he called a number his Embassy had provided him just two hours ago. It was answered on the first ring. "It's me. The old man put up no resistance. His two guests left about an hour and a half ago. One of them was your target. The other, I have no idea. I am sending some pictures of the man's face to our people in Moscow for facial recognition. Balls in your court."

CHAPTER 46

Nora's cell phone vibrated on the nightstand. She eyed its screen: 7am. She thought it might be Jim calling before he boarded the plane to return from Salzburg. Odd, but the caller ID was blank. "Hello," she said, her voice a bit gravelly.

It was Benny on the other end. "Nora, I'm so sorry to bother you at this early hour but I can't seem to reach Jim," he said with a hint of melancholy.

"Jim should be boarding his flight or in his seat already," she replied. "What's wrong Benny?"

Benny took a few seconds to compose himself before speaking. "It concerns our mutual friend, Solomon. I just received word that he and his wife died in a house fire late last night. Evidently a few hours after Jim and I had left. My friends on the scene say it looked like he succumbed to a heart attack while he was tending his fire, his wife to smoke inhalation. But I think you and I know better."

Nora shook her head slowly. She was wide-awake now as she rose out of bed, placing her feet on the floor. "I'm so sorry,

Benny. I spoke to Jim last night after Solomon called him at his hotel. Jim really took a liking to the man. Said he was an *old school gentleman*. He said I had to meet him."

"I wish you could of. Today our world is aching with the loss of Solomon." Benny suddenly changed gears. "With that said, I originally informed Jim I would perform a single favor for him. And that single favor was bringing Solomon into the fold of your little project. After I set up the meeting with Solomon I was to wash my hands and be on my way. However, the bar has been raised. Someone went too far. With the death of my friend, Solomon, I am committing whatever resources you need to get your project completed."

At first Nora didn't know how to respond. The head of Mossad was essentially saying they had his full backing. "I can't speak for Jim," she said, "But that's an extremely generous offer. Let me leave Jim a voice mail. He should only be in the air for about 45 minutes. He can call you when he lands."

"Nora, I think you should leave the hotel where you are. Pick Jim up at the airport and move to your next location. Somebody is on to you. Whether it is the Russians or someone else. It is getting dangerous. Very dangerous."

Nora thought about what Benny said for about two seconds. "Your right, we are moving."

"Sound judgement. Watch your tail."

LONG BURIED SECRETS

CHAPTER 47

Moscow

Sergei Liugo, the head of Russia's military intelligence service, sat at his desk awaiting a call from Zurich. He first looked to his watch, then the office clock. Both read 7:20am. As if on schedule, his operative called on the Voice Keeper telephone scrambler, a step down from the Russian Cryo System, but it enabled operatives to use their personnel cell phones and the call still be scrambled.

"As you requested, it is done," said Misha Zakov. "I made it look like a house fire. Both the wife and Solomon is dead."

"You have done well, Misha," replied Sergei. "I may still require your services if Lana and Yuri continue to blunder through this job. I am providing them just enough rope to hang themselves."

"I completely understand," said Misha. "I stand ready to assist."

"Good, very good. I want you to go to Bern. Check into the same hotel as our operatives. But lay low."

"I will leave as soon as I hang up. I can be there in an hour or so."

Sergei laughed aloud into the phone. "You have done enough for the past 12 hours. Wait until after breakfast and then proceed. Have an easy drive. Live a little."

"Yes, sir. As you request. I will leave first thing after breakfast."

Sergei hung up. Next he called Yuri. After five rings, a groggy Yuri answered. "How are my favorite couple?" he inquired.

Yuri took several seconds to answer. It might have had something to do with the quantity and combination of wine and vodka they were drinking the night before. "We are fine, Sergei," he replied searching for his bottle of water. He looked over to his still sleeping wife before tapping her hard on the shoulder several times to awaken her.

"Leave me alone," she protested, pulling the blanket over her head.

"It's the boss," he said with his hand over the mouthpiece.

"Damn," she said, now rising, pulling the beds sheet around her naked body.

Sergei had overheard everything that had transpired. Yuri's hand evidently did not completely cover the phone. "Put me on speaker," he demanded.

As ordered, he placed them on speaker.

"What in the hell are you two doing with my money?" Sergei demanded. "I want receipts for everything. The room, food, and from the sound of you both, drink."

Yuri and Lana looked to each other in disgust. "Yes, Sir," they both replied in unison.

"I want results from you two. You are supposed to be some of the best agents we have. Yet you both seem to be treating this as if it were one big party. Now, late last night one of the people you are supposed to be tracking, James Dieter, was in Salzburg."

Yuri looked to Lana once more. He silently mouthed, *we are screwed.*

"How come I had to hear about it from one of my field agents and not the two people I assigned to watch his every move?"

Yuri slowly shook his head realizing Sergei was setting him up. "We lost Dieter and his wife earlier in the day, but we thought they returned to the hotel soon after," he responded.

"She did, he didn't. Evidently he flew to Salzburg."

"We surveilled their room all day. We only returned to our own room around midnight. We also spread bribes around the hotel staff to assist us. They are helping us keep abreast of their comings and goings."

"Isn't that what I am paying the *both of you to do*," he yelled into the phone. "I want results or the both of you will be pulled back. Then we can see where every Swiss Franc or Euro has been spent by the two of you."

Yuri had no response. Lana spoke for them: "You can count on us, sir. We will not let you down."

Sergei's face turned a shade of crimson, his anger rising once more. "That's what you said yesterday," he roared. "Now get to work." He slammed his cell phone on his desk.

Lana looked to Yuri. "The Dieters are making us look like rookies. This stops now. From this point forward we are working 24/7."

Little did they realize but they were almost an hour too late.

LONG BURIED SECRETS

CHAPTER 48

The hotel room around her seemed to suddenly be closing in. Nora had fully digested the news about Solomon. She had no choice but to agree, the hotel was compromised. Possibly even their mission. She wasted no time in packing both her and Jim's belongings. Following Benny's advice, she did not call the porter, instead she grabbed a luggage cart to transport their bags to the front desk. Benny also told her to assume the parking valet and the front desk were all compromised. Each would have been the first to be bribed. It is an old Russian trick. One that Benny knew very well. So she followed his advice the best she could, avoiding everyone but the front desk; *she had to pay the bill*. She was able to quickly check out and hop into a waiting taxi to take her to the airport, leaving their rental car in the garage. At least she would avoid the porter and the parking valet.

Once at the airport she rented a new vehicle to hopefully lose anyone who may have been tailing them. Then she proceeded over to wait for Jim's plane to land.

With luck he would be walking out to the cabstand as she drove up.

CHAPTER 49

Lana rushed to get dressed. "If we don't come up with something our next job might be in Siberia," she said angrily.

Yuri nodded in agreement. "No more mistakes," he said.

A sudden knock at the door was cause for commotion.

"It's a little early for company," whispered Yuri. He first went to the rooms' closet, grabbing his service weapon. He now approached the door, his weapon extended. "Who is it?" He said in a calm but loud voice.

Lana also had her service weapon drawn, backing up Yuri.

"It's the parking valet, sir," a youthful voice replied from the hallway.

Yuri relaxed, lowering his weapon. He indicated for Lana to do the same. He looked out the door's peephole, seeing a young man dressed in a hotel uniform. Satisfied, he opened the door.

"Good morning, sir," the parking valet said a little too cheerfully for the time of day. "You paid me to report on the Dieters in room 584."

Yuri perked up. Lana now stood beside him at the door.

"Well, the woman checked out about an hour ago," he said eagerly. "I just came on shift and was looking at the check in-check-out log at the front desk and noticed the name. But their car is still in the garage."

Yuri reached into his pocket, handing the young man a 20 Franc bill. "Thank-you for your assistance," he said, before closing the door. He then turned to Lana. "Pack your bags. We're leaving. *Now.*"

Lana grabbed her suitcase from the closet and rushed into the bathroom. She placed her suitcase at the edge of the counter and slid in all of their toiletries.

Within less than two minutes, each of them had changed and tossed everything into their respective suitcases. Yuri then performed one last sweep of the room before closing the door behind them. A minute later they were in the lobby.

The front desk clerk nodded to them as they approached. Viewing suitcases in tow she immediately went for the checkout screen on her computer. "I take it you are departing, Sir and Madam?" She said, a smile gracing her face.

Lana was first to speak. "We understand our friends, the Dieters, just checked out, and we are supposed to meet them for breakfast," she lied.

The clerk hit a few computer keys before replying. "Yes, Mrs. Dieter checked out at 7:23am," the clerk replied efficiently.

"Did she take her car?" asked Yuri, already knowing the answer.

The clerk typed in a few additional keys. "That's strange. Our computer says it's still parked in the garage."

Yuri looked to Lana, then the clerk. "Did she happen to mention where she was going?

"Yes, I was the one who called her a taxi. She said she was heading to the airport to pick up her husband."

Lana realized Nora had an hour head start but they knew where they could find them.

"Shall I have the car valet bring your vehicle around?"

"Yes, please," he replied.

They would not get away. Not today.

CHAPTER 50

The airport terminal was essentially empty with the exception of Jim and six other passengers who were the sole occupants of the small turboprop aircraft. That was the beauty of small airports. It made for easy deplaning.

Nora stood beside her new rental as Jim exited the terminal. She waved at him. A look of surprise spread across his face, then one of worry. He sped up to meet her.

"What are you doing here? What's wrong?" he inquired, looking first to the new rental van, then to Nora.

Nora opened the side door for him to view their suitcases. "Benny called this morning. He tried to reach you but you were evidently airborne."

"Why would Benny have to call you? I just spoke to him at Solomon's home last night. And why are we packed to leave?"

Nora indicated for Jim to get in the van. "Let me fill you in on the way."

"On the way to where?" he countered.

"Wherever you think we should go after Bern. At least for a few days."

Nora then proceeded to tell him everything.

THEY WERE TEN kilometers west of the airport when Jim started speaking again, the shock of Solomon's murder evidently wearing off. "Benny said it's most likely the Russians? So we have both Dolans people and the Russians watching our every move?"

Nora kept her eyes fixed on the road. "But Benny said we could count on him for whatever assistance we need. They were his exact words," she said. "And he did get rid of the Iranians for us."

"Benny and Solomon were pretty tight. I can see how deeply his passing would affect him."

"When we spoke on the phone he had to pause a few times to compose himself."

"The death of a dear personal friend had to hit him pretty hard. However, Benny is a professional. It will soon pass."

Nora nodded. How far outside of Bern do we want to go?"

He looked at the upcoming signs. "Let's get off here and find some economy motel. I don't think our tails would look for us this far out of town. We also want to stay close to the airport with Eian, Summer, and Chuck flying in today."

They drove over a canal before they reached their exit. Jim looked out the car window at the passing scenery below them. He noted several boats passing under the bridge. Over the course of the next few minutes he came up with an idea.

"I want to move the paintings out the same way my old partner, Dan Flaherty, and I moved my father's gold bullion out of Germany a few years back. We used a barge. A vacation rental barge to be exact. Pure luxury. Top of the line."

"You sold me at luxury," said Nora. "But what about flying them out as we planned."

"Don't get me wrong. We are still going to fly the paintings to the US, but first we wait until everything cools down. We can treat it like a vacation." His mood had changed for the better since viewing the barges. Jim searched his cellphones index of numbers. "Got it!" he said excitedly. "I still have the barge salesman's name and phone number. Let me give him a call and see what's available."

CHAPTER 51

Aarburg, Switzerland

The small town of Aarburg lay nestled alongside the Aare River and State Route 22, a route notorious for trucks looking to avoid the expensive Swiss road toll system on vehicles over 3.5 tons. Outside the town, on Route 22, stood a few cheap motels and restaurants frequented by truckers. The motels were definitely not the Ritz; and the restaurants not Michelin starred, but ideal if you were looking to go unnoticed for a few days with the constant comings and goings of people.

Nora and Jim checked into one of the motels located near a restaurant. They booked four rooms in total due to their crew flying in later that same day.

Nora looked around at the room's décor. "Sure isn't the Ritz. She pulled at a piece of loose wallpaper near the bathroom. "Just standing in the room makes me want to take a shower," she said.

Jim laughed at her. "We are incognito. Nobody will look for us out here. He indicated for her to sit at the table by the room's window. He opened the curtains, letting in the sunlight. "Any better?"

"Not really. With the extra light, I can categorically say this is a dump," she said, looking around the room.

Jim joined her at the table. He broke out two plastic cups they had purchased along with two cases of beer and a case of wine from one of the towns liquor stores. He uncorked a bottle of a local merlot, pouring some into each cup.

"Isn't it a little early for the vino?" she said.

"Not after Solomon being killed last night."

Nora agreed, taking one of the cups from him. "Okay so we rent the barge. Vacation a bit. I like the sound of that but we will still need to move the paintings from the museum in Bern, to where we can rent a river barge in France. Depending on our destination, that could take maybe three to four hours."

Jim nodded absently, looking deep in thought. After several minutes, he suddenly perked up. "When you and Summer met the museum security guards at the bar, they informed you all of the guards are in one place, one room, playing video games. So if that's true, we can possibly incapacitate them all at the same time. Possibly for a few hours."

"Are you thinking some type of chemical? Maybe something in their coffee?"

"What if they all don't drink coffee? We need something that would affect them all at the same time."

"I say you call in a favor with Benny. I'm sure they have something available like you are describing."

He agreed. It was time to call Benny.

"BENNY, JIM HERE. My wife just informed me about Solomon. I still can't believe it. The two of us were just laughing and enjoying his hospitality last night. So tragic."

Benny nodded absently before replying. "As I told your wife, whatever you need from me, you will have it. Either you hurt them, or we will."

Jim understood Benny's definition of *hurt*. Usually someone, or a few, turn up dead. "That's most gracious of you, Benny," he replied. "And you know us Americans, you give us an inch and we take a yard."

Benny could be heard on the other side of the phone line taking a deep breath. "You already have something in mind, don't you? Did I walk into a trap?"

Jim smiled at Nora before responding. "A great big bear trap."

"What do you have in mind?"

"Let's start with a non-toxic gas that can incapacitate and possibly allow no memory of what transpired."

Benny typed a few keys into his computer. "Give me a second, I'm just checking on something."

"I'll wait all day if it has the possibility of helping."

A few seconds later Benny came back on the line: "Yes, we do. It's a non-toxic, canister-operated gas that comes in a variety of different sizes. Typically it is connected to a hose for use in an air conditioning intake. The operative just has to wear an oxygen mask to avoid being rendered unconscious."

"It's a pretty big museum. We might require a large canister. And how long after discharge does it take before we can safely enter the building?"

"Hold on, hold on. One question at a time, my friend. Yes, you find the museums air intake and discharge it. Remember, you are only looking to remove and replace paintings in the Gurlitt collection. The other 75% of the building is not on your agenda. We can build a gas canister to handle that one particular section. Possibly a liter sized canister will do. As far as when you can enter, well, maybe five to ten minutes after discharge. It's a heavy gas that sinks to the floor where it dissipates very quickly when it interacts with common floor wax. That's what makes it ideal."

"Sounds exactly like what we need. Now, the million dollar question: how soon can you get it here?"

"You Americans. Always so rush, rush." He typed in a few more keys, observing his computer screen. "We have a diplomatic pouch going to Zurich tomorrow. I can have the chemicals in the pouch. Once in Zurich, I have a man at our Embassy who can assemble what you will need from local manufacturers and build the actual device. I can then have him deliver it to you by 3pm. Is that convenient enough for you?"

Jim laughed aloud before responding. "I think we owe you some more drinks for this one."

Benny wouldn't hear of it. "You owe me nothing. Let's just say we are doing this for an old friend."

"For Solomon's sake."

CHAPTER 52

Bern

Misha sat in the Hotel's lobby reading the Berner Zeitung morning newspaper, having ignored Sergei Liugo's advice of a leisurely breakfast before driving to Bern. He arrived five minutes earlier. Luckily for him he had timed his arrival perfectly with Lana and Yuri's departure.

Misha eyed Lana as she departed the front desk area. He tossed aside his newspaper and, at a quick pace, caught up to her from behind. "Sergei Liugo says hello," he said in a low voice, now walking in step beside her.

"What?" she said, half turning to see Misha, a look of surprise on her face. "What are you doing here?" she demanded. "This was supposed to be our job."

Misha shook his head. "Keep walking towards your husband," he commanded. "At least you can do that without losing him. Can't you?"

Lana eyed him with contempt.

"I'm here on Sergei's orders. I have to baby sit you two."

Yuri was sitting in their car out front waiting on Lana when he saw Misha suddenly appear beside Lana. "Son of a bitch," he said to himself, instantly recognizing Sergei's pit bull. He withdrew his weapon and placed it in the doors pocket. He wanted it within easy reach as Misha drew near. Their distrust of each other first formed in Syria while Misha was his senior non-com. When, against Yuri's orders, Misha executed five Kurdish prisoners in cold blood. Yuri pushed for a court martial. Their superiors agreed and soon recommended a dishonorable discharge from the army. Misha next found a new employer in Sergei. But he never forgave Yuri for turning him in.

Lana's smile had long disappeared. Misha now held her arm as he steered her towards the car. "Get in the front seat with your husband," he said in a voice tinged with anger. "I will sit in the back and watch over you two."

He opened the door for Lana, acting all the gentlemen. After she sat down, he slammed the door shut. He then opened the rear door and quickly sat down. "Did you miss me, Yuri?"

Yuri adjusted his rear-view mirror so he would have a better view of Misha. "What are you doing here?" he said in disgust. "Prison not good enough for you?" he was alluding to Misha's stretch in a Moscow prison for beating two suspects to death with his bare hands for his new employer. Of course, Sergei had him freed after two weeks, the charges dropped.

"So you heard about that little incident?" Misha replied. "I didn't think you could read."

Lana reached out for his hand to calm him. He pointed to the doors pocket. Lana smiled in understanding.

"Drive," ordered Misha, pointing forward. "We don't have all day to find the Dieters."

"Anywhere in particular?" said Yuri.

"Go to the airport," he commanded. "When we get there head towards the rental car area."

Yuri didn't want to argue with his bosses' pet, so he drove off.

EIAN STEERED THE JET from the runway onto the taxiway while following a yellow airport vehicle with a large *Follow Me* sign attached to its rear.

Luckily for Eian it was a small airport. After several minutes he found himself deposited in the ramp area reserved for Swiss Customs. Eian waved his thanks to the airport workers in the yellow vehicle before they sped off. His attention now returned to his aircraft and its passengers, Chuck and Summer, still asleep in the rear of the aircraft.

"Rise and shine my fellow compatriots," he said over the cockpits intercom, still sounding jovial after nine hours in the air and one hasty refueling stop in Ireland. "Time to break out the passports."

Eian shut down one of the aircrafts two engines, leaving one at idle to supply power for the aircraft. He then exited the cockpit and walked to the aircraft's emergency door, pulling in on the doors handle to open it and activating the aircrafts stairs, allowing them to automatically drop into place on the tarmac.

"Is he always this much fun?" said Chuck after Eian now passed them by on the way to the plane's galley for some well-deserved coffee.

"From what Jim tells me, only when a bit of danger is involved," replied Summer. "Evidently he's a bit of an adrenaline junkie."

Chuck looked out one of the aircrafts windows to gauge the weather and noticed the Swiss customs agent approaching. "Well hopefully Jim was able to get his friend to contact Swiss customs," he said, pointing out the window, "because here she comes."

The agent came aboard as Eian was pouring his coffee in the small galley in the rear of the aircraft.

"Bonjour," she said upon entering.

Chuck waved.

Summer smiled politely. "Parlez-vous anglais?" she said. *Do you speak English?*

"But of course," she replied. "I speak English, French and German. May I please see your passports?"

Eian came out of the galley with his passport in one hand, coffee cup in the other. Summer and Chuck handed theirs to Eian, who in turn handed all three to the customs agent.

"Thank-you," she replied. "Where are you coming from?"

"Philadelphia, of the good old USA," he replied.

"Oh, I am familiar with this place. The Rocky statue. Liberty Bell."

Eian nodded. "The same."

Another agent came on board. He said something in French to the agent with the passports. She smiled at Eian as she handed the passports back to him. "Enjoy your stay in Switzerland," she said, swiftly departing.

Eian in turn handed the passports back to Summer and Chuck. "All right," he said, "we have to get this aircraft over to the transient ramp so we can unload our goods. Summer I need you to call Jim and tell him we just cleared customs. And we need that lift he promised us." He quickly pulled up the stairs and then locked the door. In a matter of minutes, they were taxiing over to the transient ramp. Another five and they were offloading their cargo to the concrete ramp as they patiently waited for Jim and Nora to show.

YURI, LANA, AND MISHA were sitting in their car outside of Bern Airports three rental car companies, all jointly located under one roof. Common for small European airports.

"Wait here," said Misha, "while I do your work for you." He exited the car and disappeared into the rental car building.

In ten minutes he was back, a smile on his weathered face. "They are now driving a white Transit van," he said. "They just rented the van within the past hour and a half."

Lana half-turned in her seat. "And how did you come across that information so quickly?"

"Easy," he replied, "I bribed the woman behind the counter two hundred francs. Now we have the license plate, make and model. And that's how it's done."

Lana rolled her eyes.

Yuri spoke up. "Now where do you want to go with your newfound information?"

He held up a new set of car keys. "First, we are driving a new rental car. This one stays here. Evidently your Dieters are already acquainted with the embassy car. Our new car is that white Opel parked beside us." They quickly transferred their bags and the Embassy bag to the new rental before Misha spoke up once more. "Let's start looking for the Dieters right here at the airport. It's as good a place as any."

"He's probably right," said Lana. "If James Dieter was in Salzburg last night, he is probably flying in this morning. Either that or the rest of their crew is flying in."

"Even your wife agrees with me, Yuri," said Misha, laughing as he spoke. "Smart woman you married."

It was Lana's turn to cringe.

He continued. "Now when I stopped at our Embassy last night they informed me that they provided you with a host of gear. So let's start with binoculars."

Yuri pointed to the trunk. "Help yourself," he said, "You have the car keys. Everything is in the black duffel bag."

Misha popped the truck open. In seconds he found what he was looking for, taking the binoculars out of their green plastic case. He strolled to the airport fence line in order to scan the entire complex. He soon turned to them, an expression of satisfaction upon his face. "Come over here," he said to both Lana and Yuri. "Look over in that direction," pointing to the southwest towards a private jet.

Lana took the binoculars from Misha, adjusting them to suit her vision. "It's them," she said aloud before offering them to Yuri.

Yuri declined to look. "Damn it," he was heard to say aloud.

"Let's go," said Misha, tossing the keys to Yuri. "Use the basics. You two are nothing but a bunch of idiots. Wait until I report this back to Sergei."

In seconds, they sped off.

EIAN, CHUCK, AND SUMMER watched as Nora drove the rental van onto the ramp and right up to where they had already offloaded their cargo and luggage.

"My apologies for our tardiness," said Jim as he jumped out to greet them. "Long story, short. We had to check out of our hotel and into a motel. We can tell you more about that along the way."

Nora followed up behind him. "How was your trip?"

Summer looked over to Chuck. "What do you say partner?"

Chuck pointed over to Eian. "That man is a raving loon. He took us down to wave height. Isn't that what he called it?"

"You have it right," she replied. "Wave height."

Eian smiled at Jim and Nora. "Just giving the plane a salt wash."

Nora busted out laughing. "Welcome to the club. He indoctrinated me a few months ago."

"And me a few years ago," chimed in Jim.

"I'm flying home commercial," said Chuck dryly.

Eian came up behind Chuck and jokingly punched him in the back. "Just testing you both. You'll be glad to know, you both passed with flying colors."

"Why? Because we didn't grab a parachute?" countered Summer.

Eian looked to Jim. "Help me, my man," he pleaded.

"Okay," Jim said. "Everybody help load. Then on the way to the motel, Nora and I will explain what transpired over the course of the past few days."

"No problem," said Chuck. "As long as he," pointing over to Eian, "isn't driving."

They all laughed aloud.

"All right you two. Let's concentrate on loading and getting out of here," said Jim. "Too many prying eyes."

YURI MANUVERED THE CAR as close as possible to the Swiss Customs building, 200 feet from the aircraft. From the safety of their car, they watched their targets load luggage and cardboards tubes into the white Transit van.

"Now we simply follow them to their new destination," said Misha assuredly.

"Easy as one, two, three."

CHAPTER 53

After checking into their respective rooms and dropping off their gear, the team gathered in Jim and Nora's motel room.

Chuck reflected on their room, taking it all in. "I didn't think this motel had a crappier room than mine. I was wrong." He paused for a few seconds before continuing: "I didn't think they had anything this crappy in all of Europe, especially Switzerland."

Summer playfully punched him on the arm. "You of all people should know we are trying to lay low for a few days. And it's a motel, not a hotel."

"There is laying low, *and then there is this place*," he replied.

"All right," countered Jim. "Let's just bite the bullet for a few days and then you can each buy your own hotel with your share if you want."

That comment caught their attention. Eian grabbed another beer from where Jim and Nora had set up a temporary bar. "Don't let them bother you, Jim. Just provide us with the rest of the plan."

Jim continued. "Okay. Obviously we had to modify our plans due to the paintings impending move. What we have, courtesy of Solomon before he passed on, is the time and date the Gurlitt collection will be moved."

"Good for us, Jim," said Eian. "Now all we require is a way in."

Chuck nodded. "That sounds like my department."

Jim held up his hands to quiet them. "Nora and I think we have that one covered. But we would like a second opinion. So we will need the three of you to walk around the exterior of the museum filming every step of the way with your cell phones. That way we will have three different cameras recording different angles."

Summer spoke up. "So you want us to act like tourists taking movies of each other but in reality, shooting the whole exterior of the museum?"

Jim tapped the tip of his nose to signal she was correct. "We are planning to hit the museum in two days. That is only one day before they plan to pull the paintings from public view."

"Tomorrow morning Nora and I will drop the three of you a block from the museum so you can start filming. After that, my lovely wife and I will drive a few hours roundtrip to France to check on the feasibility of another escape route. Right now, it's on the down low. We can fill you in that piece of the plan tomorrow night. For now, have a few drinks and relax."

YURI PULLED INTO the motels parking lot, making sure to park on the opposite side of the U-shaped lot from Jim and his crew. An empty pool surrounded by a worn metal fence lay in-between where they sat in their car, providing them with decent cover.

Misha still had the binoculars, now observing Jim's room from his vantage point in the back seat. "Besides luggage, I saw them carry in possibly eighteen cardboard tubes. Each looked to be about one meter in length. Do you think they already have some valuables with them? Maybe some paintings?"

Yuri loathed Misha. He could not believe Sergei would send him of all people to babysit them. "They didn't have time to steal the paintings yet," he replied as if scolding a child. "Don't you remember? Lana and I have been watching them for the past several days."

"That's not what I heard from Sergei. He said you two are on your way to some crappy assignment in Africa after this mission. Maybe even Siberia. You really screwed up. Or something along those lines."

Lana looked to Yuri, worry in her eyes.

Yuri decided it was time to take a short walk. He excused himself, and in one swift motion grabbed his weapon from the door pocket as he exited the car, slipping it into his pants waistband, pulling his shirt over its top.

Misha kept his binoculars trained on Dieters room.

Yuri walked around to the now open car's trunk. In seconds, he had what he was searching for. He expertly screwed on a sound suppressor to his weapon, placing his weapon back into his pants waistband before closing the trunk. He then lit a cigarette, his first one of the day, trying to settle his nerves due to Misha's unexpected appearance. The man could not be trusted. Of that, he was sure. Something had to be done, and soon.

Inside the car, Misha handed the binoculars to Lana. "Keep your eyes on the Dieter room. I'm going for a close up to see if I can hear anything." He opened his door and grinned at Yuri. "Stay put little fellow, while I go do your work for you."

"Stay here, Misha!" yelled Yuri. "We can't approach them yet. We have to observe."

"Think about that plum assignment in Africa," he said, his middle finger extended. "I don't have to listen to you. I'm taking over. I want to see if they have any of our paintings. So just sit tight. Don't fret if I come out the hero."

He swiftly turned and scaled a three-foot high fence that surrounded the pool in order to take a more direct route.

Yuri had enough of Misha's antics. He was not about to have his wife and himself put at risk by this bastard. He ran after Misha, jumping the fence as Misha was rounding the deep end of the empty pool.

"Stop," Yuri said in a low voice only meant for Misha to hear, pointing his weapon at him.

Misha turned in time see Yuri with the silencer screwed on his weapon, now pointed at him. "Are you mad?" he said. "Are you threatening me?"

It was Yuri's turn to laugh. "Does it look like I'm threatening you?"

"Go back to the car, little man," Misha said, before he resumed walking towards the Dieters room.

Yuri fired twice in quick succession hitting Misha once in the side and in the head. Misha staggered a few steps before he fell forward into the deep end section of the empty pool, and out of site.

Yuri quickly surveilled the immediate area to see if there were any witnesses. Seeing none, he hopped back over the pool fence and walked back to the car.

Lana had a look of shock on her face. "Are you crazy? What have you done? You have jeopardized our whole mission."

"I just rid the world of one less fool. He was going to turn us in for his own gain. You know it, and I know it."

"But Sergei will blame us for his death," she replied in a high voice, her hands covering her face.

"Nobody will find out. We will wait until dark and dispose of the body." He put the car into reverse and backed into another spot. "Now we simply check into a room and keep an eye on the Dieters."

To Lana, the $50,000 in euros was looking to be a wiser escape plan. And maybe a few paintings.

If they lived...

LONG BURIED SECRETS

CHAPTER 54

They had just settled in for a few drinks after Jim's mission brief. Eian was now regaling the room with some of his tall tales when there was a sudden knock at the motel room door.

Jim looked to Nora with suspicion. "Are we expecting anyone?"

Nora thought for a moment or two before responding. "The only person who knows our location is Benny," she replied.

Eian eased back the windows curtain. "Small, tan male. Doesn't look dangerous to me."

Jim nodded to Nora that it was okay.

Nora opened the door to find five-foot two-inch Rahm Mizrahi, a briefcase in one hand, his other extended in greeting. "Benny sent me," he said, before shaking Nora's hand.

Nora turned back to Jim. "We have company," she said anxiously. "One of Benny's people." She allowed him to enter, introducing him to everyone in the room.

Eian was skeptical of the well-tanned man. "You don't look like the typical Mossad agent I envisioned," he said. "When I hear Mossad, I tend to think tall and muscular." Eian finished the beer he was drinking in one long gulp, slamming down his empty bottle on the wooden nightstand.

"Then my size makes for a good undercover agent," Rahm replied. "Don't you agree?"

The room about him broke into laughter.

Rahm wasted no time in setting up shop on the room's sole table. Rahm withdrew an object the size of a small soda can out of his briefcase. Within minutes, he was explaining the ins and outs of LO-MAX-TAL gas.

"And this stuff is really dangerous in the hands of amateurs," he said looking around the room at each of them. "And in my book you are all rank amateurs." He placed the can on the table for them to view it more closely. A small metal spray nozzle lay affixed to its top, an electronic circuit card the size of a quarter visible on its side.

Eian stood up and walked over to the canister. He tapped the cans casing a few times, and then eyed the diminutive Rahm, towering a good foot over him. "Who the hell do you think you're talking to? We've handled a lot worse stuff than this crap. And another thing, I don't like being called an amateur at anything. Especially by the likes of you."

Rahm immediately realized the need to set an example in order to gain respect. With his thumb and forefinger, he applied a quick jab to Eian's larynx, just enough to make him choke for a few seconds. The distraction enabled Rahm to kick Eian's legs from the rear and force him to the floor on his stomach. Rahm grabbed Eians' arm around the wrist area and twisted it behind his back. He waited until Eian started breathing normally.

"Are we good, Eian?" he said in a low voice.

"If you get off my back you little runt," Eian spat out.

"Okay, the little runt will now let you stand up, Eian." He released him.

Eian stood up ready for a fight.

Jim jumped between them. "Eian, he beat you once. I honestly think he can do it again. He's Mossad you fool."

Everyone laughed, even Eian. "I didn't mean anything by it," he replied sheepishly.

"Shake hands," ordered Jim.

They shook hands. Eian returned to his seat, Rahm to the table where the canister sat.

Rahm continued. "Now that the floor show is over, I can get back to the reason why I'm here. Benny has instructed me to assist you in any way I see fit. After meeting you, I have made the decision to join you. But only after I make a slight change to your plans. We will not run the gas into the air conditioning vent."

Jim was ready to protest but Rahm held up his hand, smiling as he had anticipated as much. "I pulled the interior drawings on the Bern Museum. If we push our gas into the air conditioning intake, it will get caught in this neck," he pointed to the drawing. "It will slowly dissipate before it has time to reach our intended targets in the security room."

Chuck looked to the drawing. "So, what do we do now? We have to find some way to subdue the guards."

Nora spoke up. "But all of the guards will be in one room. The security room. We don't have to worry about the rest of the museum."

Rahm smiled once more. "Even better. I can place the can in the security room behind a cabinet or something along those lines. Once in place I can activate it via my cell phone to disperse the gas when needed. It will not make a sound and the people in the room will gently fall off to sleep within seconds." Rahm searched the drawings for the security room. "Okay, the drawings indicate the guard's room is 10 x 10 feet. I can mix the chemicals accordingly. Their sleep should last a good 4-5 hours. When they wake up, they will be none the wiser."

Eian shook his head, disagreeing with Rahm's plan. "And how do you intend on placing the can in the security room. Just walk in and announce yourself?"

Rahm pulled a gray coverall from his case, the name of the firm contracted for cleaning the museum embroidered on its front, a plastic identification badge attached to its collar. "Courtesy of Mossad Forgery department. With this, tomorrow morning I walk in, clean a few rooms, to include the security room where I place my can, and be on my way."

Nora was the first to speak. "Welcome to the team, Rahm," she said enthusiastically. "I think he just solved what had been, up to now, a big hole in our plan."

Jim nodded as he rose. "Okay, with the addition of Rahm, I think we are ready to move out in two days."

CHAPTER 55

Bern

Early the next morning, Jim and Nora dropped off Rahm, Eian, Chuck, and Summer a block from the Bern Museum.

"Take a taxi back to the motel," said Nora as they each scattered in different directions.

Confident in their new plan, Jim and Nora proceeded west to France.

"WHICH ONE DO WE FOLLOW?" said Lana from behind the wheel. "The van, or should we split up?

"I will get out and follow one of these clowns," said Yuri, pointing out the passenger side window. "You stay with the van."

He quickly jumped out, choosing to follow Summer.

Lana sped off in close pursuit of Jim and Nora. She was battling fatigue, with her and Yuri rising at 3am to remove Misha's body from the empty pool, the same body that now resided in the trunk of her car beside their embassy gear. She anticipated dumping him somewhere along her travels. Hopefully far away from prying eyes.

IN A MATTER OF A few hours Jim and Nora were in the quiet little French town of Pouilly-en-Auxois, 20 miles west of Dijon. The town had stood for hundreds of years on the banks of a canal that ran as a tributary from the Rhine River. With a population that never exceeded 500, unless you count the sheep, and with no castles or anything resembling something of historical significance, it was overshadowed by its larger neighboring towns that regarded it as no more than a bump in the road. But it did operate as the terminus, or beginning, depending on which way you were going, for the lucrative vacation barge rental traffic. Just like the one Jim envisioned for their getaway. It also had a public use concrete ramp, one that backed up to the canals edge and could accommodate a large van. Just like the one they envisioned could be used to unload paintings without interference from inquisitive neighbors.

This made the location ideal for Jim's plan.

Jim and Nora walked all two blocks of the towns' quaint main street, flower baskets hanging from each lamppost. They acted the typical tourist and took selfies that were sure to capture areas of interest to be utilized in their getaway. They then detoured to the towns' towpath that ran along the edge of the canal. They watched as a canal barge slowly made its way along the canal, a tourist steering from his location on its rear. The barge looked recently renovated, with its woods highly varnished, its brass ports shining in the midday sun. Two additional tourists sat on lounge chairs in the middle of the barge drinking glasses of wine, an empty bottle at their feet.

Nora looked to Jim. "I think I might enjoy this portion of the trip."

Jim nodded. "I believe you will. Now this is the town where we will load the paintings. We still have to travel to one more town to acquire our barge transportation. But first we have to rent a small building somewhere around here, preferably a garage."

LANA LOOKED TO HER gas gage; she only had a quarter tank left. She hoped they weren't going too much further as she resumed her position tailing them.

She followed them outside of town to an abandoned auto garage. She watched as they looked at a *For Lease* sign.

Why do they require a garage? She thought to herself.

CHAPTER 56

Dockside, St. Florentine, France

THE SMALL TOWN of St. Florentine sat on the lush border of Burgundy and Champagne, in the heart of France's wine country. The town's history dated back to ancient times, when it served as a fortress outpost on the fringe of the Roman Empire. Through time, it adapted and experienced not only an Italian influence in its stone and fresco architecture, but also some of a Germanic nature. It also had the dubious distinction of serving as a "backdoor hub" for vacationers, both wealthy and working class, eager for a barge vacation and waterway access to travel throughout Europe.

One that also included canal access to the town they had just visited: Pouilly-en-Auxois.

Jim eyed a group of three, twenty-five-meter-long steel barges that lay tied parallel to and against the towns dock. The barges reminiscent of its larger cousins that plowed the canals of Europe for some fifty years, giving way to tandem trucks in the late 60s. These barges were of the smaller variety used to off-load cargo from the larger barges and the cargo delivered to destinations on the shallower rivers. Most of the smaller barges eventually made their way into the lucrative tourist trade.

Nora stared at Jim for several moments, she could see a slight smile crease his face. "Is this where you and Dan rented the barge a few years ago to sneak your father's gold out of Germany?"

Jim nodded at Nora upon the mention of his late friend's name. "I still can't believe he's dead. It feels like he is standing beside me now, trying to steer us in the proper direction. I can hear his voice in my head." *We need a boat, not just any boat, a barge, a river barge.*

"Maybe he is," she said, grabbing his hand, pulling him close. "I know he's looking out for us."

Jim gazed into Nora's eyes, lost in the moment. "He's sitting up there with a bottle of Jamison, laughing his head off at what we are attempting to accomplish."

"At least he's laughing." Nora kissed him on the cheek before backing away. "All right James Dieter, tell me the rest of your devilish plan."

Jim pulled a paper map from his pocket using the metal railing to balance the map. "It's simple really. We can basically float from the town we just visited, Pouilly-en-Auxois, to here in St. Florentine using waterways consisting of rivers and canals. No police or anyone to interfere. We load the paintings in Pouilly-en-Auxois, enjoy the scenery, and have a little vacation on the side."

Nora looked first to the parked barges, then to Jim. "One question, James Dieter. After we steal the paintings, load them onto our barge, sail for four or five days on the barge, how do we get them across the Atlantic?"

Jim pointed east of the village. "A mile away is a small airfield with a 6,500-foot runway. Just the distance required for a Gulfstream 550 to take off with enough fuel to cross the pond."

Satisfied with his response, she said: "Now take me to the barges, Mr. Dieter," her hand extended. "I have to see what all the fuss is about."

JIM WALKED THE barge's topside teak deck. "This is a beauty," he said to the salesman, Monsieur Dobet. "But do you happen to remember me from a few years ago? It was myself and another gentleman who rented one of your barges."

Monsieur Dobet eyed him for a few seconds or so, a look of shock slowly taking over. "But of course!" he replied in flawless English albeit with a light French accent, "You and that crazy Irishman you were with returned my barge with bullet holes in the woodwork, the glass doors all shattered!"

Jim turned to Nora and in a low voice said, "I think I upset the little man."

"Please get off this barge," said Monsieur Dobet, his voice rising. "You ruined the last barge I rented to you. It will not happen again!"

Jim stood his ground. "Monsieur Dobet, if you will remember, we reimbursed you for the damage to fix the boat. It was judged to be a case of mistaken identity. The British Army shot up your barge. Not us."

Monsieur Dobet also stood his ground, pointing at the barge's gangway. "You are what we consider, *bad customers*. I do not want nor need your business.

Jim was prepared for such a development, pulling a wad of euros from his pocket. He counted out ten, one-hundred-euro bills, handing them to Monsieur Dobet. "This is for you. A gift. An apology. From me to you."

Monsieur Dobet eyed the money, then Jim. He gradually shook his head. "You rich Americans think you can come over and just throw your money around and get what you."

Jim counted out an additional five, one-hundred-euro bills. "To sweeten my apology." He tried to hand them to Monsieur Dobet.

He looked to Nora then Jim, then back to the office where he boss sat. "I can't accept that," his tone not as harsh as before.

Jim could see the man was about to break. He counted out five more one-hundred-euro bills. "A two-thousand-euro apology." He waved the bundle in front of Monsieur Dobet. "If you don't want it, I'm sure the business next door will take it from me."

It took all of three seconds before Monsieur Dobet grabbed the bundle from Jim, folding the money in half before placing it in his pocket. "Apology accepted," he whispered.

Nora covered her mouth as she smiled.

As if nothing had transpired, Monsieur Dobet took the lead. "If you follow me I will take you on a tour of the barge."

Jim allowed Nora to proceed first.

"This barge resembles a fully loaded motor home only she's lacking the wheels," said Nora as they walked past the kitchen or galley in *boat speak*, outfitted with a glass double-door refrigerator and stainless-steel quad-burner stove among its many amenities.

Monsieur Dobet took her comment as a compliment as he continued pointing out various areas of the barge. "And as you will notice," he said haughtily, "all of our vessels meet the highest French Maritime standards in accommodation. Our corporate office recently received three stars from your American Mobile Guide for excellence. This model in particular earned extensive praise in that booklet." Not missing a beat, he continued with the tour, one of many he had clearly provided. "This barge has two bedrooms, each with in-suite private Jacuzzi baths."

Monsieur Dobet offered Nora and Jim a quick glance in the area before hastily moving on.

He continued his pitch. "As you can see, the dining areas are exquisitely paneled with American cherry wood and equipped with the latest in the Bose surround-sound entertainment equipment. And if you'll notice the floors, we have modest oriental carpeting located throughout the barge protecting the fabulous teak wood floors."

Monsieur Dobet didn't miss a beat. "If I can direct your attention over here," he said, pointing to an elaborate digital control panel the size of a paperback book mounted on the wall. "You will notice our central air-conditioning system. It is a rarity for the European environment, but we think it's a requirement that should be afforded to our, shall we say, *higher echelon clientele.*

The salesman walked toward the middle of the barge with Jim and Nora in tow. "And as you can see, the top deck is also richly appointed in both teak and mahogany woods." He concluded the tour by the barge's aluminum gangway.

Jim removed another crisp, new, fifty-euro bill from his pocket. "Thank you, Monsieur Dobet, for an excellent tour," he said, casually slipping him the bill. "You have quite a majestic product here. I think we may want to lease her for several weeks' time."

Monsieur Dobet had an uneven smile upon his face. Most people just thanked him and were on their way. "You must promise me that you will return the barge in the same condition we provide it to you."

Jim played along. "But of course. Nothing like the last time. Scouts Honor."

Monsieur Dobet smiled at him. "Our terms are simple. You will provide us with a cashier's check for full payment in euros seven days prior to sailing."

Jim nodded. "I can pay cash if you prefer. Do you foresee that to be a problem?"

"Cash is always accepted, sir," he replied nattily. "When would you require the barge?"

"In two days. And we would need to pick it up in the town of Pouilly-en-Auxois."

"That is only 48 hours from now. I cannot possibly have the liquor and food delivered by that time. The barge would also have to be captained through 60 miles of canals, moving 24 hours a day. The logistics of such a request is too incredible. I simply cannot do it."

It was a fishing expedition, surely, on the part of Monsieur Dobet. The first big tip received, he now required a bit more bait. Jim had planned for as much.

"Monsieur Dobet, I apologize for the short notice," Jim said. "We would not dream of inconveniencing someone of your stature." Jim looked around to see if they were being observed. "Maybe we could achieve some type of understanding." He removed ten, crisp, one-hundred-euro bills from his pocket, placing them one by one into the salesman's now open palm. "Would this tend to move things along at a more ambitious pace?"

Monsieur Dobet withdrew a white handkerchief from his pocket, wiping the perspiration from his brow. Between the two tips, he would clear over three thousand euros. A first. "I will personally see to the operation, sir. You can count on me. Should you require anything else, anything at all, please let me know. *Yes*?"

"If I need anything else you are the man, Monsieur Dubet," Jim said. "And this barge has to be in Pouilly-en-Auxois in 48 hours."

"It will be waiting for you, sir," was his reply.

LANA WATCHED FROM HER POSITION ACROSS the canal as Jim and Nora chatted with the salesman. *Why are they renting a barge?* She thought to herself, snapping photo after photo of them with her iPhone. Lana now watched them walk down the gangway. She suddenly realized she required gas in order to make it back to Aarburg. Hopefully this was the Dieter's last stop and they were heading back to the motel.

Either way, she still had a body to dump.

LONG BURIED SECRETS

CHAPTER 57

Aarburg

As Jim and Nora drove into the motel parking lot, the sun had already set an hour before. It had been a long but fruitful day.

Nora smiled at Jim. "How upset do you think they will be because of the changes?" she asked. "Ten to one, Chuck is the first to erupt."

Jim nodded. "Chucks a good choice, but my monies on Eian," he said confidently. "He's been drinking. And with not much to do. A bad combo."

They exited the car and approached their room. They could overhear boisterous talking emanating from inside. "Sounds like they are having a bit of a party," said Jim. He opened the room's door, nodding to each of them as he and Nora walked in. "I hope you all had time to finish reviewing the recordings before you started the imbibing?"

"Of course we have," replied a grinning Chuck. "That's when we decided to start on these nice bottles of vintage." He pointed to four empties on the table. "The Beaujolais was excellent." The emphasis on *was excellent*.

Nora shook her head as if disappointed. "I don't think you are taking this seriously," she said, her voice raised. "We are robbing a museum in two days' time. I don't know about you, but Jim and I sure as hell don't want to get caught."

The laughter subsided for the moment as Nora looked to each of them.

Summer spoke first, keeping her tone low. "Nora, I think you may be a bit unfair in your quick judgement. We may appear to be goofing off, but we are just blowing off some steam. We reviewed all of the recordings at least 30 times. We reviewed the sewer access; the exterior of the museum; the generator; and the escape route. Only then did we start on the wine."

Jim patted Nora on the shoulder. "It's okay," he said, smiling at her. He then turned to address the group. He opened a beer for himself, then one for Nora. "I'm glad you have everything ready to go. Because Nora and I have a slight change to the original plan to fly everything out the same day as the theft."

Eian was first to protest. "We have to escape as soon as possible, Jim. The longer we stay in the area the more likely we are to get caught."

Nora quickly countered. "Jim and I think it might be best to lay low for a week or so. Raise no suspicions. That's even if the museum notices the reproductions on the wall."

Chuck pointed over to Eian. "The man's right for once," he said. "Get out while the getting is good. This from a man with plenty of experience."

The room around them started to get louder with everyone pairing off to discuss what was best in their opinion.

Jim whistled. The shrill caught them all by surprise. "Can I have the floor please?" He waited until everyone stopped speaking before he continued. "The other reason for hanging around for a week or two are simple. We have the Russians after us, and we have a partner, Mike Dolan who thinks he's getting everything we steal from the museum for his own personal gain. Hell, we might even have the Iranians after us. I don't know about you, but I have no intention of giving anything to anyone but Benny. We need time to come up with a plan to string everyone along. And I mean everybody. That's the reason why we can't return right away."

Eian nodded, followed by the rest of them. "Whatever you say is best," responded Eian, his tone changing considerably. "You and Nora lead, we follow."

Jim continued. "Nora and I have just returned from visiting several towns in France. Including one not far from where we sit. Pouilly-en-Auxois. Our plan is simple, to load the paintings onto the vacation barge and sail up a canal to a small airfield outside of St. Florentine, France, about 60 or so miles north of Pouilly-en-Auxois." Jim turned to Eian. "St. Florentine conveniently has an airport within ½ mile of the river."

Eian started to protest but Jim cut him off. "It also happens to operate a single paved runway of 6,500 feet. Which coincidentally is the minimum distance you said we would require for takeoff."

Eian smiled at Jim. "You were paying attention when I told you what I needed. The 6,500-foot runway will do nicely. We just have to stop in Newfoundland for fuel. However, that will do. My end is covered."

"I'm glad to hear that," said Nora. "One less thing to worry about." She looked to Jim, he nodded to proceed. "Jim and I will sail the barge with the paintings and allow for any mistakes to melt away. Also, if the alarm is raised every highway, railway and airport will be searched. But not the canals. Who takes a vacation barge to steal paintings? Now I'm sure you all will be disappointed but only Jim and I will be on the barge."

"What, we don't rate?" joked Chuck.

Nora smiled at him before continuing. "We obviously don't want a large group attracting attention. So Jim and I rented a car that is already prepositioned and waiting for the four of you outside Dijon in France. After the robbery, Jim and I will drop you off and you will drive the car to St. Florentine in Burgundy. We have made reservations for a block of rooms in St. Florentine. We will provide you the address when we drop you off. You can enjoy the local restaurants and wine while we transport the paintings on the vacation barge."

"That part doesn't sound half bad," said Eian. "Of course, everything is expensed to you both, correct?"

"Eian you are one cheap bastard," replied Jim. "But the short answer is yes. Nora and I are footing the bills." He pointed back to Nora. "Can my lovely wife finish?"

Eian nodded. "I concede the floor to your charming wife."

Nora smiled at Eian. "Thank-you, Eian, because this part concerns you. Once Jim and I arrive in St. Florentine via the barge, hopefully in four to five days, you will work your magic and fly us back to the states with the paintings. But first we will require you to drive back to the Bern Airport in four days and return the car to the airport. We rented it in France so there will be a hefty drop off charge. Then you simply fly the jet over to St. Florentine. Sounds easy but it's going to take a lot of planning on our end."

"Not a problem," Eian replied. "Been in worse situations."

Jim turned to Rahm. He seemed to fit right in with his team, sipping on a glass of wine.

"I accomplished my end," he said, his words a bit slurred. "Today I placed the device in the security office. If what you say is true, and all of the guards congregate in the office to play video games, it will not be a problem getting in. We are, as you Americans have a tendency of saying, *good-to-go*."

Jim nodded to Rahm. "Benny was right about you. A true professional."

Jim then turned to the group. "Now, who wants to pick up Dolan at the airport tomorrow?"

CHAPTER 58

Lana pulled into the motel parking lot not more than five minutes after Jim and Nora. Yuri was waiting patiently in their room, the curtains pulled back just enough for him to view both the parking lot and the Dieters room.

"They are moving something via a vacation barge," said Lana as she walked in the room. "It's over the border in France."

Yuri nodded. "I think they are getting close to hitting the museum," he said, still eyeing their room. "I followed the woman as she walked around the museum three times, filming every possible angle. I even saw one of their crew slip behind some shrubs where the museums back-up generator is hidden."

"So we wait until they steal the paintings, then we steal the paintings from them."

"That's the plan," he replied. "Did you dump the body?"

"Yes, I picked the most desolate section of woods in all of France for our friend."

"Well hopefully the wolves get to him before any hikers. At least they might enjoy the bastard."

"I wonder when he was supposed to check-in with Sergei?"

Yuri suddenly closed the curtain. "Who cares? The bastard is dead. Now lets get some rest. Dieter and his crew are drinking and planning tonight. Hopefully we can do the same."

CHAPTER 59

Lana and Yuri had risen by 7am, resuming their lookout duties and monitoring the Dieters room. The previous night they had waited until everyone had departed the Dieters room and the lights went out before they decided it best to rest.

All was quiet until around 2pm when Jim Dieter left the room.

"My turn. Jim Dieter is on the move. Toss me the keys."

Lana quickly tossed the keys as he walked to the door.

"You stay here and monitor their room."

IT WAS JIM'S THIRD visit to the airport in four days. He was starting to feel the effects of the endless pace he had set for himself. *Between that and the small party they had the night before.*

He noticed Mike Dolan right away in his flashy light blue suit. He had a new goon standing smartly beside him in a tight black tee shirt and jeans.

"You took your sweet time in getting here," said Dolan to Jim as he exited the van to help with their luggage.

Jim looked to his watch and smiled. "I'm five minutes late," he said. "So shoot me."

"Don't tempt me. You should have been early," he replied, his voice rising. "You should have been here waiting when we walked the hell out. It's called manners."

"Well we've been a little busy *Your Highness*."

"Just get me to my room. You can fill me in on your plans as you drive us to the Hotel. And tell me everything."

BY THE TIME THEY pulled up to the Hotel Weiss, Jim had relayed *most* of his teams plan. Dolan seemed satisfied with what they had accomplished up to this point.

But of course, he already had his people watching their every move.

Jim turned to Dolan. "I arranged for you and your, ah, associate to have suites at the best hotel in town."

"You and your team aren't staying here?" replied Dolan.

"Can't afford it," said Jim. "Can't waste too much of your money."

Dolan shot him a mischievous smile.

The parking valet approached Jim's side of the van. "These two gentlemen are staying here," he said to the man. "Can you have someone take their bags."

The parking valet said something in German into his walkie-talkie. In seconds, two porters were unloading Dolan and his goon's bags.

Before Dolan departed Jim called him over, out of earshot of his goon. "We are hitting the museum tonight," Jim said.

Dolan had a puzzled look on his face. "On the drive from the airport you said the job was in three days."

"That was for the benefit of your goon to hear, not you. I think he might be a stooge for somebody other than yourself."

Dolan was taken back by the accusation. "I trust him with my life."

"Well, I wouldn't trust him with anything of value for the foreseeable future. That is, if you want to live."

"Are you threatening me?"

"No, just stating a simple fact."

Dolan stood leaning in the passenger side window. "All right. For the moment, we will play it your way. I guess we will meet up in two days? With my goods?"

"You will be my first call," he said, flashing a smile. "After I call you, I will provide you with an address and directions for the paintings. Plan on a three-to-four-hour drive to the location. I need you and your buddy to rent a car from the hotels front desk. I already reserved your car, so they just require your payment."

"That's not a problem," replied Dolan. "Then I wish you nothing but good luck on your little heist tomorrow."

"We're going to need it," Jim said before driving away.

As he pointed the van towards the highway, he smiled to himself. "In your dreams, Dolan," he said aloud. *"In your dreams."*

YURI WATCHED AS JIM DROPPED off Dolan at the Hotel Weiss. He was well acquainted with Dolan from Russian informants in the states. Now, with Dolans arrival, he was sure Dieter and his crew were in their final stages of their theft. Dolan was the last piece of the puzzle.

At a safe distance, he now followed Jim back to the motel. He then called Lana from his cell. "Dolan has arrived and is in the Hotel Weiss. I think they are close to making their move."

Lana was still sitting in her motel room, the curtains pulled to one side, eyeing the Dieter room. "It been relatively quiet here," she replied.

"I should be there in fifteen minutes or so, unless he makes another stop."

"That's strange," Lana said interrupting him. "All of a sudden we have some activity."

What type of activity?"

"They just moved two black duffel bags from one room to the Dieters room," she paused for several seconds. "Now I see luggage being moved to the Dieters room. It looks like they are checking out of their rooms and consolidating into the Dieters room."

"They obviously won't do anything until nighttime," said Yuri confidently. "But start packing just in case. Also, go pay the front desk. I want to be ready to depart as soon as they do."

"I have the strange feeling we are about to be rich," said Lana, the excitement in her voice building. "I can feel it."

"Yes, we are," replied Yuri before repeating it once again. *"Yes, we are."*

LONG BURIED SECRETS

CHAPTER 60

Bern 12:15am

The moon was approaching its quarter mark, providing minimum low-level light. Intermittent rain showers kept down the chance meeting any nosey pedestrians, and being midweek, no midnight revelers.

As far as law enforcement, with the Swiss being the Swiss, the police patrol had driven by at precisely 12:08am, and would return on their patrol at 2:19am.

Everything was perfect for a robbery.

Jim, Nora, Summer, and Eian sat in their white Transit van parked on a side street, 20 meters from the museum. Each of them looked ready for the mission, having donned a black ensemble from head to toe before they had left the Motel.

Minutes earlier they had dropped off Rahm and Chuck by the manhole identified as having the cables that supplied power to the Museum. Nevertheless, before they did, for the fifth time in an hour, Jim had queried Chuck if he was *positive* he had drained every ounce of diesel from the generator.

Traffic was light. A mix of cars and vans were parked on the street providing them with a decent cover if a police vehicle happened to reappear, off schedule.

Nora looked out the passenger side window with a pair of night vision infrared binoculars they had purchased at a military surplus store outside of Zurich. She focused on the museum's office employee section, a corridor containing offices that separated the museums main collection from the Gurlitt collection. Old-fashioned window cages covered each of the six ground-floor windows, an inside facing padlock on each for additional security.

Two days earlier, Chuck identified one of the windows in the office corridor that looked to be the most accessible to make their entrance. He thought it might actually be slightly ajar. Chuck said bolt cutters would do the trick on the lock. He also managed to buy a similar lock in-town to replace the one they would be cutting. Everything had to look undisturbed when they departed.

"The window is still ajar," said Nora confidently, handing the binoculars to Jim for confirmation. He took a quick look before nodding to Nora.

It was time.

NORA DIALED RAHM's cell phone. "Okay," she said when he answered, "We are in position. Go for it. But remember to activate the gas at least 20 seconds or so before you cut the power."

"Will do," he replied before hastily hanging up. He motioned to Chuck to open the sewer cover. "It's go time."

Rahm helped Chuck pry up the solid steel lid with a common crowbar. Rahm heaved up the 75-pound manhole cover, rolled it to the holes side, and gently laid it down.

"In the US, this close to a museum, this manhole cover would have been welded at four points so we couldn't do what we just did," said Chuck. "You have to love the peace-loving, neutral Swiss."

Chuck removed a large can of woman's aerosol hairspray from his black duffel bag of *goodies* as he called them. "Do you know how hard it is to find this anymore?" he said to

Rahm. "In the long hair days of the eighties and nineties it was everywhere." He then pulled out a long, candle length, lighter, laying it beside the can of hair spray. Next, a handful of bare copper wire strips, each about two inches long, laying them beside the can and the lighter.

"Ready to make some trouble?" said Chuck, a wide grin on his face. He grabbed the can of hair spray and lighter, and then he laid flat on the street so he could better reach the bundle of wiring two and a half feet below the street level. He was ready. Chuck looked up at Rahm awaiting his signal.

"Go," said Rahm.

Chuck snapped on the lighter but nothing happened. He did it several more times to no avail. "You have got to be kidding me," he said. "It worked fine just this afternoon." He tried it several more times.

Rahm used his cell phone's flashlight app to shine its beam on the lighter in order to aid Chuck.

Chuck was cursing loudly by now.

"You have to keep your voice down," said Rahm, "you might attract attention."

After five minutes, Jim called Rahm's cell phone. "What's going on?" he said. "Power should be out by now."

"We are having trouble with the lighter," Rahm replied. "Gives us another minute or so." He hung up with Jim. "Let me see the lighter," he said to Chuck. He took the lighter from Chuck to examine it. After several seconds, he found the problem. "You must have hit the edge of the manhole when you leaned in. The lighter is in the off position." He moved the black plastic piece to the ON position before handing it back to Chuck. "Go for it."

"Don't I feel like the dumbass," said Chuck sheepishly.

He resumed his position of laying on the street, his head and arms in the manhole. Soon there was a whooshing sound with the hairspray spray igniting. The smell of burnt rubber insulation soon filled the air. "Almost through," said Chuck. He burned off a wide section of rubber only to reveal the plastic-coated cable below it. "Give me the second can from my bag," he asked of Rahm. "Used up more than I thought I would." Rahm handed him a second can and in seconds the whooshing sound resumed. Another 20 seconds and he extracted his upper body from the manhole. "Done," he said, grabbing his copper strips. "Stand back," he said, "You never know how these things will blow."

"Wait a second," said Rahm. "I have to activate my gas can. We need those security guards knocked out before the power goes out." He dialed a number on his cell, waiting until he heard it connect. "We give the gas a little time to do its thing and then you can finish," he said.

Chuck stood up and extended his right hand over the uncovered manhole, directly over the now exposed wiring, awaiting Rahm's signal.

Rahm looked at his phones clock, patiently waiting until 20 seconds went by and the gas had time to incapacitate the guards. "Go," he said.

Chuck dropped his copper strips on the bare wires then quickly darted away. In seconds they heard a series of pops, followed by arcing, then the area went dark. "Done and done," said Chuck. He walked over to replace the manhole cover. "Call Jim," he said. "Inform him both power and the guards are out."

FROM HIS SIXTH-FLOOR suite, Dolan sat alone staring out his floor to ceiling window, eyeing the Bern Museum, looking for anything out of place. He was soon rewarded when the lights went dark in the museum. *That has to be the start of things*, he thought.

In celebration he walked over to the suites mini bar and removed a small bottle of Scotch. He poured it in a crystal glass over two pieces of ice and walked back to his seat by the window. He raised his glass in toast before sipping the drink.

"I'm about to be very rich," he said aloud.

LANA SAT BEHIND THE STEERING wheel of their car, Yuri in the passenger seat. They were parked a block from where Dieter and his associates sat, parked, in their white van. Suddenly the lights in the museum went out. "That's it," said Yuri. "They are going for it."

Lana turned to Yuri, grabbing his hand in excitement. "We are about to become very rich," she said.

JIM PICKED UP ON the first ring. "Are we good?" he said.

"Get going," replied Rahm. "Chuck and I will be right behind you. We just have to replace the manhole cover."

Summer, Nora, Eian, and Jim exited the van as the rain started to pick up. Each carried two, six-inch wide, three-foot long cardboard tubes similar to what architects used for carrying large drawings, only these contained the reproductions. Jim also carried a standard toolbox containing box cutters, mini-flashlights, a crowbar, screwdrivers, a hammer, and tubes of glue. In his other hand a heavy-duty bolt cutter. They cautiously approached a group of ground-floor office windows, each covered in a box like metal cage that Chuck had identified earlier as being their best chance to enter the museum. They were located between the older Museum and the new Gurlitt wing. They looked more like your ordinary office windows, not ones that possibly stood between them and billions of dollars in paintings.

They approached where a window was slightly ajar. The same one Nora had noticed from the van. Evidently the person who occupied the office had left their window slightly open, maybe an inch, to provide some air for his or her plants, the plants laying against the window. "You have got to be kidding me," Jim said. "Only the Swiss would do this. I guess they think the five-armed guards inside would be enough of a deterrent."

Jim raised the bolt cutters and in one swift motion cut through the lock. He opened the cage and next carefully pried out the screen. When he was done, he simply pushed the window the rest of the way up, cautious not to knock over any of the plants. He then carefully placed the screen in the office. "Don't forget. We have to replace this screen when we leave," he said back to those assembled. He then grabbed several of the plants from their spot on the windowsill, handing them back to Nora and Summer. "Wait until I get into the office, then hand them back to me," he said.

Jim pulled himself through the now open window and into the office. He made quick work of placing the rest of the plants on the floor. "Let's go," he said to Summer, Nora, and Eian. They handed him first the plants then their cardboard tubes and toolbox before he helped each of them into the small office.

Chuck and Rahm approached just as Summer entered through the open window. She helped Chuck in, he in turn helped Rahm.

Chuck pulled the window cage shut.

"That was quick," Chuck said to Summer.

"Window was open just a crack just like you said it would be," said Summer.

"Same thing happened to an art museum back in Boston in the nineties. A nice $500 million job for somebody."

"Close the window," Jim whispered from his position now at the closed office door. "Don't need anyone seeing that baby wide open." Satisfied, Jim opened the office door slightly, looking out onto the darkened hallway that separated the two galleries. They knew the guardroom was only 50 feet away directly across from where they now stood.

Rahm walked up to Jim and whispered, "If they are in the guard room, trust me, they are out of commission. Let me go first."

Jim backed up. "Be my guest," he said before handing him a pen light.

Rahm cautiously stepped into the hallway. He first looked to see if the motion sensor lights were out. The loss of power would have also deactivated the floors weight sensors. Satisfied, he jogged the 50 feet over to the guardroom. Once there, he placed his ear to the door. Hearing nothing, he opened it slightly knowing the gas would have dissipated by now. He counted five guards all asleep, four with video game controllers still in their hands. He turned back to Jim and signaled the coast was clear by flashing his light on, then off, then on. Rahm hastily closed the door and rejoined the group.

Jim was busy handing out tools of the trade: a box cutter, a flashlight the size of a pen, and a straight slot screwdriver to each of them. "Everybody knows which paintings they are assigned to take and replace with the reproductions. We practiced this a number of times in the motel. We take them off the walls and pry the nails from the canvas's. We ease the canvas off the frames, replace them with our reproductions, and tack the paintings with the original nails. You then lay each of the paintings on the floor, one on top of the other until you have your assigned number. Then roll them up in one big roll and place them in the assigned cardboard tube. Everyone good with that?"

Each of them nodded, having heard it for the umpteenth time, first in the motel, now here.

"All right," Jim said as he checked his watch, "we meet back right here in under one hour. Check your iPhones, set your alarms. No more than one-hour, people. Now go!"

IN FORTY-FIVE MINUTES, they started filtering back one-by-one. First Summer, then Chuck, Rahm, Eian, with Nora bringing up the rear, meeting back at the office where they had first entered the museum.

"I can't believe how exciting this is!" said Summer. "Here I am the head of one Museum, breaking into another Museum!"

"Well hopefully you don't want to take this up as a side job," said Chuck. "Take it from me, you wind up getting caught at one time or another."

"Oh this is it for me," she replied. "I'm one and done. All of these paintings shouldn't be on display to begin with. They deserve to be with the families that they were stolen from during the war."

"And that's one of the reasons we're here," said Jim as he collected each of the cardboard tubes holding the paintings, each tube containing between seven to nine paintings layered one on top of the other, then rolled up to fit into the tube.

Jim handed each in turn to Nora.

As a final quality check, Jim asked Chuck and Summer to walk the floor and take one last look at each of the reproductions. While they walked the floors, Jim had Eian and Chuck perform an inventory check on all of their tools to make sure they were leaving with everything they brought in. He also asked Rahm to return to the security office to monitor the sleeping guards. In addition, he had to pick up his gas canister he hidden behind a cabinet. No evidence could be left behind.

In 15 minutes, Summer and Chuck returned. "Everything looks perfect," Chuck said. "Nobody should be able to tell the difference. *At least for a while.*"

Summer concurred. "The paintings each employ a disturbance sensor for when the paintings are removed from the wall, but they will automatically reset when the power comes back on."

Jim nodded. "So nothing should look out of place when the guards wake up or when the power comes back on? No lights flashing or alarms going off?"

Summer smiled at him. "No, nothing like that. This museum put too much emphasis on foot patrols walking around ready to phone in any disturbance. And we all see how well that works," pointing over to where Rahm looked in on the sleeping guards.

"Okay," Jim said, "I think it's time to get the hell out of here." He waved over to Rahm. "Let's go," he said.

Rahm closed the door and ran over to where they were now starting to exit the building through the window they first entered.

"Jim," he said a bit out of breath from his jog. "I understand German and I just heard on the guard's two-way radio that the power company had repaired the electrical line and were preparing to turn power back on in five minutes."

"The floor sensors will be activated in the office if we don't hurry," Jim said to everyone. "Let's go people."

Nora was first out. She took the toolbox Jim handed her, then the cardboard tubes. Summer soon followed, then Chuck, Eian, and Rahm. Jim carefully placed each of the plants in their rightful spots, and then handed the screen to Rahm. "We have to try and place that screen back in after I close the window," he said. After he exited, he then placed the last two plants in their spot on the windowsill. Jim adjusted the window down to its previous position when they first entered. Rahm then handed Jim the screen. Luckily for them, it fit nicely back into the metal slots with no trouble.

Suddenly power came on as he finished adjusting the screen.

"We are sitting ducks out here," said Rahm anxiously.

Jim pointed over to the truck. "Everybody head for the truck," he said. "I'll follow in a few."

Each hastily walked to the truck with their tools and cardboard tubes in tow.

Jim hurried to extract the new lock from his pocket. He then pushed the cage back into place over the window, making sure to place the lock on the interior side of the cage. "And that's how a successful robbery is done," he said to himself. He then rushed back to the van, the side door held open for him by Eian.

"Let's get out of here before the cops make their rounds," Eian said as Jim jumped in.

Chuck looked to his watch. "That should be in about four minutes," he said, having observed their schedule over the course of the past several nights. "They are both very efficient, and very predictable."

Two blocks away they noticed the yellow sirens of the Axpo Municipal Electric company workers trucks as they concluded their repairs on the brilliant work Chuck had performed on the wire bundles.

In minutes, Nora maneuvered the transit van down to the main boulevard, and in a short distance they were on the highway and driving west towards France.

Over one billion US dollars' worth of paintings lay rolled up in cardboard tubes beside Summer and Chuck in the back seat.

Eian leaned over to Rahm in the seat beside him. "Did that really happen or did I just dream it all?" He said, a grin on his face from ear-to-ear.

Rahm looked to Eian with a hint of seriousness about him. "You enriched the lives of many people today," he said. "Now if you are lucky enough to live another day, maybe you can collect."

LANA NOTICED THE POWER come on first. "I hope they get out of there quick," she said. "That's our money as much as theirs."

Yuri saw them come into view, the black clad figures running from the museum to the van. "Start the engine, Lana," he said. "We have to stay behind them."

As she was ready to pull out, Lana noticed a police car approaching at a high rate of speed from behind them. She made a quick decision and pulled out into the narrow road, in doing so blocking the police car from getting by.

The police car skidded to a stop only feet from their car. The police now applied its cars sirens, in essence ordering them to clear a path on the single lane road.

Lana rolled down her window. "I'm so sorry," she said in German to the two officers in the car.

"What are you doing, Lana?" asked Yuri. "You will get us caught."

"I'm giving them some time to get away," she replied. "We know what type of vehicle the Dieters are driving, the police don't."

A loudspeaker barked an order in German to clear a path.

Lana waved out the window in acknowledgment, backing into her spot once more.

The police car sped past them, lights blazing, before turning in the opposite direction of the Dieters.

"Now we catch the Dieters ourselves," said Lana.

"Quick thinking. And that's why I married you," said Yuri. "Now go. Hurry."

CHAPTER 61

From his vantage point in the hotel, Dolan saw the black clad figures running from the side window to the awaiting van. He soon noticed the lights were back on inside the museum.

He took another sip of his Scotch. *Feels like a live crime drama,* he thought.

As he saw Dieter and his crew drive away, he noticed a car pull out into the street directly into the path of an approaching police car, temporarily blocking them from squeezing past. When the confusion ended, the police car drove up to the stop sign and turned right, driving past the front of the museum as they angled down a separate side street, evidently on another call.

There was no Museum alarm.

They did it! he thought.

They actually did it!

DOLAN HAD JUST DRIFTED OFF to sleep when his cell phone abruptly rang on his nightstand. "Hello," he said, his voice raspy.

"Dolan," said Jim. "I didn't mean to wake you but its time."

"I understand," replied Dolan. "You said something earlier about providing me with directions to our meeting spot."

In under a minute Dolan had directions and a time to meet. By 5am he and his goon had checked out of the hotel and were heading to France.

LONG BURIED SECRETS

CHAPTER 62

02:21am Bern Switzerland

Each of the Museum guards woke from their gas-induced slumber within seconds of each other. Four of the five still had game controllers in their hands; the fifth had been watching the other four play their games when each had drifted off.

They never realized what had transpired.

Now with the power restored, the wall of 20 LED monitors in front of them showed various locations around the museum. All undisturbed. The two LED monitors the guards had been using for their video game were experiencing the snow effect. "I must have dozed off for a second or two," said one guard to the others. "Why don't you reset the screens for our game."

In seconds they were playing another round of *Assassins Creed,* none the wiser.

LONG BURIED SECRETS

CHAPTER 63

Vicinity of Pouilly-en-Auxois, France

As previously arranged, Jim and Nora drove the white Transit van to an empty auto garage they had leased two days ago on the outskirts of Pouilly-en-Auxois. At the same time they rented a Range Rover Defender and parked the vehicle inside the garage in order to make it look like as though the property was in use.

It was early morning as they swung the garage door open and pulled in, out of sight. Nothing around but freshly plowed farmers' fields. They had been driving for a solid three and a half hours since they had stolen the paintings, their only break coming when they dropped the team off at their prearranged rental car. Soon they each went their separate ways, promising to meet in four to five days.

Jim now maneuvered the van so the trucks rear was facing the Range Rovers rear. "Let's get the ones we identified out of the tubes and the fakes in their place," he said. "First let me close the garage door."

YURI AND LANA HAD followed Jim and Nora from the museum, careful to maintain some distance, but not too careful to lose them. They now drove past the garage in their car as Jim was just lowering the garage door. They continued another 1,000 feet before they parked their car just out of site, in the relative safety of a tree line. From the shelter of their car, they observed the garage with a pair of binoculars.

"How long do you want to stay here?" queried Lana.

Yuri looked at her, a grin on his face. "Let's give them a little more time before we approach."

IN A MATTER OF MINUTES they had exchanged 45 of the most expensive paintings with the second set of reproductions painted by Summers group. That left five original Old Masters they would use as bait for Dolan, all placed in one cardboard tube and marked with a thin black line. This on the chance that Dolan brought along an art expert with him. *Of course, the five Old Masters provided to Dolan would be the ones worth the least amount of money.* A small sacrifice to save the remaining forty-five paintings. The rest of the reproductions were rolled up, nine to a cardboard roll, and readied for Dolan.

Jim patted the cardboard tubes. "Now you know why I wanted double reproductions of each painting," he said, a broad smile on his face. "The high-end reproductions for the museum, and the low-end ones to fool Dolan."

"What can I say," said Nora, "you are a genius." The sarcasm in her voice evident.

The originals were laying in a separate set of cardboard tubes in the cargo area. Time was of the essence with Dolan due at any minute.

Nora kissed Jim on the cheek before she climbed into the Range Rover. "Be careful when you meet Dolan. I don't trust that bastard any more than you do."

"Don't you worry about me," he said, holding up a Glock 9mm, a gift from Benny, "you just get the real paintings to our first canal stop. I can handle Dolan and his crew."

"Love it when a plan comes together."

"And we get the bad guys in the end, right?"

Jim walked over to the garage door, looking through its horizontal row of glass windows to make sure nobody was around. He waved to her as he pulled up the door.

"Get the rest of the supplies and I will meet you in a few hours."

"THERE GOES A RANGE ROVER," said Lana. "It looks like only the woman is driving.

"We stay with the van and Jim Dieter," replied Yuri. "Quick, duck down," he said as the van turned towards them, driving by without slowing.

They waited until Nora had driven by, then exited their car, weapons drawn, running up to the garages back wall.

NO MORE THAN FIVE minutes had elapsed since Nora had departed when Jim heard a car approach, soon followed by two doors slamming shut.

Okay, only two people, he said to himself. He placed the 9mm Glock at the small of his back as insurance. He never trusted Dolan, nor liked him.

The garages side door opened as Dolan walked in with his goon. "Jim, I knew you could do it with a little proper motivation," said Dolan, his bleached teeth shining brightly. He indicated for his goon to open the vans rear door.

His Goon walked over to the van, opening its door. He unscrewed each container. Satisfied. "Looks like the paintings are here, boss," said the Goon.

Dolan kept his eye on Jim as he went for a peak himself. "Where's that pretty little wife of yours?"

"She's getting some supplies," he said. "But like I told you earlier driving in from the airport. We could only get fifty of the paintings. Any more would raise suspicion. Don't worry, they are all there," said Jim. "We have no need for your paintings."

"I'll take fifty and still be very rich," said Dolan as he randomly picked a tube, the one that just happened to have the thin black line, sliding out the paintings. He laid them on top of the other tubes. He pulled out an eyepiece and a pencil flashlight from his pocket, before leaning over the first Old Master on top, looking in detail at the artist's signature. He then looked at the remaining four. He looked up after the last painting, smiling at Jim. "I'm satisfied. Your boy Eian, his slate is wiped clean."

Jim shook his head. "No, it's not that easy. I want you to call your people back in Philly and tell them, now. A deal is a deal."

Dolan tossed the keys to the rental car to his Goon. "Load these tubes up and put them in the trunk of the car."

LANA WATCHED AS THE goon loaded the paintings in the rental car. "We follow Dolan now," she said matter of factly.

"No," replied Yuri. "I follow Dolan. You follow Dieter. I think he still has something up his sleeve."

Lana was about to speak but Yuri raised his hand in order to silence her. "I'm aware you won't have a car. But the town is only ½ a mile from here. You said Dieter was by the docks a few days ago. I am betting he will return to the docks. Unfortunately, you will have to walk to town."

He kissed her on the cheek before he ran off to their car, leaving her to tail Jim.

On foot.

DOLAN PULLED OUT HIS cell phone, in a matter of seconds he was connected to his moneyman back in Philly. "Wipe the slate clean on Eian. The man has paid his debts. All contracts rescinded on him. He is not allowed to gamble in any of our establishments. None of them." He hung up just as quick. "Satisfied?"

"That's all I needed. I particularly like the part about him not being allowed to gamble in any of your establishments. You better beat feet out of here." Jim directed him towards the door.

Dolan stopped him before they reached the side door. "You still owe me the airport information. The one where my buddy Eian is supposed to fly us home from," he said.

Jim smiled at him. "You are correct," he said, handing him a piece of paper with the name and address of an obscure airport no more than 20 miles from where they stood. "There is a Gulfstream 550 waiting for you two. Eian is making the aircraft ready for a flight back to Philly as we speak."

"You have done well, Jim. If you ever want to make some extra cash, contact me."

"I'm semi-retired after this one but thank-you just the same."

YURI HAD LEFT LANA at the garage and returned to the car waiting for Dolan to depart. He took a roundabout approach so Dolans goon would not see him. Now, from the safety of his car, he watched as Dolan and Jim said their good-byes. Dolan surprised him by turning away from town and proceeding back the way they had driven in.

Yuri wasted no time in turning around his car and following his new prey.

CHAPTER 64

Six miles east of Dijon, France

Dolan was driving the car, following the detailed instructions his Goon was reading off to him, the same ones Dieter had provided to them earlier.

They now exited the main highway at Orgeux in order to drive the backroads to his destination: the small airport at Bretigny.

Yuri followed them from ½-mile distance, careful not to spook his new prey. He had overheard Dolan and Dieter in the garage says something about an airport, so maybe that is where they were heading. He hoped so. An airport would present many opportunities to overtake Dolan and his Goon.

The Goon pointed over to Dolans left. "There it is, boss," he said matter of factly. "That's the smallest airport I have ever seen."

Dolan turned in, now driving on a gravel road, a solitary hanger in the distance. "I guess we head for the hangar."

Yuri watched as Dolan turned in. Once the location and its solitary hangar presented itself, he immediately sensed opportunity. "Those paintings are coming home with me," he said aloud to an empty car.

CHAPTER 65

In the aircraft hangar at Bretigny, Benny sat in a darkened office space located on the hangars second floor off to its left side. From his vantage point, he had a perfect view of the well-lit, Gulfstream 550, parked just below him. He also had a large window to the outside that allowed him to watch as a car approached from the main road.

Benny watched as Dolan drove up in his car and parked outside the hangar, soon approaching from the hangars side door. Of course, Benny had amble warning of Dolans expected arrival time with Jim Dieter calling him 30 minutes ago.

Dolan cautiously opened the hangar door peaking in. "The jet is in the hangar," said Dolan to his Goon. They both walked into an area bathed in light, the Gulfstream sitting before them.

Inside the hangar, Dolan walked up to the plane, its door open, steps down. "This has got to be ours," he said to the goon. "Anybody here?" he yelled.

From inside the aircraft a female voice said "hello" in reply.

Dolan walked up the steps and into the plane. "Eian, where are you?" he said looking into the cockpit.

In the aft section of the eighteen-person capacity jet sat a man and a woman dressed in pilots attire. "Good afternoon," said the woman. "You must be, Mr. Dolan," she said in an accent he couldn't quite make out. "Slight change of plans regarding your friend, Eian. I am your pilot, Margaret Thistle, and this gentlemen is my co-pilot, Reese Ahlstrom."

YURI NOW APPROACHED the same side door to the hangar that Dolan and his goon had walked through. He opened the door and peaked in, seeing Dolan and his Goon up in the aircraft. He crept up to the plane's nose, gun at the ready.

He could hear the pilot and co-pilot introducing themselves.

Yuri crouched under the aircrafts nose, out of view, awaiting his prey.

What he didn't realize was Benny already noticed him from his second-floor perch and fed the information to the co-pilot via his in-ear mike.

The pilot led Dolan and the Goon back down the aircraft steps. "Let's go over the route," she said pointing to a table covered with two flight maps. The co-pilot stayed on the aircraft in accordance with Benny's new instructions.

Yuri stood up from his concealed position, his weapon pointed at the pilot, Dolan, and the Goon. "Stop where you are," yelled Yuri as he walked around to the front of the table where the maps lay.

"Who the hell are you?" yelled Dolan. His goon reached for his weapon, Yuri shot him in the head before he could extract it from his waistband, falling hard to the ground. Dolan looked to the pilot for help, then Yuri. "Calm down there, friend," said Dolan. "May I sound to impertinent by asking who the hell you are?"

"I work for the Russian government, Mr. Dolan," replied Yuri, walking over to remove Dolans weapon from the small of his back. "These paintings are going to Russia, where they should have gone many years ago."

Dolan once again looked to the pilot for assistance. Sensing none, he continued his negotiation. "Let's make a deal." He was not about to let his prize get away, or at least what he perceived to be his father's legacy. "There's plenty for all of us."

After hearing the Russian announce himself, the co-pilot pulled an Uzi from his flight bag in the cockpit, making his way to the doorway. His pilot signaled to him with a nod. That was all he required. The co-pilot let loose with a quick burst that killed Yuri instantly. Dolan instinctively dove for the ground. After several seconds, he realized he was not the target.

"You can get up now, Mr. Dolan," said the pilot, she now also brandishing a gun.

Dolan looked surprised. "What, everybody has weapons around here?"

The copilot now approached Dolan, a pair of plastic tie wraps in his hands. "Why don't we put these on?" he said.

The pilot smiled at Dolan as the cuffs were placed about his wrists and feet. "We work for Mossad, Mr. Dolan," she said a matter of factly. "Those paintings are not yours. They belong to a lot of different people, most of whom, if not all, are dead."

Satisfied they were, indeed, alone, the pilots opened the hangar doors and drove Dolans car to the side of the aircraft. In a matter of ten minutes, they had transferred the paintings from Dolans car to the plane.

Benny now made his appearance. "Good morning, Mr. Dolan," he said. He walked around the aircraft's nose to see Dolan sitting on the floor.

"Who the hell are you?" he spat out. "Its like Times Square around here."

"Allow me to introduce myself. Benny Machaim. Head of Mossad. Maybe you have heard of us?"

Dolan looked over to his dead Goon, then the Russian. "I guess I'm next to die?"

The pilot shook her head as she walked over to Dolan, kneeling down in front of him. "No, you will not die," she said. "Our boss," she pointed over to Benny, "said to leave you with five of the paintings. He said not to be too greedy and leave you with those of least value." She dropped a cardboard tube at his feet, one with a thin black line on its outside. "Have fun."

"You can't leave me like this," implored Dolan.

Benny ignored him as walked up the steps onto the plane.

The pilot nodded. "Your right," she said before going into the plane and returning with a glass of water. "Drink this and you will rest for a bit. Just until we are gone."

"I'm not drinking that," he blurted out. "That could be poison for all I know."

"You are not that lucky, Mr. Dolan. Drink it and you live, don't, you die." She now held a 9mm to his head.

He begrudgingly nodded. He drank it slowly. In a matter of minutes, he was in a drug-induced sleep.

The co-pilot laughed aloud as he readied the aircraft for take-off. "He is going to wake up with one hell of a headache."

"At least he is waking up," said the pilot in reply.

"Well, we need someone to blame for the robbery."

FROM THE COMFORT of the Gulfstream, Benny spoke on his cell phone with his counterpart in the French Directorate-General for External Security, informing him that there was the possibility the person, or persons, who robbed the Bern Museum were at the Bretigny airport.

CHAPTER 66

Dolan woke up to view the aircraft gone. He was still a little groggy from the concoction he was forced to drink. He blinked a few more times to clear his head. He sat up and kicked at the cardboard tube that lay at his feet. He then viewed the dead Russian and his goon. "This doesn't look good," he said aloud. The Israelis were kind enough to leave behind the Uzi that killed the Russian. Placing it strategically near Dolan. He now could be blamed for their murder and the art heist.

He was not having a good day.

In the distance the sound of sirens could be heard, and they were getting closer by the minute.

Dolan easily removed the plastic ties that had bound him, having been partially cut by the Israelis' before they departed. He struggled to his feet, still experiencing the side effects of the drugs. He staggered towards the hangars side door hoping to escape. He managed to get about ten feet away when five *Gendarmerie Nationale* cars pulled up, their tires screeching to a stop. Out poured 20 agents of the National Police force, all with guns drawn, each scouring off in different directions.

Dolan stopped, a smile creasing his face, as two agents forcibly pushed him to the ground. They spoke in French, pointing to the bodies, wanting to know what happened.

"I don't speak your language," he spat out to the one nearest him.

"You are American?" the first officer replied.

"You're damn right I am. Moreover, I know my rights. I want an attorney. *A good one.*"

The second officer opened the cardboard tube. "These are definitely from the art theft in Bern," she said.

The first officer rolled Dolan over. "Art theft and murder. You will be lucky if you ever see the outside world again."

Dolan closed his eyes, realizing he had been royally set up.

CHAPTER 67

Pouilly-en-Auxois, France

Jim had abandoned the van less than two blocks from the canal, leaving its keys on the passenger seat, secretly hoping someone would just steal it. He removed his travel bag and walked the remainder of the way to the canal.

He still had plenty of time to meet with Nora. She had several shopping duties to complete before meeting him at their agreed location.

Jim waved to the salesman. "Bonjour, Monsieur Dubet," he said in greeting, his travel bag slung over his shoulder as he approached the vacation barge. The barge itself barely visible due to a two-meter-high concrete canal wall that performed double duty: keeping the earthen bank from falling into the canal, and providing a walkway alongside the canal that traversed through town. "You are a man of your word."

Dubet was dressed in a cheap brown suit coat and matching slacks, his hair slicked back. "You required your barge here in record time, and yes I am a man of my word. Of course, it required some extra euros. But in the end, everything is okay."

Jim walked down the aluminum gangway onto the barge, his hand extended. "Is the barge ready to go?"

"Stocked with everything you asked for. The Galley has provisions to last you for a few days. Basic foodstuffs and such. In addition, you have enough diesel fuel to make the entire journey without the need for a pit stop. I topped off the tank myself not more than ten minutes ago."

Jim withdrew an additional ten, hundred-euro bills from his coat pocket. "This is for you, my friend," handing the bills to Dubet. "My wife and I appreciate all you have done."

Dubet quickly pocketed the bills as though expected, without saying a word. "Where is your lovely wife?" He said, looking to the gangway, then Jim. He was obviously eager for another look at his shapely wife.

"I'm meeting her in the next town. She's picking up some additional items we might need for our trip."

Jim ushered Dubet to the gangway. "I don't mean to be rude but I am trying to get underway as soon as possible. We have a tight schedule to keep. Can you provide me a hand and untie my bow lines?"

"All part of the service," Dubet said. In a matter of minutes he had unslung the lines with ease. "Au revoir," he said in French, *Good-bye*. He stood on the side as he watched Jim motor the barge up the canal, waving back to him. Satisfied, he continued back to his car, parked at the edge of the waterway. With the extra thousand euros Jim had provided he could place a bet at the casino in Dijon. Maybe double his money? He looked at his watch. He still had time to reach the casino and then make the drive back home. As he was about to put his keys in his car door, a woman approached him, seemingly out of nowhere. Dubet dropped his keys in surprise.

"I am so sorry," she said innocently, her accent sounding Slavic. Possibly Russian. "I did not mean to surprise you." She reached down and picked up his keys before handing them to him.

Dubet stood admiring Lana. "No. no. Not a problem. You did not surprise me," he said. "I was simply shocked by your beauty."

Lana rolled her eyes. How many times had she heard that line? She thought it would stop once she married and had a gold ring on her finger. She continued. "I was just hoping you could tell me who was on that barge, and possibly their itinerary?"

Dubet was taken back for a moment. Obviously she wasn't interested in him. "Who are you?" he replied with contempt. "And why do you need to know who my customers are?"

The woman produced a pistol, on its end a silencer. "Because I asked you nicely," she said. "But if you like, I can also be a real jerk." She aimed the pistol at Dubet's knee. "Need I ask the question again?"

Dubet looked to Jim's progress, the barge already at the opposite edge of town. He instantly thought back to the last time he rented a barge to Jim. It was to him and his Irish hoodlum friend. They returned it wrecked. Bullet holes in the woodwork. Glass windows shattered. He had even heard rumors that two dead bodies had been found on board. Now he had the strange feeling it was about to happen all over again. "I rented it to one James Dieter, an American on vacation."

"Just one person for such a big barge? Who would do such a thing?"

Dubet shook his head meekly. "He did not share his plans with me. You know how Americans can be."

She fired a shot by his foot. With the silencer attached, it sounded similar to a metal ball dropping in a hollow metal tube.

He jumped back.

"The next one is in your knee."

Dubet looked down at where the bullet had dug itself into the dirt. He managed a slight smile as he said, "He is meeting his wife further up the canal."

"How far up the canal? Don't toy with me."

"I really don't know. As I said earlier, he did not share his plans with me."

Lana shook her head, then turned and fired a bullet into his driver's side window, the bullet causing the window to spider around its hole, before imbedding into his passenger seat. "Again, how far up the canal?"

Dubet looked at the damage, before realizing he could be next. "I think he mentioned the next town up," he said submissively. "Please, I am but a salesman. I don't make much money on these rentals. I told you all I know."

The woman nodded in understanding. It sounded reasonable enough. She produced a hundred euro note, holding it up for him to see. "What is the name of the barge?" She continued.

"La Belle," he said, his voice quivering. He studied her for a quick moment. He noted she was someone he would have liked to have met under different circumstances.

She handed him the bill. "If you tell anyone of our little conversation, I will make you a cripple," her weapon pointed at Dubet's knee. "I also know where you do business. Now give me your car keys and then go over to the canals edge."

"What?"

"If I say it again, you will be limping."

He handed her his car keys.

She pointed to the canal with her weapon. "Go."

He walked over to its edge.

"Jump in," she commanded.

"But this is a new suit," he pleaded.

Lana aimed her weapon at his knee. "Well, it's an ugly new suit," she said, a smile upon her face. "And it's going to have a hole right where your knee is if you don't jump."

Lana watched as he jumped in. She lost sight of him due to the floodwall but was soon rewarded with the sound of a splash when he hit the water. Satisfied, she jumped into his car and drove off.

Dubet heard the woman drive off in his car. "I don't believe this," he said aloud. "Every time I deal with that crazy American, James Dieter, this happens to me!"

As he struggled to climb out of the canal's muddy waters, his first instinct was to run. He did not want to get involved. He realized he had to at least warn Jim. But how? He patted his pockets. A soggy lump in his jacket indicated he did not lose his cell phone to the canal's waters. However, would it still work? He depressed the *On* button and to his surprise, it powered up. Soon he was able to locate Jim's saved cell number and within seconds, the call was going through.

CHAPTER 68

Aboard the *La Belle*, along the canal

Piloting the barge brought back memories of his last trip with Dan. How they had enjoyed the French countryside and the wine. Way too much wine. He laughed aloud at the thought of Dan opening a bottle when Jim wouldn't let him steer the barge. Then he sat out on the deck with several bottles in plain view of Jim. *Too bad you can't drink and steer*, he said, sitting back in his lounge chair, enjoying his first glass of the day. That was enough of an enticement for Jim to finally relinquish the wheel.

Still can't believe he's dead.

The ring of his cell phone snapped him back to reality.

"Mr. Dieter," said Monsieur Dubet, his voice sounding high shrilled. "I have some bad news for you."

"I just left you 10 minutes ago. What in the hell happened in the meantime?"

"Somebody approached me after you left. They were very rude." He was flustered. "I mean to say, *a woman accosted me*."

"Slow down. You were accosted? Why don't you call the police?

"She was asking questions about you."

That caught his attention. "Slow down and tell me the details."

"I was walking back to my car and a beautiful woman, Russian I think, from her accent, approached me. She had a gun with what I think was a sound suppressor screwed on its end. She wanted to know who was on your barge."

"I guess you held out for as long as you could before telling her?"

"She shot my car window! She put a hole through it! Then she said my knee was next. That's when I felt I had to provide her with something."

"So she knows my name? The boats name? And where I plan to stop and pick up my wife?"

Dubet paused for several seconds before he responded. "Yes, on all accounts. I am sorry Mr. Dieter. But the gun, it was pointed at me. And she was very attractive. I can't forget her long black hair, slim, high cheekbones."

Jim shook his head. "Was she alone? Anyone else with her?"

"No, she was alone."

"Which way did she proceed?"

"I was in the canal when she drove off in a flash after you. In my car! She stole my car," his pitch rising. "She might be approaching you as we speak. Please don't get her mad. And do me a favor. Please, please, return the barge in one piece this time. I say it once again, please!"

Jim paused for several moments before he responded. "But that's why I purchased insurance, Monsieur Dubet."

CHAPTER 69

Lana focused on the road that ran parallel to the canal, taking time to scan the canal when she entered a straightaway, looking for the barge, La Belle.

He can't be that far, she thought to herself. She knew the vacation barges only could muster a top speed of about six kilometers per hour.

She now deliberated whether she should go after the wife first, or Dieter? The barge salesman said the wife was going to meet Dieter along the canal or possibly in the next town.

Entering a straightaway, she hit redial on her cell phone, hoping that Yuri would tell her he had the paintings. It went straight to voice mail. I hope he is having better luck than I am, she thought.

JIM MANEUVERED THE barge over and adjacent to a clump of trees and shrubs that grew out of the canal's embankment. Not necessarily an ideal area for parking a 10-ton barge but these particular trees and shrubs looked like they would provide just enough concealment from the road. Satisfied, he shut down the engine and turned off all of the barge's lights.

Then he called Nora.

LANA DROVE ALONG THE canal road, and past the location where Jim had already pulled the barge in, not noticing a thing. The heavily forested portion of the canal provided him excellent concealment from the road.

Lana had already changed her mind, deciding to focus on Jim Dieter's wife, Nora. According to the barge salesman, she would be waiting in a position further up the canal or possibly the next town.

She recalled her time spent at the GRU Academy. Her instructors would always insist they attack the weakest link first. Neutralize one, and the rest would soon follow.

Lana chose Nora as the weak link.

Jim would have no choice but to come to her.

WHEN NORA DIDN'T PICK up Jim had no choice but to leave her a voicemail. He knew she might still be driving, or had merely left her phone in the new rental. He waited five minutes and then called her a second time. She picked up on the third ring.

"Where are you?" he said in a controlled voice.

"What, no hello?"

"Listen. Hear me out. Somethings come up. There is a female Russian Agent possibly coming to your location. I think she is the same one from Bern. The barge salesman called me to tell me of his run-in with her after I pulled away from the dock."

"That's not what I wanted to hear right now. I just pulled into the spot where you planned to load the paintings. It's really dark here, between the tree's canopies, and what looks like a nasty storm approaching."

"Get out of there, now! Drive back towards town. I am no more than ½ mile outside of town. When I see you approach I will turn on the barge spotlight and point it towards the road."

"I'm on my way. But don't you think the Russian will see me driving in the opposite direction?"

Jim paused for several seconds. "You're right."

Nora looked up towards the road. "I already see a car's headlights coming towards me from town. It could be the Russian now."

"Get out of the Range Rover. Hide somewhere. I'm coming to you. I should be there in 10 minutes."

Nora quickly exited and sought shelter in some underbrush.

LANA NOTICED THE Range Rover on her left as she drove by, it parked by the canal, about 25 meters off the road. She intentionally drove by before choosing to turn around in the middle of the roadway about a half a kilometer away. She thought it best to drive without lights, turning them off, as she doubled back.

Lana drove slowly, stopping just out of view of the Range Rover, and in the middle of the canal road, leaving her engine running. She now reached for her AK-47, releasing its safety, placing it in her lap. She then turned on the cars high beam lights as she steered in directly towards the Range Rover, placing the car in neutral, she aimed the car straight for the Range Rover before jumping out, rolling on the ground with her machine gun.

JUST AS JIM ASKED HER to do, Nora was hiding in some underbrush on the edge of the canal, awaiting his arrival in the barge. Hopefully he would arrive before the Russian did. She thought she heard an engine chugging away in the distance. *That has to be Jim*, she thought.

Then she heard another sound, one much closer, possibly a revving car engine, quickly followed by a metal-on-metal crunching sound.

LANA QUICKLY SPRUNG up with her machine gun pointed towards the Range Rover. She cautiously approached, her weapons wooden butt expertly tucked into her shoulder, the weapon leading the way. She had hoped to surprise whoever was in the vehicle with her *controlled crash*. Her cars engine sputtered and died as she walked past where it had rear-ended her target, proceeding to the driver's side of the car. Luckily, a fallen tree had stopped forward progress of the Range Rover or it would have been pushed directly into the canal, paintings and all. Lana kept her weapon pointed at the driver's side as she used one hand to pull open the door, stepping back in case anyone was waiting inside.

FROM HER HIDING SPOT, Nora viewed Lana as she sprung up and walked towards the vehicle.

Nora realized she was cornered and had no choice but to attack. Carefully she approached Lana from the heavily forested side along the canal, trying her best to maintain cover as she watched Lana open the driver's side door.

Nora looked around for a weapon of some sort, settling on a small, two-to-three-kilogram, round rock. When Lana poked her head in the van, Nora sprung on her, the rock over her head.

Lana heard the snap of a tree branch and turned in time to see Nora but not before the boulder smashed into the left side of her head. Lana managed to let off a quick burst of her weapon before falling unconscious to the ground.

JIM HAD JUST ROUNDED a turn in the canal and could view his meeting place with Nora. He also saw the front of the Range Rover parked dangerously close to the edge of the canal. He signaled with a flashlight, two long, one short. When she didn't respond, he tried once more. That's when he first heard a burst of an automatic weapon. He tried calling her cell phone. No answer. He went below for his own weapon, a 9mm Glock.

He wasn't about to go to a gunfight empty-handed.

NORA FELT SOMETHING hot hit the right side of her head as she fell to the ground on top of Lana. Both Lana and Nora now lay intertwined, bleeding, both unconscious.

JIM MANEUVERED THE barge into the earthen bank of the canal, about 100 meters from where the van was parked. He wanted to make sure the area was secure and Nora was indeed okay. He swiftly secured the barge to a rather large ash tree. He then jumped to the soft ground as he silently moved off to where Nora should be waiting for his arrival.

His arm was extended with his 9mm Glock leading the way.

He had no intention of walking into an ambush.

AFTER SEVERAL MINUTES Lana woke. For a split second, she wondered where she was. A heavy weight was crushing her stomach. She looked down to see a bloodied Nora laying across her midsection. She pushed her off and attempted to stand up. As she tried to rise dizziness forced her back down. The last thing she remembered was something heavy hitting her across the head. Lana felt her head and her hand came away red. She then looked to Nora, her right side bloodied. *Looks like we both got a blow in before passing out*, she thought. But Nora looked worse off, possibly dead. She hit Nora a couple of times with her fist. No response. Lana had to get up. She realized the barge would be appearing at any moment. She eased Nora off to the side before using her machine gun as a crutch, pushing on it to aid her in standing. Once up, she held onto a small tree for several seconds to try and maintain her balance. Slowly she was regaining her motor skills. The canal was only 10 meters away. She knew she had to reach the waterway to look for the barge.

JIM PUSHED THROUGH THE heavily wooded area the best he could. As he approached the Range Rover, he noticed a figure moving towards the canal, their back to him. *Was it Nora?* The trees heavy canopies and the approaching storm turned day into night, not presenting him with a decent enough view to make a determination.

Then he noticed a car had rammed Nora's vehicle.

He eased himself out of the woods near the canal road. It looked to afford him a better vantage point. He searched for a possible second figure but could only view the one down by the canal. The figure looked to be leaning up against the Range Rover for support, scanning down the canal. Apparently looking for him and the barge.

He expertly maneuvered down towards the figure, using the line of trees as cover, easing in and out to his advantage. He stopped to reassess. Should he try and call Nora once more? But if he did and she wasn't the figure down by the river, would it alert them?

He had to get closer so he could determine if it was Nora or not. Moving to within five meters of the rear of the car, he stumbled over something soft. First he looked at the figure down by the canal to make sure he wasn't overheard. Satisfied, he leaned down and saw it was Nora, her head bloodied. She was unresponsive as he shook her several times.

"I think she is dead, Mr. James Dieter," said a women in a slight Russian accent. She stood only meters from where Jim cradled his wife, her AK-47 pointed at Jim "I shot her when she attacked me. I must say, she did not go without a fight. Now, please get up. We have work to do."

Jim softly kissed his wife, gently laying her body on the ground. At this moment nothing mattered to him. Not even his own life. "You are obviously here after the paintings. Why couldn't you just be satisfied with just taking the Range Rover and its contents? You had to kill her?"

Lana looked surprised. "Are you telling me the paintings are in the vehicle and not the barge?"

Jim looked down at Nora, his weapon still in his hand, hidden under Nora. "That's exactly what I am telling you."

"Get up," she commanded.

Jim rose, discreetly laying his weapon beside Nora's body. "You can kill me now. Why wait?"

"Who said I was going to kill you? I am under explicit orders not to hurt anyone."

"Yea, I noticed," he said, pointing down to Nora's body.

"That was unfortunate, she attacked me first. But I can promise no harm will come to you if you cooperate."

Jim could see she was a true professional, keeping her distance so he could not charge her. Weapon at the ready.

"Keep your hands where I can see them please."

Jim raised them a little higher.

"I require you to get in my car and see if it you can still start it."

Jim opened the door and sat in the driver's seat. He turned the keys and tried to turn the car over several times to no avail. He held his hands up. "Battery looks to be damaged. She won't start."

"Keep trying, or I won't require your services anymore."

Jim tried several more times, to be rewarded with a clicking noise in response before it randomly started, reeving loudly, a cloud of black smoke emitting from its tailpipe.

"Back it up to the top of the road. No further or I will be forced to shoot you."

He turned the cars lights on in order to aid him. Lana also helped him with hand signals as he backed the car up to the road.

"Now the Range Rover, please."

Jim walked down to the vehicle, its front tires precariously near the edge of the canal.

"Don't even think about it. You drive into the canal, and I promise that your wife's body will be so desecrated they won't even know if it was male or female."

He now realized how a dog felt on a leash. The Range Rover started with no problems.

Lana aimed her machine gun at Jim. "Just back it up away from the canal." After 5 meters, she stopped him. "Okay. Out. You handled that too easy. I would have expected a little more of a fight from a former US Navy SEAL."

"What can I say, you took all of the fight out of me when you murdered my wife."

Lana looked back to the car parked by the road. She had just enough room to squeeze by. "Please, I require you to walk back towards the canal."

Jim did as ordered."

"Now step in."

"What?"

"Step in until the canal water is up to your waist."

She fired a short burst at the dirt in front of him to help with his decision.

"Okay. You don't have to go all mad Russian on me."

"I don't have time to play around. Now in."

Jim hesitated just a few seconds, waiting until she had opened the vehicles door.

"In the water," she demanded, followed by yet another short burst from her machine gun.

This time Jim just smiled at her, "Check the ignition."

Lana felt for the vehicles keys. "You bastard. Where are they?" She demanded.

Jim held them up in his right hand, playfully acting as though he would toss them in the canal. "And this is why I didn't have to fight you earlier. I used my brains and not my brawn."

"Hand them over," she demanded her tone not as harsh as before. "Or I will have no choice but to shoot you."

THE LAST BURST from Lana's gun caused Nora to stir. Her cheek and head felt as if they were on fire. She reached for the side of her head and felt her wet, sticky, matted hair. Of course the blood being the cause of the wet part. She quickly realized head wounds always produced a lot of blood. She then felt Jim's 9mm beside her. "How did this get here?" She tried to rise but her pounding head forced her back down. Nora overheard Lana's demands for Jim to step into the canal and realized she had no choice: she had to get up no matter what.

If she did not, he would be dead.

For that matter, they both would be dead.

LANA SLOWLY PROCEEDED to only a few meters from where Jim stood. "I know the canals not that deep. If you think that tossing the keys in would cause me additional heartache I promise you I will find them and you will join your lovely wife over there, in the afterlife."

NORA OVERHEARD Lana's last comment. It was now or never. She tried to stand up, using every bit of her willpower, grabbing onto the same tree Lana had used earlier to steady herself. Blood was now rushing from her head. She felt woozy, lightheaded. She had Jim's weapon in her hand. She was seeing double for the moment. She shook her head in an attempt to clear it. She closed her eyes for several seconds; she opened them, doing this several times. After a minute or so, the double figures had disappeared.

LANA AIMED THE machine gun at Jim. "Any last wishes?" she asked.

Jim realized his predicament. He had only one option available to him. He mentally counted down before he attempted it.

Suddenly, four rapid shots rang out.

Jim dove into the canal.

Nora managed to stagger up to where Lana's body now lay, dead, firing two additional shots into her head for good measure. "Who's the boss now, bitch?" she yelled at Lana's dead body. "You should have made sure I was dead before you left me to rot!"

Nora looked to the canal, searching for Jim, before scrambling to its edge. "James Dieter, don't you die on me!" she yelled, hoping she would not be rewarded with his body floating to the surface.

She waited patiently, yelling his name.

Jim slowly rose out of the water, first only the top of his head was visible, then his eyes. He was a good 10 meters further down the canal from where he first went in. He was obviously hoping to use the canal and its tree-lined banks to aid in his getaway.

"James Dieter, you better not die on me now," screamed Nora. "You're not getting away from me that easy."

Jim heard Nora screaming his name. Upon seeing her, he stood up in the shallow water, the water was only up to his lower chest. "Down here," he yelled.

He ran back through the shallow water to where she stood, a wide smile gracing his face. He struggled up the canal's muddy banks, slipping several times, before he gained a foothold, climbing to the top. "I thought you were dead," he yelled excitedly. "You're alive!"

Nora fell to the ground. "And I thought you were dead!"

Jim laid down beside her, cradling her head in his arms.

"I'm okay," she said. "I think I might have lost a little blood. But the hell with me, I thought she shot you!"

"Are you kidding me? I've had people aiming at my sorry ass all over the world. Each and every time they missed. Including this time. I guess it helped that I dove into the water. She didn't expect that move. But let's take care of you, shall we."

She squeezed his hand in acknowledgment. "I just need some rest."

"The bullet couldn't enter that thick skull of yours." He brushed back her hair in order to get a better look at the wound. He quickly tore off his shirt, using it to dab at the wound. "Keep pressure on the wound," he said. "We have a medical kit on board the barge."

"Go get the barge. Bring it here and load the paintings. We need to get out of here before somebody shows up."

IN A MATTER OF 30 MINUTES, Jim had loaded the barge, buried the body of Lana, and set fire to both the van and car to get rid of any evidence.

They were 10 kilometers up the canal by the time the fires subsided and burned themselves out. The wreckage itself would take two weeks to find before hikers stumbled upon it.

LONG BURIED SECRETS

CHAPTER 70

Aboard the Barge La Belle

Nora stood beside Jim in the barge's wheelhouse, a white bandage covered the left side of her head. Luckily she didn't require medical attention for her wound, just a good cleaning, ten butterfly stiches, and a glass of whiskey. Of course it helped the pain subside but she still felt as though a truck had run over her.

But it was better than being dead.

Daylight was beginning to break as Jim steered the barge down the narrow confines of the canal. With the aid of the barge's single headlamp, he was able to put 20 kilometers between where they loaded the barge with the stolen art, and their present position.

A loud whistle originating from the kettle in the barge's galley informed them tea water was ready. Nora tapped him on the hand. "I have it, Captain," she said, saluting him.

"At least you know your place, crewman," he said in jest. "My apologies, *crewwoman.*"

"Did you want to wear your tea, or drink it?"

"Definitely drink it," he replied in a humbler tone.

In minutes she handed him a cup of strong Irish tea.

"I added honey, no sugar," she said, "just the way you like it."

Jim winked at her. She smiled in turn. He noticed she was starting to regain her color after putting him through a fright.

"Just the way I like," he responded. "Here, I think it's time you took the helm. Just steer her down the middle."

As Jim removed his hands from the wheel, Nora took his place. "I can do this," she beamed. "First time for everything. Take a picture of me behind the wheel."

Jim took out his cell phone, snapping a quick picture.

"Check another thing off my wish list," she said, a smile gracing her face.

Jim kissed her on the cheek. "I had no doubts."

"What do you say I steer this baby until we reach our first lock, then some breakfast?"

"Already ahead of you. Next lock is in 3 kilometers. So, at our present speed, we should be arriving in about 30 minutes. Just pull in before entering the lock and we can eat."

"Well just the same, I'm famished. How about you cook us a real American breakfast."

"Let me see what our French host left us, and we can go from there."

CHAPTER 71

St. Florentine

After four days of cruising, stopping at wineries, fancy restaurants, or just luxuriating in the beautiful countryside, Jim and Nora arrived at their destination a full day ahead of schedule. They returned early because Jim felt guilty with the two of them basically leaving Summer, Eian, Chuck, and Rahm to fend for themselves.

"James Dieter," began Nora, "you really know how to show a lady a good time."

"I bet you could have stayed out for a few more days, couldn't you?"

"Days? How about a few more weeks?"

Nora tossed a mooring line to an older gentleman who obviously worked for the barge company as Jim expertly docked the barge.

Summer was waiting at the docks for them, the barge company having informed her they were coming in early.

"WHY IN THE HELL didn't you keep your cell phone on?" yelled Summer, shaking her head. "Jim, you of all people know you should maintain communications."

They had just placed their bags and the cardboard tubes on the dock when Summer confronted them.

"Please, calm down," said Jim, looking around at who may be listening. "Wait until we get away from this public area."

Nora ran over to comfort Summer, her now crying. "What happened?" asked Nora, hugging Summer. "Tell us what has you so upset."

Summer wiped her eyes with her shirts sleeve. "They killed Chuck," she replied in a much lower tone. "They just straight up and killed him for no reason at all."

Jim and Nora each grabbed their things, Summer helped, as they walked away from the docks. They strode over to an empty park, Nora and Summer sitting on a park bench. Jim chose to stand.

Nora patted Summer on her back in reassurance. "Tell us what happened," she said, in a soft tone. "Tell us everything."

Summer stopped crying. She took several deep breaths to calm herself. After a few minutes she spoke. "Eian drove the rental car back to Bern early this morning, just like we planned." She paused to once again compose herself before turning to Jim. "I didn't sign up for this," she said in a loud voice, pointing at Jim. "You said it was going to be an easy three-week job. Easy money. I could pay off my kid's tuition."

Jim pulled her up from the bench, hugging her. At first she struggled to pull away, then she grabbed him in return, crying as she did.

"It's okay," Jim said. "Get it all out."

Nora joined in on the hug, the three of them standing there, in an empty park. To anyone from afar, it looked like a joyful reunion.

She stopped crying, easing away from Jim and Nora. She resumed sitting on the bench, determined to finish her story. "As I said, Eian left with the rental car to return it to Bern. He picked up the plane soon afterward." She looked to her watch, "About three hours ago, he called us before he left Bern and said he would land here in less than 45 minutes. So Rahm, Chuck, and I met him when he landed at the little airport outside of town. But another aircraft was already parked in front of the hangar. A Russian one. The only reason we knew it was Russian was because Rahm noticed the make and registration of the aircraft. It looked deserted, so we just waited." She paused, looking directly at Jim. "They knew we were coming."

Jim kneeled down beside her. "Who knew we were coming?"

"The Russians," she replied. "Someone by the name of Sergei Liugo. He said something about being the head of Russia's military intelligence service."

Nora touched the bandage on her head. "We already had a run-in with them four days ago. Or one of their associates."

Summer put her hand to her mouth I shock. "I was so distraught I didn't even notice you had a bandage on your head."

"They took a shot at both of us," said Jim. "Luckily, we are alive. But what happened to Chuck?"

"We were waiting for Eian to land when the Russians emerged from the sole hangar. Five of them, each with handguns, walking straight towards us as Eian landed the plane. They took up positions behind us. Eian pulled up beside the Russian jet and parks. When he exits the plane, the Russians gather us up and ordered us into the hangar. Once inside, they told us to sit on the floor. And that's when this Sergei Liugo fellow walks out of one of the offices."

Jim nodded. "I'm familiar with the name but not the person. I heard he is a really nasty person to cross."

Summer continues. "He walks right up to Chuck. Tells him to get up. Extends his hand to him. The Russian then took Chuck out of earshot. He shook his hand and with the other raised his handgun and placed a bullet in his head."

"That's ruthless bastard!" exclaimed Nora, looking to Jim for support.

Jim turned to Nora, patting her back. "It was evidently a message meant for Nora and myself."

Summer rose up from the bench. "The head Russian sent me to tell you to either bring the paintings to him at the airfield or he would kill Eian next. Then he would hunt the two of you down and sliced you into a hundred pieces. His words, not mine."

Jim's next move was to call Benny.

BENNYS GULFSTREAM 550 landed at St. Florentine's airfield only two hours after Jim called. Benny chose to stay in Europe, knowing the Russians would attempt something like what Jim described to him. And on that chance, he had held on to Dolan's five Old Masters and forty-five low-end fakes knowing they would come in handy once more.

Benny could be courteous and a gentleman, or a brute force assassin when required. He usually left it up to the opposition to decide. Unfortunately, he had been dealing with the likes of Sergei Liugo for far too long. Especially the crooked ones. He knew Sergei was in it for the money, and money alone.

The pilot pulled up and parked beside Eian's leased Gulfstream 550 and the Russians Embraer Phenom 300. The little airfield had never seen so many high–end jets at one time.

JIM, NORA, AND SUMMER waited until they viewed Benny's jet park before they dared approach the rear of the hangar, away from where the attention would be directed towards Benny's aircraft.

Jim had his 9mm Glock at the ready.

He would have to be Benny's sole backup.

ONE RUSSIAN STAYED inside the hangar to guard Eian and Rahm. The remaining five, including Sergei, went out to see who dared approach.

Benny casually walked down the steps of the aircraft as if he owned the airfield. He viewed five Russians with handguns all pointing in his direction. "Gentlemen," he said, a smile gracing his face, "Can't we be civil about this?"

"Who the hell are you?" demanded Sergei, walking up to the diminutive Benny.

"Benny Machaim, head of Mossad," he said, his hand extended, in the other he held aloft his identification. "And you must be Sergei Liugo, head of Russia's military intelligence service or as they are better known, the GRU."

Sergei viewed Benny's identification before handing it back to him. He then chose to shake Benny's hand in the greeting of a fellow spy. "What is the Mossad doing here in this little backwoods area? Especially one that is temporarily in my jurisdiction?"

"Your jurisdiction?"

"As I said, temporarily. What the French don't know won't hurt them."

Benny nodded in understanding, before pointing back to his plane. "A little bird told me you require some artwork?" he said, a smile upon his face. "Some very expensive artwork."

"You! He said in a demeaning way. "You are responsible for that magnificent heist in Bern?"

"Let's just say I am a neutral party who is brokering the deal for that very expensive artwork."

Sergei turned to his men. "This little man wants to give us our paintings."

Benny pointed over to the aircraft hangar. "It's simple really. You turn over to me the people you are holding in the hangar. Then you get your paintings."

"Simple as that?" he said skeptically.

"Simple as that. No monies. No information. Just your prisoners."

Sergei turned back once more. "Boris, bring the prisoners out here," he commanded.

In a matter of minutes Eian and Rahm were standing behind Sergei.

Benny waved to the pilot in his aircraft, signaling for them to bring out the paintings.

The co-pilot and pilot carried the cardboard tubes from the aircraft, laying them on the concrete in-between Benny and Sergei. They then retreated back to the aircraft where, out of sight, they readied for the exchange by arming themselves with Uzi's.

Sergei pushed Eian and Rahm forward. "Fly away little birds," he said sarcastically.

Eian turned, ready to strike Sergei, but Benny grabbed him, pushing him towards the plane. "Another time, another place," Eian replied.

Sergei smiled at him. "Anytime, Irishman."

Eian and Rahm boarded the aircraft. When they stepped inside the co-pilot handed each a Jericho 941 pistol. "You might need this," he said.

Sergei called for his art expert to come forward. As the man approached the cardboard tubes, Benny also approached, looking for the tube with the thin black mark on it. He noticed it lay the closest to Sergei. Thankfully, the expert selected that tube first, holding it up for Sergei to view.

Sergei nodded.

The expert opened the tube, extracting five rolled up paintings, gently laying them on the tarmac, one on top of the other. He placed a monocle to his right eye as he surveyed the paintings one by one. "Beautiful," he said repeatedly. After the fifth painting he turned to Sergei. "These are originals."

"Excellent," replied Sergei. "Now open the rest of the tubes," he demanded of his expert.

Benny's heart dropped. He tapped the left side of his leg twice, a sign to his pilot and co-pilot in the aircraft to take up shooting positions for eliminating Sergei's men. Benny then turned and nodded slightly to Jim in his distant position behind the hangar.

JIM TURNED TO Nora and Summer. "That's the signal Benny's in trouble. I need the two of you to go into the hangar and be prepared for what comes next.

Jim started walking alongside the hangar, seeking a decent shooting position that wouldn't put him in a crossfire with Benny's people.

AS THE EXPERT opened the next tube, Sergei suddenly called him off. "No," he said. "On second thought, we must have trust."

Benny relaxed for the moment.

"Don't you agree, Benny of Mossad?"

Benny nodded. "I totally agree. We must have trust."

Sergei commanded his men to load the cardboard tubes with the paintings onto their aircraft. Satisfied, he next turned to Benny. "Until we meet again," he said. "Possibly under different circumstances?"

"Yes, until we meet again."

He bid one last farewell to Benny as he boarded. In a matter of minutes they were buttoned up and ready to be airborne.

Jim, Nora, and Summer walked over to where Benny stood. Rahm and Eian had already exited the aircraft and joined the group as they observed the Russian jet taxi into take-off position.

Eian was the first to speak. "So let me get this straight. We let the Russians take the five originals and forty-five reproductions in exchange for Rahm and myself?"

Benny smiled. "A small price for peace."

The Russian jet took off with a roar just overhead of them.

Eian continued. "They are going to be pissed when they get back to Russia and find out about the fakes. They might be coming after us? Maybe even you and your famous Mossad?"

Benny pointed to the aircraft. "Let us ponder that thought for a moment, shall we?"

They each watched as the jet gained altitude, climbing ever higher on its way back to Moscow. The aircraft looked brilliant with its gleaming white fuselage, on its tail the Russian national colors. Suddenly there was a bright flash, then the Russian jet exploded, the explosion shredding the aircraft into many small pieces, the pieces now falling to earth like confetti, many miles away.

Benny looked to his small group. "Time makes all problems disappear. *Well, time and explosives.* As you are now probably aware, we placed explosives in one of the cardboard tubes. Obviously of enough intensity to take down a fuel laden aircraft."

Eian turned to shake Benny's hand. "I like your style, Benny. You people in Mossad don't mess around. Remind me to never get on your bad side."

Benny looked over to Jim, nodding to him as if saying, *and that is how it is done.*

Jim nodded in return before speaking. "I think we have something for you back at the hotel. Forty-five Old-Master's."

"I think you do," replied Benny.

CHAPTER 72

Benny sat on the hotel room's sofa beside Jim and Nora. He had requested Summer and Eian acquire an expensive bottle of Champagne, his treat, for a toast. Rahm had already driven the original paintings back to Benny's jet and was waiting their return to Israel.

Benny reached down beside the sofa and pulled up a brown leather pilot's briefcase, one that was basically two times the width of a normal briefcase, handing it to Nora. "I am providing this to you, knowing that you would take better care of it than your husband."

"Heavy sucker," she said before placing it on the floor in front of both her and Jim.

"What, you don't trust me anymore?" said Jim sarcastically. "I'm hurt."

"I trust you with my life and have done so on several occasions. But for this one event, it's your wife's turn."

"Do I open it now?" Nora said excitedly.

Jim stopped her. "Are you kidding?" he said in jest. "You saw what he did to the Russians. Who knows what's in the case."

Summer and Eian knocked softly on the rooms half-open door, and walked in. "Champagne anyone," said Summer, holding up a bottle of Louis Roederer Cristal Brut for them to see.

Eian chimed in. "With the price we paid, they even tossed in five free glass flutes. Oh wait. I'm sorry, for what Benny is paying."

Summer handed the bottle to Benny. "You paid an arm and a leg for it, you get to pop it."

Eian handed each of them a glass.

A loud pop signaled Benny was successful. He poured each of them a generous glass of the expensive French Champagne, then his own.

"May I propose a toast?" he said, seeing no objections, he continued. "To our dear departed friend, Chuck."

They all joined in. "May he rest in peace." Each took a small sip.

"Blah," said Eian. "Tastes bitter. How do you drink this stuff. For one thing it cost more than most people make in a week. I'd personally rather have an Irish Whiskey or a Guinness."

Summer tried to take his glass.

He protested. "I didn't say I wouldn't finish it."

Everyone laughed.

Benny rose once more. "A second toast," he said. "To my friend, James Dieter. One of the few people I trusted to come up with an efficient plan and assemble a very capable team, to pull this operation off."

They each took another sip.

"When I deliver the paintings you rescued to our people in Jerusalem, it will be to a grateful nation," said Benny. "Hopefully it will set off a worldwide firestorm in the press demanding the Swiss return the rest of the paintings and drawings originally stolen by the Nazi's."

Summer nodded as she raised her glass. "I will do my best as the University of Pennsylvania museum curator to create such a stink," she said, a wide smile on her face. "I will also contact some of my friends in similar positions and ask them to do the same."

Benny raised his glass. "That is all we can ask. If we can keep it active in the press, the profiteers won't be able to hide under any rock in the world." He sipped his champagne before pointing to the pilot's briefcase. "And now I would like Nora to open the briefcase."

Summer looked at each of them. "Is it ticking?" she said in jest.

Eian was excited. "Open it, Nora," he said.

Nora rose from her seat before reaching down and picking up the case, placing it on the room's bed. She looked to each of them. "I don't hear any ticking," she said, smiling.

Benny pointed to the case. "I would never do something like that to a friend." He paused for several moments before continuing. *"At least not when I am in the same room."*

"Nice one," replied Eian.

Nora pulled up the cases two leather flaps so only she could she what was inside. Her eyes went wide. "Oh my," she exclaimed, before upending the heavy case and dumping its contents on the bed for them all to see.

Out came 100, bank-wrapped bundles of one-hundred-dollar bills, each bundle representing $10,000, for a total of $1million US dollars.

Jim was first to respond. "That's a lot of money!"

Benny nodded. "There was a reward for the forty-five paintings you rescued." He pointed to the bed were the money lay. "That is only a simple down payment of the reward."

Eian jumped up from his chair, walking over to the bottle of champagne, filling up his now empty glass.

Summer laughed at him. "I thought you didn't care for the champagne?" she said.

"I need it to steady my nerves, my dear. I think my ears are about to hear something that will enrich my pockets greatly."

Jim shook his head at Eian's antics. "You never surprise me Eian."

Benny continued. "You are entitled to another $9 million to be delivered to a place of your choosing. This so you can escape those horrible American income taxes."

"And there it is," said Eian in celebration. "It's the winning lottery number; the slot machine payout; the Ed McMahon delivery of the Clearing House check all rolled into one. *Ka-ching*."

Nora walked over to Eian. "Pour me some of that champagne."

Jim and Summer joined them. "Same for us."

Benny declined as he rose from his seat, walking over to the door. "With that Dolan character in prison, Sergei and his crew dead, and Sergei's two Iranian agents dead, I'm assuming that leaves no one to harass you."

They all rose in unison. "It's been a pleasure, Benny," said Jim. He and Eian shook Benny's hand.

Jim said. "You will have to come over to the US sometime and vacation on our yacht."

Benny smiled. "You mean the one you inherited from your former partner Dan? In the Florida Keys? I think he called it the *Irish Rebel* or something along those lines. Docking at pier number 17?"

"Why did it not surprise me that you already knew," replied Jim.

Benny pointed to Eian. "And you, stop the gambling, and take care of my friends. No more trouble from you. Do you hear me?"

"Loud and clear," said Eian. "I'm done tossing away money to line somebody else's pockets."

"If I hear you are gambling again, I will personally see to it that your money disappears faster than the casino can take it."

Eian held his hands up in surrender. "Done and done."

Nora and Summer both grabbed Benny, each kissing him on a cheek.

"If only my wife could see me now," he said. He waved, and then he was gone.

CHAPTER 73

Florida Keys

Jim was topside on his yacht *Irish Rebel* preparing to sail to Panama for the winter months. It was something he had been looking forward to for these many past months since the Bern job.

Nora was below in the dining salon finishing her article on Nazi art theft during WWII, this for the Chicago Tribune on-line edition. Sadly for her many fans, it was to be her last article due to her impending early retirement. She had enough awards, enough business travel, and experienced enough nonsense from her boss. That and her husband Jim had simply requested her too.

Jim had no desire for his wife to work through her pregnancy.

The Bern museum never realized their precious paintings were missing; or they never chose to reveal to the public that reproductions now hung in their place. That was until Benny began the arduous task of returning the forty-five Old World masters to the original owners' families; for the original owners were all dead. In a bold move, he even held a worldwide news conference to discuss the theft, in effect daring the museum to push for prosecution. He also went on to state that the museum still held hundreds of stolen paintings either on view or in storage.

True to her word, Summer started a campaign involving her fellow Museum curators, in effect challenging the Swiss government to return the paintings to their original owners' families. Each of the museums threatened to isolate all Swiss museums, not just the Bern Museum.

Between Nora's article, Benny's disclosure, and Summer's challenge, the art world was suddenly in an uproar, demanding their return.

It was if six million voices from the past had all spoken up in unison.

It wasn't long before the Bern Museum experienced difficulties with both donors and patrons, forcing them to declare bankruptcy. Its assets soon confiscated by the Swiss government and moved to Zurich for protection, placed in a vault 200 feet below street level.

Just like Benny said they would do.

Summer was soon able to quit her job as a Museum curator and, fulfilling a life-long dream, opened her own gallery in the affluent suburbs of Philadelphia. It didn't take long before her Gallery became well-known for its owner's unique ability to perform private jobs for many of the area's wealthy clients.

After all, she was acquainted with more than a few artists who specialized in forgeries.

Zhang and his wife took their newfound monies and decided it best to close their lunch truck operation and open a white linen, Chinese food-dining establishment in downtown Philadelphia. His former crew of *helpers* joined as minor partners.

Of course, all of the artwork in the restaurant was hand painted by Zhang.

Chuck's daughter received an anonymous, full-ride scholarship to Temple University. She was also gifted a new luxury car, and a three bedroom condominium only blocks from campus. She would also receive a $25,000 stipend each year until her 30th birthday. The donor said in their note that her father had helped them achieve something no one thought possible.

Moreover, that her father should be thought of as a hero, not an ex-con.

And Eian, well, he found himself in a high stake poker game in Monaco. Of course, he had brushed aside Benny's stern warning not to gamble. However, he could not resist the temptation. In Monaco, Eian made it to the final round where the pot had grown to an incredible $22 million euros. With lady luck on his side the entire tournament, in what would be the final hand, he found himself holding three jacks. Of course, Eian being Eian, he went all in. As each of his ten opponents lay their cards on the table, Eian knew something special was happening. No one could beat his hand! He won and finally broke his losing streak.

The following morning Eian visited the Bank of Monaco to check on his winnings only to find his money had somehow vanished. The Bank informed him their computer systems were hacked in the middle of the night but in an unusual set of circumstances, only his account was affected, none of their other depositors. That is when Eian remembered Benny's last words to him, *'No more gambling or I will personally see to it that it disappears'.*

Eian couldn't even afford to pay his hotel bill, one that had grown to over $40,000 euros during the length of his stay for the poker tournament. The hotel soon had him arrested for non-payment. As he was being processed, his jailor inquired as to whether he wanted to make a phone call for representation. He quickly replied yes.

Can you please dial the number for one James Dieter in the Florida Keys?

THE END

Amazon Best Selling author Francis Joseph Smith has traveled to most of the world during his tenure in the Armed Forces and as an Analyst for an unnamed Government Agency, providing him with numerous fictional plot lines and settings for future use. His experiences provide readers with well-researched, fast-paced action. Smith's novels are the result of years of preparation to become a fiction writer in the genre of Clancy, Griffin, Higgins, and Cussler.

Smith lives with his family in a small town outside of Philadelphia where he is currently in work on his next novel.

Made in the USA
Las Vegas, NV
22 November 2023

81357231R00203